A Heartless Laird

Clan Ross
Book One

Hildie McQueen

Copyright © 2019 by Hildie McQueen
Print Edition

Published by Dragonblade Publishing, an imprint of Kathryn Le Veque Novels, Inc

All rights reserved. No part of this book may be used or reproduced in any manner whatsoever without written permission, except in the case of brief quotations embodied in critical articles or reviews.

Additional Dragonblade books by Author Hildie McQueen

Clan Ross Series
A Heartless Laird

*** Please visit Dragonblade's website for a full list of books and authors. Sign up for Dragonblade's blog for sneak peeks, interviews, and more: ***
www.dragonbladepublishing.com

Note from the Author

Clan Ross was well known for being led by a string of cruel and unsavory lairds during the late fourteenth and throughout the fifteenth centuries. A couple of the lairds were imprisoned, and the king ordered their deaths. This is not the clan I will be writing about.

The fictional Clan Ross will be a bit different. Although my lairds and warriors will be brave and brutal fighters, the actions of the characters will be explained and their reasonings will have cause, to them at least.

1580 Highlands of Scotland north of Inverness

All the while Scotland wars with the English, there is another war in the northern Highlands, a clash of two ferocious clans. Clan Ross and their mortal enemies, Clan McLeod, have ravaged villages and families all in the name of revenge.

Chapter One

Thundering of horses' hooves vibrated the ground as the warriors retreated from the blood-soaked battlefield. A gust of wind blew over the field as if fanning over the dead and injured would add a sign of life continuing despite the errors of man.

Two clans had battled fiercely, the battle ending by the fact neither side could continue, their arms barely able to lift the heavy weapons.

The McLeod had called a retreat after spotting more fighters approaching from the direction of Ross lands. The reinforcements were mostly the injured warriors who'd been left behind and ordered to come later. But they were large in number.

There were other men who happened to head by. But they were not part of either clan, simply a group of warriors headed back to their homes after fighting the English. After months of battling, the men were desperate to return home to loved ones and cared little what happened between warring clans.

Clan Ross remained behind at the battlefield, claiming victory on that day where both sides had suffered almost equal injuries. Unlike other clashes, there were not as many dead. It was a miracle that only about a dozen men remained on the ground since the fight had been ruthless, everyone out for blood.

Today's battle was over; the war far from it.

Malcolm Ross' thirst was not quenched. As a matter of fact, dissatisfaction at the lack of a clear victor made him growl in frustration.

Atop his steed, the bloody yet proud Highlander took in the field, his gaze moving from the battleground on past to the forest.

Avenging the recent slaying of his father, Laird Ross, would take more than a few winning battles.

The vision of his father being speared through the midsection formed in his mind every night. Malcolm had not been present, but he'd demanded to hear every sordid detail. Since then, he'd dreamed of it almost nightly until it was as if he'd been present. He had a clear picture of how the youngest son of Laird McLeod had run his father through, injuring him mortally. The vision replayed in his mind daily.

In Malcolm's opinion, it was his father's demand from the grave that his death be avenged. Malcolm was sure of it.

The loss of their laird had cut deeply through every member of Clan Ross, the mourning prolonged by the knowledge of how unprovoked his slaying had been.

A proud, strong and fair leader, his father had been revered.

Now, the helm of responsibility weighed heavily on Malcolm's shoulders for he could never begin to fill the void his father had left. And for that, he despised the bastard responsible.

It didn't matter that he could possibly die in his quest to avenge his father's death. Malcolm would continue to fight and would never be satisfied until Ethan McLeod lay bleeding and dying at his feet.

And even then, if no one remained standing, would the ravine-deep hole within his chest ever heal?

It would not be an easy feat, of that Malcolm was well aware. However, the McLeods had to pay with a higher price than he and his clan had. One way or another, he'd have revenge and he was more than willing to die if required.

A bird called out from a nearby tree, bringing Malcolm out of his musings and he let out a long breath. Scanning the remains of the battle, he didn't notice any movement from those on the ground.

Several horses along with the injured lay still in the muddy field. Just then, carts neared as people arrived. Malcolm assumed they were a mixture of both clans. Once climbing down from mounts and carts, they moved with caution as if expecting to be attacked. A fair assumption as a wounded man acting out of instinct and self-preservation could be lethal.

An old man seemed more focused on the animals than the injured men. He walked to a horse and stabbed it in the heart, effectively putting it out of its misery.

Battlefields had a stench that filled the nostrils. Blood, excrement and sweat mixed with dirt wafted up when the breeze blew.

Every time the wind passed over the area, the smell was carried toward where he was. Malcolm didn't bother covering his nose but continued his vigil.

It had been a particularly grueling fight, one that had definitely hurt his enemy and he was assured in knowing many more of them had been hurt worse than his own. Clan McLeod would not seek retribution for a fortnight at least and that was too long in Malcolm's estimation.

The fact it would be a while before he could seek the battlefield again disappointed him.

However, there were far too many injuries and, admittedly, his own warriors were exhausted and required rest. Having battled for months since his father's death, even the reinforcements from smaller clans were showing signs of fatigue.

Having sent his warriors home, Malcolm and two guardsmen kept watch over the healer who'd come to search for signs of life in those presumed dead. A waste of time in Malcolm's estimation but he allowed it since it meant a great deal to his people. If one of his brothers lay amongst the injured, he too would demand for a healer.

So, he reined in his impatience and ignored his own injury and remained upon his steed, standing guard.

Nearby, there was a horse hitched to a wagon upon which four bodies were already piled. He glanced to it for but a moment, not wanting to ponder overly long at where he may end up one day soon.

Would he, too, end up in a pile of bodies, on a cart driven by an old man to be buried?

Despite the somber moment, he chuckled at the thought. Then he narrowed his eyes upon noticing an injured man lift his hand to get the healer's attention. Someone was alive.

From the profuse amount of blood still spewing from his midsection, the unfortunate warrior would, in all probability, not survive. The healer and one of the guards dragged the man near the same wagon upon which bodies were being placed.

Malcolm didn't bother dismounting to see who it was. His men were loyal to the end. This warrior, like those piled on the wagon, had fought valiantly and expected no special treatment.

More movement caught his eye. Two women and a young man emerged from the trees. Probably scavengers.

Then again, by the speed in which they scurried from one man to another, they were probably looking for a loved one.

The trio searched for signs of life and didn't rifle through clothing nor did they remove shoes. It was then that he noticed a cart left beside trees from where they'd come. He didn't recognize them. The group was either a trio of healers for Clan McLeod or idiotic Good Samaritans.

"Ride through the field and to the edges of forest once more and check for injured men," Malcolm ordered his guardsmen. They immediately rode off to do as instructed.

One of the women pushed hair back from her face. From the distance, it was hard to make out her features. However, by her body language, she was distraught as she knelt next to a fallen man. Then the other two lowered next to fallen men. Each quietly touched the faces of the dead men and positioned their hands across their chests.

The older woman called to the others and they scrambled to a fallen McLeod. The trio then tore away the man's tunic and inspected him. If the man was alive, he wouldn't be for long.

"Aye, Laird," the healer motioned for him to come closer. "Could use a hand."

He urged his horse closer and dismounted, recognizing the injured man as a one of his guardsmen, a good fighter. Young and brash Ian McElroy was a likeable sort that had an easygoing nature. However, once on the battlefield, his sword skill was without reproach. Now the man was pale and still. However, his chest lifted and lowered, showing that he remained alive.

"Will he live?" Malcolm asked, not particularly caring to hear the truth. "Ye must hurry about yer tasks. I cannot continue to remain here much longer. There is much I must do."

"I am not sure, be he deserves a chance. It will be just a moment, if ye can help me load him onto the wagon." The older man's flat gaze met his.

Malcolm looked to the healer's wagon. The man had managed to load four bodies with the help of a young skinny lad who was red-faced now from the exertion. "Where are ye putting him?"

The healer shrugged. "Atop the others I suppose."

Ian had passed out and would hopefully remain so until they arrived back at the keep. If he survived the trip, then there was a possibility for recovery. By the looks of his bloodied body, he'd been hacked in the side and his left arm was almost severed. The man would lose it in all probability. And yet, the healer didn't seemed fazed at the fact that Ian would have no doubt preferred to die than to live the rest of his life as a maimed man.

Together, they lifted the injured man and made their way to the wagon. Once they neared, the healer motioned for Malcolm to lower

Ian to the ground. "I'll move the bodies over."

"He can come in our wagon." A singsong voice came from behind and Malcolm whirled around, his right hand on his sword's hilt.

The greenest eyes he'd ever seen met his. The woman lifted her chin just a bit in a show of bravery, but the slight trembling of her hand told the truth. "I will care for him. I am a healer."

"Are ye a McLeod?" Malcolm snarled. "If so, be gone with ye."

If possible, her chin lifted a bit more. "Nay." Then she quickly added. "Neither am I a Ross." Disdain dripped from the words. "Ye were about to toss him in a wagon with dead men." She looked about to cry, her gaze moving to the injured Ian.

"Very well," Malcolm acceded. He wanted to leave. Pain seared his injured side and his tunic was getting bloodier by the moment.

Perhaps the fair lass was romantically involved with Ian. If so, she'd take good care of the warrior. "Where do ye live?"

"The village there past the trees," she replied, no longer paying him much heed. Her full attention on Ian, she'd lowered to her knees and brushed the warrior's hair back from his face. For some strange reason, the action annoyed Malcolm and he huffed impatiently.

"Send word of how he fares. I will ensure his father is aware." He turned away toward where his horse was.

"My name is Elspeth," she said, and Malcolm wondered if she spoke to him or to Ian. He looked over his shoulder and, once again, was struck by the beauty of her deep pools of green. Like the darkest shadowed foliage around her, they held the promise of danger and adventure. Malcolm tore his gaze away for a moment. Realizing the tactical error, his gaze snapped back to her face. This time, he focused on her mouth. That turned out to be an error as well.

She swallowed visibly. "Elspeth Muir." Motioning with her head toward the older woman and young man who watched from a safe distance, she let out a soft sigh. "They are my grandmother and my brother, Conor." The duo hitched their chins much like she'd done upon meeting him. Obviously, the Muirs were a proud people. It was something he respected, and he nodded in their direction in acknowledgement.

"Send word," Malcolm repeated, not wanting to remain longer. There was much to do as the new laird of Clan Ross and dawdling or holding a long conversation that did not involve strategy was a waste of time. Also, the pain was becoming unbearable.

When he mounted and started on his way toward his keep, Malcolm looked over his shoulder. The Muir trio had already loaded Ian onto the back of their wagon. While the brother guided the horses, the grandmother and Elspeth rode beside the injured man. Both were hunched over Ian, seeming to be working on saving his life.

If Ian survived, he'd not be able to fight again. With only one arm, it would be impossible to protect himself in battle.

Malcolm wondered what he'd do if the same sort of injury happened to him. It didn't take him long to admit he'd continue to fight. However, unlike him, Ian did not have the need for revenge coursing through his veins.

Interesting that the Muirs had come to search for injured men. It was also possible they'd come with the sole purpose of finding Ian. If the lass had preoccupied the warrior, then he deserved the outcome. Women were a distraction fighters did not need during war.

He searched his brain considering if any of his men were involved in any kind of romantic liaisons. There were two he'd often seen in what looked to be a relationship. If so, they'd be ordered to end the attachment. It would be the topic of discussion with his leaders upon his return.

Relationships by his warriors would be banned until they conquered Clan McLeod.

CHAPTER TWO

THE WAGON SWAYED from side to side as they traveled the uneven terrain back home to their small village of Kildonan, near an inlet of Loch Broom. Deep in the forest, the tiny village had escaped the clan clashes by being so secluded.

Struggling to keep the wounded man stable, Elspeth and her grandmother rode mostly in silence. Finally, they traveled on a somewhat level road.

"Ye shouldn't have spoken to him," Elspeth's grandmother said in a harsh whisper. "He is a ruthless, heartless tyrant."

Elspeth had to agree with her grandmother's assessment of Malcolm Ross. By the uncaring way he'd responded to her request to take the injured warrior, it was evident he'd not cared one way or the other if the young man lived or died.

There had not only been disdain upon looking over the dead and injured, but also a sort of detachment. The man did not care for his own people or what happened to them. As a matter of fact, she was sure the only thing that motivated him was war and conquest.

"I must admit, he was intimidating and..." she considered her next words. "Hollow, as if missing a soul."

Her grandmother shook her head. "Malcolm Ross is evil incarnate.

There has been nothing but death and destruction since his father, the fair Laird Ross, died. Ye are correct, he has no soul."

"He is the laird now. I am grateful he is not our laird, but even our family has suffered because of him." Elspeth proffered a cloth and wiped the injured man's face.

"However, ye are right, he did not seem to care whether this man lived or died." Elspeth studied the young warrior. "So young, all of them dying."

"And for what," her brother chimed in. "So that the lairds can boast of a triumph over each other."

"It should have been him instead of this young man." Her grandmother brushed the injured man's hair away from his face.

"Grandmother. We are a family of healers, caretakers. Never should we wish injury or worse on anyone. Even someone as misguided as Malcolm Ross."

They resumed the trek in silence until arriving at their cottage. Her father and older brother, Gil, hurried over to help unload the unconscious man.

"Boil water," Elspeth ordered as they made their way to a room on the side of the house where they tended to the injured. "I need someone to help me."

While waiting for the water, Elspeth hurried to a table next to a shelf replete with herbs she'd picked and dried. Mixing a tincture of ground hemlock, bryony, henbane, and whisky, she stirred the vile-smelling liquid and poured it into a small cup. Then she turned to Ian, who remained unconscious. She'd begin the procedure while he was unaware and, hopefully, he'd remain so.

There was shuffling and footsteps as her friend Ceilidh walked in. "I came to help. Saw yer arrival from my window." Her friend's gaze went to the injured man and she blanched upon seeing all the blood. "Is he alive?"

"Aye, but not for long if we don't help him." Elspeth handed Ceilidh a stack of clean cloths. "Come, hurry, help me."

She removed the temporary bandages and inspected the angry gash. From the foul odor, his insides had been pierced. Elspeth motioned for her brothers, who walked in with two buckets of steaming water, to come closer. Then she instructed them to pour some into smaller vessels to cool.

In the meantime, she and Ceilidh set aside threads, needles and small knives made for her by her father who was a blacksmith.

Gil narrowed his eyes at her. "A Ross this time?" He spit on the ground. "Should have left him to die." He didn't wait for a reply, but instead limped away.

Her brother's left leg, stiff and unbending, made his gait encumbered. Just two months earlier he'd almost lost the leg due to a wound he'd received after being recruited to fight with the Ross.

Gil's injury was what had drawn Elspeth to go to the battlefield and fetch those injured. Like the young injured warrior, without intervention, Gil would have certainly perished.

"Do ye know his name?" Ceilidh interrupted her thoughts. "He's quite badly off."

"Ian is what I heard. In all probability, he will not live. We will do our best to help him."

With precise movements, Elspeth dipped a cup into the boiled water and tested it to ensure it had cooled. Then she began washing out the wound. Once that was accomplished, she reached into the gaping hole, hoping to find the precise location of where his insides were cut. Finally, she was successful and pulled out the affected portion. "Needle and thread."

Ceilidh looked about to faint. "I do not know how ye can do that." Nonetheless, morbid curiosity kept the lass present. She helped Elspeth by wiping away blood and washing the affected areas as instructed while Elspeth stitched.

"Now to sew the wound closed," Elspeth announced. "Once that is done, we will bind his midsection tightly."

A loud animalistic howl made them jump. The warrior had come to. There was a crazed look about him as he attempted to sit up while the women tried to keep him from it.

"Stop at once, ye will hurt yerself," Ceilidh spoke into his ear. "Ye are safe. Stop."

The man was much too infirmed to hear reason and he continued to struggle. Elspeth flinched when a portion of the newly stitched wound tore open.

Ceilidh raced to the doorway. "Gil! Conor!" Thankfully, her brothers arrived before more damage was done. They held down the now weakening man.

"Hold his nose," Elspeth ordered and Ceilidh did so that she could pour the tincture down the man's throat. Thankfully, he swallowed the entire contents of the cup.

It was a matter of minutes before, once again, he was unconscious.

"I have to remove his left arm. Please bind him to the table." As much as she wanted to not do it, the hand was already purpled from lack of blood.

Her brothers ran a thick strip of fabric across the injured man's chest and upper thighs and bound him to the table.

Once Ian was tied down, ensuring he'd not move if he regained consciousness, Elspeth began cleaning the wounded arm. Bone and muscle had been hacked through, leaving only a bit of tissue that kept the limb attached. She quickly cut through the flesh and dropped the severed portion, just above the elbow into a bucket.

"Oh," Ceilidh swallowed. "I do believe it's best I sit." She swayed, but managed to fall delicately into a chair. "What a horrible sight."

Her poor friend regularly helped even if she didn't always have the stomach for it. Elspeth smiled at her. "I can do the rest alone. Best ye sit and not faint and injure yerself."

"True, ye would leave me laying there." Ceilidh eyed the bloody floor with a look of pure disgust.

Elspeth returned her attention to Ian's left arm. Once she released the tourniquet, bleeding would begin. She had to singe the wound. There was no other way to ensure the man didn't bleed to death.

She raced to her father's shop, grabbed an iron from the fire and hurried back to the injured man. Her father barely paid her any mind. He was used to her healing practices and purposely put the blunt iron into the fire in case she needed it.

"I hate this part." Elspeth lifted one of the bandages and tied it around her face to cover her nose and mouth. Her gaze moved to Ian's face. "Poor man."

She'd make sure he'd drink the tincture regularly to help with the pain. However, it would not be enough and Ian would suffer greatly for a few days.

Despite how hard Elspeth had tried to spare the wounded man, he let out an inhuman howl when she singed the wound closed. Ceilidh did her best to calm him by stroking his shoulder, but he thrashed and cursed at them. Blinded by the pain, he strained against the bonds to the point that Elspeth wondered if he'd break free.

A true warrior, he was used to pain so Ian remained awake, even when they poured more tincture down his throat. He sputtered and screamed for them to release him.

"Ye would not make it far," Elspeth informed him calmly. "Please settle or ye'll make the wounds worse."

His bloodshot eyes slid from her to Ceilidh. "Who are ye? I will kill y…"

"Enough of that nonsense," Ceilidh said, pushing his head down onto the table. "We need to put ye in a proper bed, but we will not if ye're acting like a crazed fool."

He frowned, and squeezed his eyes shut, face scrunching up from the pain. "Where am I?"

"Kildonan," Elspeth informed him, wringing out a wet cloth. "Yer laird is aware ye are here."

"He passed out," Ceilidh replied, taking the cloth and wiping it over the man's sweaty face. "Mercifully."

"I'll go get my brothers to move him to the cot." Elspeth hurried from the room. "Ian has a long recovery ahead. Hopefully, his mood will improve."

CEILIDH STUDIED THE warrior's face, keeping an eye to ensure he didn't wake and catch her off guard. He seemed to be fully passed out, but she knew the tricks some of the warriors played. She'd helped Elspeth enough to know. Her stomach churned at the grotesque smell in the room. As soon as they moved him to the cot, she'd dash out for fresh air.

After rinsing the cloth with cold water, she returned to the task of cleaning him. His neck, upper chest and then down to his stomach. It was best to wash the injured man before moving to the cot to ensure he would be comfortable.

His body was formidable. Muscular and honed for battle, there wasn't a spare bit of fat. She lifted his right arm and washed it, her gaze steadily on his face.

The warrior was handsome; she'd not deny it. However, at the same time, he was intimidating and by the way he'd cursed them just moments ago, she wouldn't trust him for a single moment if left alone with him unrestrained.

Ceilidh cleared her throat and returned to the basin. She poured out the water and refilled it with freshly-boiled water from the hearth.

Now to wash his bottom half. She wasn't shocked by nudity. After months of war, she had seen more than any unmarried woman should.

Most men cared little about modesty, especially when injured and in pain. Although she did her best to keep her gaze averted, more times than not, it was quite embarrassing if the injured man was awake. Some made crude remarks, which earned them a very specific threat. Interesting how threatening to do harm where she washed often quieted them immediately.

With a long breath, she turned to Ian and pulled the blanket down. She dipped a fresh cloth in the warm water and looked.

"Goodness," she whispered, her hand shaking just a bit as she continued the task of cleaning him.

There was a healed scar that ran down the side of his upper right thigh.

She made quick work of her task, doing her best not to stare at the rod nestled in thick dark hair. It was worth noting his manhood was spared any injury.

She covered his midsection and finished the task of washing his legs and feet. When the task was completed, once again the water was poured out and fresh water poured into the bowl.

Elspeth, her closest friend and confidant, learned everything about healing from a traveling monk. The man had insisted on the unorthodox practice of washing every little thing, from wounds, to tools and the injured person's body. Although bothersome, Ceilidh had to agree it made sense.

"Once we move him, I'll clean up the room, Ceilidh," Elspeth said, entering with her brother and father following.

The men helped to roll the injured man to his side so that Ceilidh and Elspeth could finish washing him. Then they moved him to the cot and tied his ankles and right arm to rails that had been built and connected to the bed. After too many incidents with wounded men fighting and attempting to run away only to injure themselves further, they'd come up with a way to keep them in bed.

"Only one today, seems odd given we heard the fighting was brutal," her father commented.

"Everyone else was dead. The only other survivor was taken by the Ross' healer." Elspeth used a hand brush to scrub the now empty table with lye while boiling more water to rinse it off.

Ceilidh swept the floor and scooped bloody bandages into a bucket. The women worked quickly and efficiently.

Her younger brother, Conor, would be spending the night there and Elspeth wanted to be sure he would not be subjected to stench.

"Is he awake?" Elspeth's grandmother entered with a bowl of steaming broth. "I thought he'd be hungry."

All three turned to the cot where the warrior winced in pain, watching them through narrowed eyes.

"Not sure ye want to go near him with hot soup, Grandmother," Elspeth said. "He's very angry."

Ian moaned and, once again, squeezed his eyes shut.

Ceilidh neared the cot and placed a hand on his shoulder. "Would ye like more tincture?"

"Bu…bucket," Ian said.

"Ye'll have to release his arm," her grandmother said, noting that he'd turned a ghastly shade of green.

No sooner did they untie his arm did he turn and expel into the proffered bucket.

Ian continued until he was dry heaving. "I…I do not want more of that vile liquid."

Before she could be warned against it, Ceilidh wiped Ian's mouth and held a cup of lukewarm water to him. "It is only water."

He took water into his mouth and spit into the bucket and then drank another entire cupful. To Elspeth's surprise, he didn't try to untie his legs but fell back into the bed and groaned.

Elspeth neared and his reddened gaze met hers. "Ye're wasting yer time. I am dying."

Chapter Three

Unsteadily, Malcolm paced in the great room, unable to settle after a day of battle and speaking to the leaders of his army of warriors. The men needed rest and many had injuries to heal from.

"Come back to the kitchen," his sister, Verity, called out as she stormed in. "I need to stitch the wound closed."

Where was everyone? The room was empty except for a servant boy, who swept the floor without much interest on the far side of the room. The boy's eyes darted between him and the door, no doubt considering escaping if Malcolm were to lose his temper.

"Where is Tristan?" he said, waving his arm across the room. "Kieran?"

"Upstairs. They bathed, were tended to and bandaged and are probably in their chambers getting much needed rest." Verity took his arm and guided him back to the kitchen. "Ye're drunk."

He would have argued, but when he stumbled sideways, he decided against it.

Once in the kitchen, he was shoved into a chair. Several women gathered around as Verity and Moira, the cook, began tending to his wounds. Malcolm wanted to argue that it was a waste of time, but since there was no choice but to wait for a few days, he may as well ensure to be in the best of health for the next battle.

Moira looked over her shoulder. "Give him some tincture."

"I don't need it," Malcolm growled. But he was caught by surprise when someone grabbed his head from behind and tilted it up.

"Open yer mouth," Verity ordered as she poured a mixture of whisky and herbs down his throat.

He sputtered, but swallowed most of it. Just moments later, he could barely keep his eyes open.

"Call a couple of men to come and to take him to his bedchamber." Moira's words seem to come from a far distance and Malcolm shook his head. "I can't sleep. Too mu…much to…do."

⟫⟪

THE AROMA OF roasted meats made Malcolm stir. It was dark outside and he wondered how many hours he'd slept. Admittedly, he was too comfortable to move and although he was hungry, he was more exhausted.

Every bone ached as he turned to his side and looked to the doorway. On a table next to a chair was a tray of food. From the steam wafting from it, it hadn't been there long. Whoever had sent food didn't wish him to leave his chamber.

He didn't have to guess. His mother, ever the tyrant whenever he or his brothers were injured, had probably locked him in.

She shouldn't have bothered, Malcolm thought, sliding from the bed. He had no desire to do much more than eat and sleep. In the morning, he'd start anew. Battle plans had to be made and scouts sent out to spy and find out how the McLeods fared.

While he ate, the green-eyed woman back at the battlefield came to mind. *Elspeth.* He narrowed his eyes toward the window. Whoever she was, it was a foolish pursuit she was on. Traveling to battlefields to find the injured would one day lead to finding herself at the end of a sword. The wounded were often brutal in their last attempts to survive.

The green eyes floated in his mind. She was a fair lass, one of the prettiest he'd seen in a long time. Not that he'd noticed much lately. He had more important things to concentrate on than a woman. Women were a distraction he didn't allow.

The direction of his thoughts reminded him to set a new rule against any kind of relationships. Once the war was won and his father avenged, he'd allow more freedom. But for now, no one would be distracted by the frivolity of a relationship with a woman.

Whores were available for what men needed. There was no reason for the heart to be involved.

Once he finished his meal, he relieved himself, rinsed his hands and face with water from a basin and fell back into the bed.

Within moments, slumber claimed him and he didn't hear the servant enter to take his plate away and empty the chamber pot.

"WHAT IS THIS I hear about no relationships allowed?" his mother screeched much too loudly the next morning. After being plundered with whisky and whatever herbs Verity had mixed in, Malcolm's head felt heavy.

"I won't be talked into changing my mind, Mother," he said, motioning for a servant to refill his cup with water. "It's best for our warriors to concentrate on the task at hand, which is…"

His mother leaned forward so she could look him in the eyes. "Listen to me, Malcolm. Ye cannot control people in that manner."

They sat upon the high board waiting to break their fast. Moira was late with the meal this morning and Malcolm was quickly losing his patience. Was the world suddenly slowed for some inexplicable reason?

His mother continued unabated. "Yer sister must marry. Arrangements were made prior to ye becoming laird," his mother insisted.

"We cannot very well have a wedding when now ye're against relations."

He wanted to pound his fist on the table, but given the sensitivity of his head, not to mention the watering of his mother's eyes, Malcolm decided against it. "Mother, Verity can marry soon. But not right now. I am sure the bridegroom can wait a few months."

Lady Ross was an imposing woman, used to having her way and unyielding. It was quite obvious Malcolm's strong-willed nature came from her.

"There will be a wedding in a fortnight as planned. I care little for what ye say." His mother jumped to her feet. "Do not dare to try to stop it either."

Once again, she pinpointed him with a steady glare. "Yer Da arranged for it and I will not have ye ruin plans made by him." She stepped down and headed toward the kitchens. "Why is our meal not prepared?"

"More ale," Tristan's deep voice boomed as Malcolm's brother held up his cup to a servant. The second-born son was neither like he nor Kieran, the youngest, in the least. Seeming to take each day as if it was new, he rarely held resentment and was quick to forgive. At least he had been until their father's death.

Nonetheless, although fierce in battle, Tristan never showed any sign of a bad temper nor did he act as if anything was different upon returning home afterwards. It was puzzling to Malcolm who had an easier time relating to Kieran who was currently brooding into his cup. The youngest hated returning from battle, preferring to stay out and await the next.

If there was a complete opposite to Tristan it was Kieran, who was as frightening as he was fair of face.

Kieran's face seemed to take most by surprise upon seeing him. Even men who were not interested in the same gender would often gawk whenever Kieran entered a room.

Although his beauty may have attracted people, his dark personality repelled them. Kieran was rage personified. He hated everything and everyone, barely tolerating his own family on most days.

It had been Kieran who'd been there on the day their father was killed. On the youngest of the Ross' son's shoulders was the boulder-sized burden of guilt. Although no one faulted him, Kieran carried the responsibility of his father's death. In the months that followed, he'd become distant and angry to the point of rage.

Servants marched in with trays of steaming food. A red-faced Moira rushed forward with a tray and came straight to the high board. "My apologies, Laird. Time got away from me. I tried to hurry the food and ended up with a burnt disaster." The woman babbled, apologizing while serving Malcolm and his brothers.

"Tis not words we need right now, Woman," Kieran snapped.

Annoyed at Kieran, Malcolm narrowed his eyes in his brother's direction. If there was a soft spot left in Kieran, it had always been for the sweet cook.

"Do not be distressed," he told the woman who looked about to cry. "We eat now and that is what matters."

"Thank ye, Laird," Moira replied and approached Kieran slowly. "More bread, dear?"

Kieran looked first to Moira and then to the floor before standing and rounding the table. So tall that he towered over most men, Kieran bent to look down at the diminutive Moira and placed a hand on her shoulder. "Forgive me."

The woman sniffed and nodded, then headed back to the kitchen.

"There's no need to apologize to a servant," their mother snapped, sitting down to eat. "Everything is horrible since yer father left. Nothing is the same."

Tristan huffed. "Father did not leave. He died."

The same argument occurred regularly. Their mother not seeming to accept that her husband was gone and Tristan annoyed about it. It did little good to correct her. She pretended not to hear.

Like the others in the family, his mother had also changed in the last couple months. She was bitter and resentful, constantly complaining or demanding things. His sister wasn't much better. Verity, who'd always been a spoiled, immature girl was now almost tyrannical.

Malcolm almost laughed at considering the battlefield was a respite compared to life at the keep.

"We must speak of the wedding." His mother resumed their earlier conversation. "If we don't proceed as planned, the Munro will consider it a slight on our part." From where she sat at the end of the table, Verity watched intently. Obviously, she tried to gather what her future held. Her face reddened and she jumped from her seat, the chair flying backward.

"I don't wish to get married. There is no need for it at all," she yelled. "I choose to remain here."

Malcolm didn't bother scolding her. Little good it would do. Instead, he looked to his mother. "If there were to be a wedding, it would be the perfect opportunity for the McLeods to attack. We can use it as bait."

At Verity's triumphant expression, his mother scowled. "Go to yer room, Verity. I am tired of yer outbursts."

"I will not until I know for sure what will be done. This is my life…"

Malcolm met Tristan's gaze and then motioned to Verity with his head. Within moments, their sister was swooped up and carried away to be locked in her chamber.

"What if it's a discreet affair, without much in the way of feasting or music? She and I and perhaps a guard of eight can travel to…" his mother persisted.

Malcolm had enough. His food had become cold and he pushed the plate aside. "Good plan, Mother. What a perfect way for us to trap the McLeods than to send ye and my sister as decoys. Of course, ye'll probably die before we reach ye, but that is obviously a price ye are willing to pay for this wedding to take place."

His mother blanched. Without a word, she left the room.

CHAPTER FOUR

IT WAS AN unusually warm day and Elspeth was glad for it. Gathering herbs in the forest meant hours in the dank, cold shade with only trickles of sunrays that managed to get through the thick canopy of branches. Walking along a narrow path, with her basket dangling from her arm, she let out a contented sigh and looked up to the tree branches at a loud ruckus of birds chirping.

Not too far from the loch, she considered it would be a wonderful day for a swim and perhaps after gathering herbs, she'd suggest it to her unhappy escort.

Over her shoulder, she spied Conor, her younger brother, who by the annoyed expression wished to be anywhere but there. He hated going with her and guarding as she harvested herbs, often pronouncing it a waste of his time. The lanky young man bent over to pick up a branch and threw it.

Conor wanted to learn blacksmithing from their father, hoped to one day take over, but between the constant trips to the battlefields and escorting either her, their mother or grandmother, he rarely had time to himself. It was almost enough to make Elspeth feel bad except that, in her opinion, he was not exactly suffering and, besides, he already spent plenty of time with their father.

"Hurry up, will ye? Tis getting late and I would like to help father this afternoon," Conor said, throwing a stick and then bending to pick up another.

Elspeth rolled her eyes. "We've just arrived."

Doing her best to ignore her brooding brother, she continued picking the herbs she'd been taught to use.

It was strange how the plants grew in some of the same spots that her tutor had indicated even a year after he'd suddenly gone. Elspeth took a breath and lowered to a tree stump, her gaze moving across the underbrush.

Conor neared. "How do ye know which plants to pluck?"

"My teacher, a traveling monk, taught me everything."

"Who?"

Elspeth was glad he asked questions. Perhaps he'd allow her to linger longer. "Grandmother and I came for walks and often sat with him. He would point out plants and tell us the healing properties."

They'd first met on a day while out in the forest, and she'd been startled by a wild boar. Fearing for her life, Elspeth had raced as fast as her legs could carry her toward her home. Unfortunately, having to run in circles to avoid the angry beast, she'd become disoriented and lost.

Suddenly, a man wearing a hooded tunic, which was tied at the waist with a rustic belt, appeared out of nowhere. Elspeth had rushed to him insisting he run, but he'd calmly turned toward the boar and stared down the raging beast. The animal had snorted several times, pawed at the ground and then to her surprise, turned and trotted away.

"How did ye do that?" Elspeth had asked, trying to catch her breath. "I thought it was going to kill me. I am sure it had every intention of it."

"I doubt it," the monk had replied gently. "The beast is ensuring ye are aware of his territory."

"By chasing me and goring me to death?" She'd been incredulous.

The monk was short and slender, with a heavily-bearded face. Other than bright blue eyes, it was hard to tell what he looked like. Waving a hand as if presenting her to the forest, he'd motioned to the trees. "Come. I have something to show ye."

Not trusting the stranger, she'd taken a couple of steps back. "I must go home. My brothers are no doubt searching for me now." Elspeth had looked around in an attempt to get her bearings. "Which way to the village?"

Instead of a reply, the monk had moved to a patch of greenery. "When boiled, the leaves will cure stomach ailments."

When she remained silent, he'd moved to a different plant, that one more of a bush. "This plant, when dried and mixed in ale, will render a good night's sleep."

Despite trepidation at first, Elspeth remained for a long while as he pointed to different plants and explained their healing properties. He seemed tireless and, although enthralled, her head spun from too much information.

"I must retrieve something to make sketches," she'd said, interrupting him. "I cannot remember all of this."

He'd nodded in understanding. "Return tomorrow." The sparkling blue eyes had made her smile. "Try to avoid the boar." He pointed with his right hand. "Yer village is in that direction."

For a long time after, Elspeth had met the monk and he'd taught her about healing as she sketched the different leaves and drew pictures, writing simple words to explain what the plants did. Elspeth barely knew enough to write basic things, so she depended on pictures and hoped her sketches would be enough to remember everything he'd taught her.

Sure her parents would not approve of meeting with the man alone, she'd recruited her grandmother to accompany her.

Over time, she became sought after to heal the sick, provide aid to those injured and even helped her grandmother deliver babies. Her gift of healing was something she enjoyed.

Since the battling of clans, her father insisted Conor accompany her to gather herbs, which was bothersome since he had little patience for it.

Elspeth mused at how, since the war between clans had begun, her sense of accomplishment in healing had ended. The fulfillment of helping those in need lost its luster in the face of the clan battles. Yes, she still wanted to help the wounded and injured, and did her best to get there in time to save lives. However, the needlessness of it all made her downhearted. That men did this to one another was heartbreaking.

Upon spotting a rather large patch of herbs, she crouched down and placed her basket on the ground.

"Conor, can I borrow yer knife?" When there was no reply, Elspeth looked up to find the rascal had left. She huffed in annoyance. Not that she was scared to be in the forest alone, but more because her father threatened that she'd not be allowed to forage without Conor along.

"Conor?" she hissed and waited. The wind in the trees and rustling of leaves were accompanied by another sound. Splashes. It was the unmistakable sound of someone swimming. Her brother must have gone for a dip.

"He cannot very well watch over me from the loch," Elspeth said, lifting her skirts and stomping toward the water's edge. She searched the ground for a stick or a stone to throw at her annoying brother. Triumphant at finding a short, thick branch, she put her basket on the ground, crouched down and snuck toward the water's edge.

Hiding behind a fallen tree, she rose up just enough to peek over it. A long arm extended out of the water followed by a second. When he dove, his bottom lifted out of the water and then disappeared.

Elspeth's lips curved. When he turned around, she'd throw the branch and hit him right on the rump. Giggling, she moved closer, this time hiding behind a bush. Once again, he swam back in the opposite direction and when he dove, she threw the stick with all her might. At the satisfying "whomp", she fell to the ground laughing.

There was splashing, cussing and wild slapping as he came out of the water.

Elspeth could barely get her breath. "Th-that…is…wh-what…ye g-get for not wa-watching over me." She couldn't see past the tears of mirth.

A shadow came across her, but she couldn't stop laughing long enough to look at him. Conor was silent, probably figuring how to get her back. But he would never lay a hand on her. Their father had never allowed it.

When pulled up by her arms and thrown over a shoulder, she sputtered. "What are ye doing?"

Since when had Conor gotten so strong? He headed to the water, carrying her with ease. Elspeth bounced on his shoulder. "Conor, put me down this instant."

"I am not Conor," the man said. Then without hesitation, he tossed her into the loch.

Eyes wide, all mirth evaporated. She turned while in the air and caught a glimpse of who'd thrown her just as she hit the water. An entirely naked Malcolm Ross stood on the bank with a murderous expression.

Stunned at the situation, Elspeth was not prepared for what happened next. She hit the water hard and sank like a stone. Although she could swim like a duck, it was impossible to untangle herself from the long skirts that floated up and over her head. She struggled wildly, attempting to free herself in a rising panic.

Not only had she just hit one of the most feared warriors with a stick, but now said man was probably taking great satisfaction in watching her being drowned by her own skirts.

Malcolm stared at the water and waited for the woman to emerge. Bubbles came to the surface and he narrowed his eyes. Was the minx up to another trick? Why hadn't she surfaced yet? He walked closer ensuring to keep his distance but, at the same time, trying to scan across the water to see where she was. Once again, bubbles surfaced in almost the same location.

It dawned on him that she'd been fully dressed and, no doubt, the thick wool dress made it hard for her to swim. He cursed and dove in.

Sure enough, she was just a few feet in over her head with the skirts around her arms, shoulders and head. She was struggling fiercely, so much so that when he grabbed her, it was hard to keep from being hit. He pulled her none-too-gently from the water and onto the shore where both lay spent. She coughed and sputtered. He sat up and watched to make sure she could breathe.

"Ye," she sputtered. "Almost drowned me." Coughing, she rolled to her side, her body shaking with each round of hacks and sputters.

"And ye could have hit me in the head and done the same," he retorted, unsure why he remained and didn't leave. There wasn't time to be wasting with the woman who'd obviously wanted to kill him.

"I thought ye were my…brother," she said breathlessly. "Besides, I did not aim for yer head."

Not wishing to hear anything more, he stood and pulled her to her feet. Her gaze roamed down from his face and to his body. It was entertaining that her cheeks turned a bright crimson. "Ye should not be here."

"It's my land."

Her eyes narrowed. "Tis closer to my village."

Malcolm went to where he'd left his tartan, picked it up and wrapped it around his midsection. "Go away."

"Do ye not want to know about Ian?" she asked, seeming to search for something else to be angry with him about. "He is yer warrior, is he not?"

"I assume he is alive," he began, and then deciding against asking anything else, stopped speaking.

"Aye he is. But very ill."

"I did not expect he would live."

"Still may not. Ye could see about him." She narrowed her eyes. "Instead of frolicking."

"I do not frolic."

She lifted an eyebrow, her green eyes going dark. "I have no desire to argue with ye."

"Away with ye then," he replied airily.

"Will ye not apologize then?" With feet planted apart, she placed fisted hands on her hips.

The woman was dripping wet, the clothing plastered to every curve. Round, plush breasts high on her chest may as well have been on full display as her soaked white blouse and chemise did little to hide them. His gaze lingered on the pert tips that beckoned a man to suckle.

She would make a good bedmate if she were the kind to allow bedding without commitment.

Malcolm was about to propose a tryst when she slapped him so hard his head snapped to the right and his neck popped.

"Ye are despicable," Elspeth yelled. Lifting her sodden skirts, she did her best to hurry away into the forest, but shuffled more than sprinted.

Running his hand down his face, Malcolm let out a long breath. He looked toward where she ran off noticing she'd left her basket behind. Served the wench right.

The corners of his lips inched up, just a bit, and he rubbed his jaw as she disappeared. If it weren't for the fact women were a distraction, she would be worth pursuing.

Chapter Five

Clyde McLeod sat forward in his seat on the high board as several of his guards entered the great room.

"Laird, the messenger has returned." The guard hesitated and looked to Ethan, his youngest son. "He's dead."

"We have our answer then." Alec, the older son, stood from the table. "We have our damned answer." He groaned in frustration. "The Ross will not stop until they see every single one of us dead."

"Or we kill them," Ethan, the younger son, replied, slamming his fist on the tabletop. "I do not understand why we…"

"Cease talking at once," his father interrupted. "It is because of yer rashness that we find ourselves in this impossible situation."

Ethan would not be quieted. "Why do ye consider it impossible? We can fight, we are not weaklings."

Alec had had enough. His brother refused to see the consequences of his actions as a detriment. Quite the opposite, he seemed to take pride in having killed Laird Ross.

"Ye killed their laird, the father of some of the best warriors in our region." Between clenched teeth, he continued. "Clan Ross is twice our size, their warriors outnumber us."

The laird motioned the guard closer. "See that the messenger's family is rewarded. Take two men to his home and assist in the burial."

"Aye, Laird," the guardsmen left to their miserable task.

Clyde turned to Ethan, motioning to the departing men. "That is what ye've caused. Go with them. Ensure ye remain quiet or I will see that ye are whipped and thrown into the dungeon."

Ethan's eyes narrowed, but he stood and went after the guards.

"If they do not allow even a messenger, how can we possibly get them to agree to a meeting?" a member of the council asked.

"Perhaps deliver a missive with an arrow?" another proposed.

Alec studied his father's weary expression and let out a breath. "Up until that day several months ago, we'd lived in relative peace with Clan Ross. My mother and Lady Ross had even formed a friendship. Perhaps that is a possible way to reach out to them. Send a woman to speak to Lady Ross…" He stopped speaking.

"We can declare ourselves as surrendering?" an older man, member of the council said. "Twould be a loss of pride for our clan, but will save many lives."

Scouts had reported seeing Ross warriors on the outskirts of their land. At only a few weeks since their last battle, it seemed their enemies itched for another confrontation.

They were forced to protect their people and their livestock or chance starving once winter came. Already, two farms and several small villages had been razed to the ground. The people who'd come to their home to find shelter lived there now within the keep gates. There was little room left, but more would be welcome rather than left to die.

"Prepare our warriors," Laird McLeod said in a weary tone. "Ensure to send only the strongest and best this time. Guard our southern border where the Ross' were seen. Our men are not to engage until approached. For now, we will try to keep from fighting."

He turned to his wife as she entered. For days, she'd been helping the healers and looked weary. "Come, Wife, I must ask something of ye."

As his parents spoke, Alec paced. He was too tense to remain seated and his mind whirled with possibilities at what to do about the current situation. In his heart, he knew the only thing that would satisfy Malcolm Ross would be to see his own father dead and it was something he'd not allow.

Up until this point, Clyde had remained behind when they'd gone to battle. However, his father hated it and would not continue to remain behind in the keep while his men fought.

There had to be a way out of the situation. That they were considering sending a woman to relay a message was not only dangerous, but also not the best way to go about gaining their people's trust.

There had to be another way.

Gwyneth, a comely woman he'd often bedded until recently, darkened the hallway and beckoned him with both hands. By the rapid motion, something was amiss.

"Can ye spare a few moments?" she asked, her eyes moving from his face to the back garden. "A woman is in the kitchen garden and asks to speak to ye."

He let out a breath. The last thing he needed at the moment was to be bothered with two women who wished to find out which he favored the most. "I do not have time…"

Gwyneth didn't bother to hide her annoyance. "I told her that, but she insists."

"Very well," he replied and looked over his shoulder. His parents continued speaking, while the council members held separate conversations.

Hoping to hear what the woman had to say to be over in quick time, he stalked down the short hall and on past the kitchens. Upon spotting him, his dog got up and stretched lazily. The hound was at his side when he walked out and into the garden.

A blonde woman stood, a shawl pulled tightly around her too-thin shoulders. Blue, tear-filled eyes met his for a moment and then she ducked into a quick curtsy.

"I thank ye for coming out," she said in a hoarse whisper that made him lean closer to hear. "I must ask ye for assistance."

"What happened to ye?" he asked, expecting she was ill and needed asylum. "Are ye ill?"

"Nay, I am not." A cough and shiver told otherwise. "I require yer help in finding my brother…" Her eyes welled up with tears. "He is all I have, ye see. He came here to ask for work and has not returned."

"What is his name?" Alec asked, his stomach tightening as he already knew the reply.

"Daegen," she said in a shaky voice. "He is blond, we…favor…"

The messenger. Somehow, she and the group headed to her home had missed each other.

Alec took a fortifying breath. "Come inside. Eat." He touched her shoulder and led her into the kitchen. "A bowl of food and warm drink," Alec instructed.

When she sat and looked around in astonishment, Alec lowered to a chair. "What is yer name?"

"Paige," she replied, taking a deep drink of the warm cider. "My brother and I live near the loch."

"Yer parents?" he asked, wondering who the party headed to her home would find.

"Only my grandfather remains. He is at home awaiting my return." She eyed the plate placed before her. "If it is agreeable, may I take this home to him?"

"Eat," he instructed and then met the cook's gaze. "Prepare a basket of food for her to take."

Her gaze rested on his for a moment and he couldn't help but notice how lovely she was. "Ye are kind."

While she ate her fill, Alec waited. It would be soon enough that he would have to tell her about her brother's unfortunate death. The young man had arrived two days prior, eager to be of assistance. From what he knew, her brother had volunteered to go to the Ross' lands, claiming to be friendly with them. Now, he wondered if it was true.

"I must return. Perhaps my brother is home now." Paige stood and Alec walked out with her.

He took her by the shoulders turning her to face him. "Yer brother is dead. He was killed this morning. He was very brave. Went to Ross lands with a missive."

Thankfully, he caught her before she collapsed in a heap. Her legs gave out as she absorbed the information. Alec pulled her against him as sobs racked her slight body. She clenched the fabric of his tunic like a kitten fearing the touch of its mother.

"No. It cannot be. No." Paige pushed back and wiped angrily at her face. "Why him? Why did ye send him?" Her bloodshot eyes pinned him, her face transformed with fury. "Ye purposely sent him to his death."

There was no use in arguing. For it was true. It hadn't been him who'd sent the messenger, but it may as well have been. "I am truly sorry," he said, meaning it. Then without thinking, he reached forward and wiped her tears with his plaid. "Do not cry."

Seeming shocked by his actions, Paige remained as still as a stone, only a sniffle here and there. Her breathing remained ragged and he knew she was wondering what would become of her family now. They'd obviously depended on her brother for food and, given her thinness, it was apparent he'd been struggling to find work. His willingness to volunteer for the task of messenger was further proof of how desperate their plight had become. The clan war had a debilitating effect on his people and Alec decided if anyone would go to the Ross and ask for a truce, it should be he.

"Come, I will escort ye home." He looked directly into her eyes. "It would probably be best for yer grandfather and ye to come here to live."

She nodded, seeming to run out of energy. "May be the best for my grandfather is old and ill."

The need to take care of her grandfather was obviously more precious than her pride as she allowed him to take her by the elbow. "Wait here in the garden," he said, guiding her to a bench. "I will retrieve my horse."

Paige sank to sit, all life seeming to have gone from her. Anger filled Alec knowing his brother did not care one bit at the consequences of his actions.

Just moments later, with her slight frame against his chest, they rode the short distance to Paige's small cottage. The party including the guards and Ethan remained. As the two men dug a grave, Ethan stood by, his expression impassive.

The men stopped to gauge the threat of his nearing. Then upon recognizing him, they relaxed. He rode to the front of the cottage, dismounted and assisted Paige down. She rushed to where they'd laid her brother and began to sob anew. An old man emerged from the cottage, a slight smile on his craggy face and eyes that no longer saw what truly happened. "Ah, I see ye have come, Clyde," he said, calling Alec by his father's name. "It took ye long enough to seek revenge on my beating ye last time we played." The old man chuckled then looked to where his granddaughter was crying. He shook his head.

"Come now, dear. Fix our visitors something warm for their bellies. I grow quite hungry."

Alec reached for the sacks that hung from his steed's saddle. "I bring food. Perhaps ye would like a bit of wine?"

The old man chuckled, allowing Alec to guide him to a chair beside the front door. There was a well-built overhang that would shield people from the elements and both chairs and table that were under it were also very well made.

Paige's brother had obviously been a good carpenter, by the looks of every part of the sturdy structure. It was a shame he would not be building anything now.

CHAPTER SIX

MALCOLM ENTERED THE great room to find his brothers and his cousin, Aiden, seated as his uncle, Gregor Ross, paced, stalking from one end of the room to the other.

Upon noting Malcolm, Gregor glared in his direction. "There was no need for such savage action. What have we become that we slaughter a messenger without allowing him to speak?"

Unsure of what exactly had transpired, he settled into a chair and motioned for a servant to bring him drink. The girl hurried over with a tankard and filled it to the rim. "I will fetch some cheese and bread, Laird," she whispered and hurried away as if afraid of him.

He watched her go, immediately disregarding her. There were more important things to worry about, obviously by the way his uncle now slashed across the air with his right hand, effectively shutting down any arguments that either Tristan or Kieran raised. "Tis not the way yer father would have wanted it."

At hearing this, Malcolm stood and walked to stand on the other side of the table where his brothers, Aiden and uncle had gathered. "What happened?"

It was Aiden that replied. "The McLeods sent a messenger. Our archers killed him upon seeing the McLeod plaid upon him."

Malcolm slid his gaze to Kieran. "Our archers? Or was it ye, Brother?"

As usual, the much too beautiful face shuttered. Kieran shrugged. "What does it matter?"

"It matters," Malcolm replied, pounding a fist on the table. "If they were to offer a truce, we would ask that Laird McLeod and that dog, his son Ethan, give themselves to us."

"They would not do it," Kieran replied, tearing a piece of bread from a freshly made loaf that the serving wench had brought for Malcolm. "Why waste time listening to drivel?"

Their uncle's dark brown eyes flashed angrily to him. "This," he motioned with his hand to Kieran, "is yer creation. Clan Ross has become an army of heartless heretics who care little for humanity."

"Tis vengeance and I do not care the cost as long as we capture the bastard son of a whore who killed my father," Malcolm replied in a flat tone. The words he'd often repeated stood hollow in the air.

No one responded. It was as if they'd grown weary of the same sentence repeated each time their council met.

Gregor rose to his full towering height and shook his head like a hound fresh out of water. "Tis not what my brother would want. It is not the way of Clan Ross." His voice boomed. "I understand vengeance and was glad at first to beat their warriors in a battle showing our anger. However, although Clan McLeod is smaller, it will be a long time before any war with them is over."

The middle brother, Tristan, had always been the peacemaker, and although a warrior to be feared, he was the most levelheaded of the three brothers. "Uncle, ye must understand how we feel. It was the McLeods who provoked us. It was them who came onto our lands when father was visiting a farmer. It was them who slaughtered him without provocation."

"I do understand," his uncle replied in a tight voice. "I, like ye, also wished to show our fury. However, after all these months of battle, they remain steadfast and willing to defend. Aye, I know we can beat them…"

"However?" Malcolm, who'd seated again, asked, leaning forward to place an elbow on the table.

His uncle lowered his voice. "We are losing too many men, are almost equal in injuries and losses. If we send more men and use our entire army, it would be a massacre and what will be won by that?"

Malcolm waited for a response to his uncle's words to come from within. There was not even a slight stirring in his chest. Neither sadness nor foreboding filled him. There wasn't a heaviness at knowing more would die, nor was there any sense of jubilation at the knowledge they would probably win.

"I want that bastard dead."

"Then send someone to kill him. But stop this war. Declare a truce. Obviously, they admit that we have the upper hand else they would not send a messenger."

Malcolm began to eat the cheese and bread, his mind returning to the scene at the forest. The woman, Elspeth, seemed to hate him. He cared little what the villagers thought about him and yet a part of him wondered if a truce of any kind mattered at this point.

At noticing his father's empty chair, his heart hardened and he narrowed his eyes. "We fight again at dawn."

His uncle's shoulders rounded and he lowered to a chair, defeated. Malcolm didn't care that it wasn't his uncle's fight and yet it should be. Did the man not care that his own brother was slaughtered for no real reason. That amidst defending his people, the youngest son of Laird McLeod had taken no mercy and sliced him from one side of the abdomen to the other?

Guards came, seeming to know orders awaited, and Kieran went to them. "We must prepare."

His cousin, Aiden, stood and stretched. "I will alert my men. Best go to see about my other needs as well." He flashed a smile and left.

"Whoring will not make ye a better fighter," Tristan called after him. Then seeming to think on it, stalked to a long table where serving women cleaned. He took one and threw her over his shoulder. The startled woman yelped, but soon relaxed, her head bouncing as Tristan took the steps two at a time up to his bedchamber.

Malcolm sat back and stared at his uncle and two remaining guards. "Have our scouts returned?"

One of the guards, the one who'd taken Ian's place, shook his head. "Nay, but I expect them at any time."

"Good. Once they do we will discuss our plan."

"When will it cease?" His uncle spoke again, his voice tight. "When not just every warrior, but yer brothers lay dead?"

He considered it for a moment. Would he feel anything? Did it matter who lived and died around him anymore?

Malcolm felt absolutely nothing.

THE CLASHING OF metal against metal, screams of both men and beast filled the air. Malcolm caught sight of a young fighter vomiting while attempting to hold his midsection, blood oozing through his fingers. Whether he was a McLeod or a Ross was impossible to say as the fighter's clothing was covered with blood and mud.

Malcolm turned to defend against the downswing of a sword and rage filled him at recognizing his opponent. Face twisted in a sneer, Ethan McLeod thrust forward, intent on spearing him through the midsection.

Malcolm moved sideways and swung his sword straight across with all his might. The bastard needed to die just like Malcolm's father had.

But Ethan was a worthy opponent, easily evading the strike and countering with a strong swing of his own.

The swords hit so hard that both of their arms shook. "Go to hell," Malcolm exclaimed, thrusting forward.

Once again, Ethan evaded and blocked. They swung more times until Malcolm lost his footing when another fighting duo fell against him. When he turned to defend against Ethan, the man was gone.

Before Malcolm could go after him, a different McLeod warrior attacked.

As the battling continued, out of the corner of his eyes, Malcolm caught sight of Tristan fighting an opponent almost as huge as his brother. Tristan was a relentless warrior who'd never been beaten in battle. He was as agile as he was immense. That fact often threw his opponents off.

Kieran was out of sight, but present nonetheless by the many who fell after being struck by an arrow.

"Retreat!" a man called out and the McLeods ran toward their mounts and into the forest, some chased by Ross warriors.

Malcolm raced after them, furious at noting Ethan was being tossed across a horse's back. The idiot had been injured. All he could do was pray it was a mortal wound.

Then and only then did Malcolm fall to his knees, exhaustion finally allowed to make its appearance. He took a shaky breath, his arms and legs quivering as the energy of the battle ebbed from him.

Too dazed to care, he watched as men hurried to and fro searching for survivors. There didn't seem to be many as the battle had been evenly matched. On both sides, they'd not cared to maim or injure but only to kill. So many months of fighting had brought out the lack of emotion that normally came when taking another human being's life.

The tactics had changed. Malcolm wasn't sure when, but they had. In the beginning, there had been many injured. Now the dead far outnumbered the injured. And those who were injured were left because they would not survive.

If Clan McLeod had taken Ethan, it was only because he was the laird's son. So that he could die in his father's presence.

A part of him wondered if that would be punishment enough. Would it cause the thirst for vengeance to ebb at knowing Laird McLeod would stand by uselessly as his son died for his own actions that caused a war between clans?

Hoping his legs would keep him upright, Malcolm stood and went to find his horse. Hopefully, the beast had survived. The animal waited near a bush, its massive hooves pawing at the ground. His steed was bred for war and as battles continued, it seemed to grow stronger and more energetic.

Other than a shallow wound to its hindquarter, Malcolm's horse was uninjured. He patted the animal's big head. "Time for a rest, Rab."

It was then he noted a small wagon. It was the same one that had taken Ian away, which meant Elspeth was there somewhere.

Malcolm whirled around, not knowing why. Amongst those that lay about, he spotted her making her way about gingerly, squatting every so often to inspect someone.

Suddenly, she stumbled backward, her gaze crossing the distance between them. It was then he noticed her hands clutching her upper chest. She'd been stabbed. The injured man had mistaken her for an attacker.

Malcolm raced to Elspeth just as she collapsed.

Chapter Seven

When Conor burst through the door, he was so breathless it took a minute for him to formulate words. Ceilidh went to the doorway to peer out, expecting a wagon with injured. Instead, it stood empty.

"Where is Elspeth?"

Conor's mother and grandmother came to see what occurred and stopped at hearing her question, their eyes wide.

Conor looked between them and shook his head. "She was injured, stabbed by a wounded man." He gulped and attempted to continue, but was peppered with questions one after another.

"Why didn't ye bring her?"

"Go back and get her."

"Tell me where she is?"

"Go on, Boy, talk," his mother urged, shaking his shoulder.

"The Ross Laird took her," Conor finished weakly. "He would not allow me to intercede."

There was a shocked silence. It was Ceilidh who spoke first. "Why would he do it?"

"They spoke the last time we were at the battlefield," the grandmother said thoughtfully. "Perhaps he means to take her to their healer."

"That useless old man?" Conor spat. "He cannot possibly be of help. I came to get ye, Grandmother. We should go to her."

"It's so dangerous," his mother replied. "Everyone who goes there does so knowing an archer could mistake them for a McLeod and spear them through the heart."

Everyone retreated to his or her own thoughts for a brief moment.

Finally, Elspeth's mother spoke. "How bad was the injury?"

Conor shook his head. "From what I could see, he stabbed her in the shoulder area."

"Perhaps a shallow injury." The woman wiped a tear. "My poor girl."

Elspeth's mother looked to the doorway. "We cannot tell Gil or my husband. They will rush there without care for their lives."

Everyone nodded in agreement. Finally, Ceilidh held up a hand to get everyone's attention. "I will speak to Ian; he may be well enough to be transported there. In exchange, we will retrieve Elspeth."

At the idea, everyone brightened.

Elspeth's mother's pleading gaze met hers. "Go speak to him. Hurry. We will make the excuse to my husband that ye and she, along with Conor, went to take him back to the keep."

Upon entering the sick room, Ceilidh lost her bravado. She'd never actually spent more than a few moments alone with the warrior. Although injured, he was intimidating. His gaze snapped to her when she entered, the blue-green eyes, the color of the loch in the late summer, not wavering.

She neared his bed, her gaze going to his injured midsection. It was too soon to move him. They were putting his life in danger to save Elspeth.

"How fare thee?"

Ian seemed surprised by the question and grimaced. "Well."

It was obviously a lie, but she let it pass and went to a side table to mix the herb tincture Elspeth had taught her to make for pain. "We need to take ye to Ross Keep. However, I am worried it may be too soon."

When she turned, he was studying her. "I will survive."

Although he didn't ask, she felt compelled to explain. "Elspeth was injured today at the battlefield. An injured man plunged a knife into her."

His eyes widened just a bit. "Tis a dangerous thing she does by going there." Seeming to collect his thoughts, he frowned. "Where is she?"

"Yer laird took her."

"Malcolm? Why would he…" He stopped himself from continuing. "So ye wish to exchange me for her."

It was a statement, not a question but she replied. "Yes. Her family…we want her back. We need to treat her."

"She will not be harmed. Our healer is well practiced."

Although she wanted to believe him, she knew firsthand how cruel Clan Ross was. "Ye cannot expect me to believe that."

"Tis true. My laird would never harm a defenseless woman." He shifted as if to move and groaned in pain. "I will need help."

She met his gaze and something in her chest shifted. He was the most attractive man she'd ever seen. Even with only one arm, he was formidable. "I feel badly. Ye are not healed enough."

Ian lifted a shoulder in a shrug. "I can remain in bed there the same as here."

Ceilidh neared with a cup in which she'd mixed the herbs with ale. "Drink this. It will help with the pain of moving ye."

Their hands touched as he took the cup. His gaze passed over her face and then down to his left where the sleeve of his tunic hung limply.

It would take time for him to become accustomed to the missing limb. She wanted to reassure him that regardless of it, he would heal and become as strong as before.

"Do ye plan to go to battle upon healing?" she asked as a form of assuring him she didn't see him as an invalid.

For a moment, she wasn't sure he would reply. Finally, he nodded. "I wish to, yes."

"I was hoping ye would say no." Ceilidh smiled. "However, men can be so stubborn."

He let out a breath. "Without a woman to ensure we remain controlled perhaps, aye."

Emboldened by his banter, she pretended to ponder his words. "Sir, tis not true. Ye do what ye wish at all times. I can see that in yer gaze."

His lips curved, just a bit. She waited for him to drink every drop of the liquid and remained by as his eyelids drooped.

Suddenly, his eyes opened and he met her gaze. "Ye are quite lovely. Why is it ye are not married?"

Ceilidh wasn't sure how to reply. By the unfocused way he watched her, the herbs had taken effect and it loosed his tongue. "Perhaps I am waiting for a fierce warrior to carry me off."

When his brows furrowed, she wanted to laugh. It was taking time for the words to filter.

"I would carry ye off."

A chuckle escaped. "No, ye would not. I am far too independent for ye."

"My wife will nay be a woman with no opinion. I like yer way."

He would probably have no memory of what they'd said. Ceilidh nodded. "Very well then. Once ye recover, I will await to be taken away."

Ian's eyes fell closed but his lips curved. "I will not fail."

Just a few moments later, his mouth went slack as he fell asleep.

"We will be gentle with ye," Ceilidh whispered when his head lolled to the side. Then as gently as she could, she pushed the hair on his forehead aside and placed a light kiss upon the warm skin.

When Elspeth's father and older brother entered to help move Ian, she watched them without speaking, as she wasn't sure what they'd been told. The grandmother oversaw the transport of Ian, her eyes meeting Ceilidh's conspiratorially.

Finally, Ian was placed in a pile of blankets and covered with furs that were tucked into his sides to keep him comfortable and, hopefully, from jostling too much.

Conor went to the bench and pretended to be aggravated. "What is taking Elspeth so long?"

The grandmother went to her son and grandson. "Can ye come and assist me in moving the kitchen table? I want to scrub the floors."

The trio went inside and Ceilidh hurried to the back of the wagon. She wrapped a shawl around her shoulders and over her head in the hopes that if either of the men looked out, they'd mistake her for Elspeth.

"Go slowly," she instructed Conor. "We can't jostle him too much."

Over his shoulder, Conor gave her a worried look. "I pray we make it there and back without Da discovering what we are doing."

CHAPTER EIGHT

THE MISTS GAVE way to a sunny day as Aiden peered out over the loch. His dark gaze moved from across the wooden view. As usual, other than an occasional bird, the vantage point from his bedroom was useless.

If he truly wished to see more, it would have to be from the rooftop where archers maintained constant guard. He went there every other day, not too often as he didn't wish to raise suspicions as to why he was so interested in the surroundings.

Cursing, he turned to the bed. Upon it, his cousin lay, fast asleep. Verity was nothing more than a conquest. A means to an end. They'd been sleeping together for only a few weeks and already he'd grown bored with her.

Clinging and demanding, she pressured him daily to go forth and ask for her hand in marriage.

If not for not wanting to wake her, he would chuckle. His cousin, Malcolm, would not only laugh him out of the room, but also send him to be whipped for daring to touch his precious sister.

Idiot.

His father was no better. Always bowing to the laird, never in charge, but more of an advisor. It churned his stomach to watch the man follow behind the laird like a dog in need of a spare morsel.

Verity stirred and so did his manhood. Perhaps he should take his frustrations out on the woman. He marched to the bed and yanked the coverings off of her nude body.

"Get on yer hands and knees," he ordered without ensuring she was fully awake.

She frowned, her dazed eyes meeting his. "What?"

Not waiting for her to say or do anything else that would annoy him further, he pulled her to the edge of the bed and rolled her to her stomach. "I said get on yer knees."

"I'm not awake and a bit sore from last night..." she said and then whined when he yanked her up to the position he wanted her in. "Shut up, Verity."

Her wide eyes met his over her shoulder. "What are ye doing?"

Taking himself in hand, he nudged at her entrance. "Taking ye as I want. Fucking ye until ye cannot take more."

Not waiting for her to be prepared, he thrust into her until fully seated and then pulled out and repeated the movement.

The sounds of slapping as their bodies collided made him even harder and he dug his fingers into the soft flesh of her buttocks, holding her in place as he pounded into her. He wanted to punish her, to take out his fury on who represented the family that he was dependent on.

Verity's mewls made him angrier. The bitch was enjoying it. She let out a loud scream as her sex constricted around his hardness. Aiden wanted to pull out and not finish, but he'd gone past the point of no return.

Once again, he took hold of her hips and thrust in once, twice and a third time. Just as he came, he pulled out and spilled his seed onto the bed.

Fully spent, Verity collapsed, her breathing labored. Aiden stalked back to the window. How he hated his lot in life.

THE INTERIOR OF the room was so very different than her bedchamber at the village and Elspeth did her best to not gawk as they waited for the healer to appear. Her wound had been washed out as she'd directed and then to her chagrin, the servant girl had refused to sew it closed. Elspeth eyed the door with suspicion. She'd not allowed any type of pumice to be stuffed into the wound.

For his part, Malcolm paced from one side of the room to the other, often barking orders and ignoring requests that he sit.

A woman entered and walked to him, her hips swaying a bit too much in Elspeth's estimation.

"My laird, would ye like me to arrange for a bath in yer chambers? I can accompany ye there if ye wish."

The darkened gaze met hers for a split second before landing on the woman. "Nay. Go and leave me be."

When the woman turned to Elspeth, her eyes were like daggers. "And who is she?"

Instead of replying, Malcolm took the woman's arm and none-so-gently pulled her to the door, opened it and pushed her out. "Go see about my bath."

He turned back, his gaze moving over her. This time, it was not like back at the loch when it had been more than obvious what was on his mind. No, this time there was concern. "I should send a messenger to yer family."

Elspeth gasped at considering she'd not thought of that. Surely, everyone at home was fretting and her poor mother probably feared the worst.

"That would be most appreciated." She couldn't bring herself to add "my laird" as he wasn't over the village where she lived. Neither was it McLeod territory.

Instead, the area where her village lay was part of Clan Urquhart, who rarely bothered to oversee them. The arrangement suited both the older laird and the villagers just fine. They didn't have to provide but a small payment yearly and the clan chieftain left them be. It was, however, not a good thing at a time like this when two warring clans surrounded the village.

Finally, the healer entered the room and Elspeth found herself enthralled by the man's speech. His words melted over her, the deep, melodic tones like none she'd ever heard.

"Where are ye from?" she had to ask as the man inspected her wound and, seeming satisfied, called for needle and thread.

"I come from a land across the ocean. Spain."

She didn't understand how it could be that such a man would end up in Scotland, but neither did she ask, as he did not seem inclined to give any additional information.

The stitching was painful and Elspeth found herself crying openly as he sewed and stretched the skin closed.

To her surprise, Malcolm held her free hand and spoke to her in low tones. "I thought ye to be tougher and not cry over a simple needle prick."

She frowned at him. "I am not a fragile creature," she snapped. "However, this hurts."

"No more than a bite from a wee flying creature," he retorted.

Did he really compare the tearing of flesh by a thick instrument to a simple insect bite?

Elspeth wanted to push him away, but flinched when the healer dug the needle in once again. This time, she cried out and sniffed loudly. "Go away, Malcolm Ross. Ye are not helping." In direct contradiction, she squeezed his hand harder when the healer pulled the string through.

How many times had she done this very same thing to others? Most warriors hadn't bothered to flinch as she'd sewn their wounds shut. Either they'd thick, unfeeling skin or she was, indeed, a weak creature.

"Malcolm." A man entered the room and Elspeth thought she'd died and gone to the ever after.

He was the most perfectly formed, most beautiful human she'd ever seen. Whoever it was had golden hair that formed a halo around the exquisiteness of his face. With thickly lashed hazel eyes, a square jawline, perfectly formed nose and lips, he was what she imagined creatures from heaven were like.

The man was the same height as Malcolm, but his shoulders were wider and he had a strange almost distant way about him. His eyes moved to meet hers. They were flat and without any kind of emotion.

"Someone is here to see about yer patient." The golden being's upper lip curled in distaste. "Should I ask the servants to prepare for a festival of some sort?" Sarcasm dripped heavily from each word.

"Nay." Malcolm looked to her. "This ignorant brute is my brother, Kieran."

Kieran didn't bother to acknowledge her. Instead, he concentrated on Malcolm. "What do ye wish to do?"

"Have someone escort them here." Malcolm walked out with his brother and she could hear murmurs from outside the doorway. Unfortunately, they spoke much too softly and she was unable to make out what was being said.

Moments later, Conor and Ceilidh burst through the door. Just behind them at the doorway was the handsome man from before.

"Ye are alive!" Ceilidh rushed to her and took her hand. "I was so worried."

"No need," Elspeth replied, noting that Kieran had left. "I plan to leave immediately and return home so that Father and Mother do not worry overmuch."

Conor looked over his shoulder to where Malcolm had disappeared. "Yer father thinks ye came to bring the injured man. We brought him here. And yer mother knows we came to get ye."

"What?" Elspeth sat up and grimaced when her wound protested. "He is not ready."

Ceilidh let out a shaky breath. "He did well and is being transported to a chamber. They are about to fetch the healer."

As much as she wanted to feel bad, at the same time, Elspeth was glad her parents were not fretting about her. "That was a good plan." She smiled at her dear friend. "But we must return immediately."

"This chamber is wonderful," Ceilidh said as she walked in a circle. "Have ye ever seen such luxury?"

"Nay and we won't again." Elspeth slipped to the edge of the immense bed, not wanting to know whose it was. A part of her acknowledged it was probably Malcolm's. Her wound throbbed and she looked down to the floor, wondering where her shoes were.

A servant walked into the room, the slippered feet silent on the plush rugs. "I bring food and warm cider." She placed a tray upon a table. "My laird insists ye eat before leaving."

Cheese, bread and meat were piled on the tray. Next, the servant returned with another tray with three cups. "Tis a brew made with yarrow root, Mistress," the maid said as she placed the cups down.

Conor and Ceilidh neared the trays just as raised voices sounded. Conor whipped around to the door. "I will see if something is afoot. Remain here."

Elspeth frowned. "I am sure it has nothing to do with us."

"Perhaps I should go see if there is some sort of misunderstanding," Ceilidh said, wringing her hands. "Could it be Ian is not doing well?"

It was obvious to Elspeth that Ceilidh had become attached to the injured warrior. Although endearing, she doubted the feelings would ever be returned. The Ross clansmen were not the sentimental sort.

"Go see, but be careful. We must leave immediately." No sooner were the words out of Elspeth's mouth did Ceilidh rush from the room.

It occurred to Elspeth there was nothing wrong with her feet and she may as well get up, find her shoes and prepare to return home. If she'd not passed out after being stabbed, she wouldn't find herself in this predicament. If something happened to Ian, she'd not forgive herself.

"Where is she?" a voice boomed. "Ye will answer for this."

The voice was familiar and yet so out of place. Elspeth felt a shiver travel down her spine to the bottom of her feet.

There was more murmuring of deep voices and she leaned forward in an attempt to decipher what was being said.

At a thud at the door, she started, her wide eyes locked to the wood. Dear God, if it was who she suspected, what would the consequences be?

Without thought, she climbed back upon the bed and grabbed the bedding, holding it up like a shield, her eyes glued to the door.

Then it was as if time traveled at a slow rate. The door burst open. First, her father entered followed by Malcolm. After that, her older brother walked through the doorway and, lastly, the same angelic man who'd been there earlier, Kieran.

"What is the meaning of this?" Her father's bulging eyes moved from her face to sweep across the bed. "Why are ye upon the bed like a wanton?"

Elspeth's mouth opened and closed and before she could say anything, Conor interrupted. "She was injured. Laird Ross brought her here to be healed."

"Upon his bed?" Her father's words seemed to echo, or perhaps it was that she'd not considered how it looked.

Slowly, she lowered the bedding to show that she was dressed. It was then she realized her blouse had been torn open so the healer could care for her wound. Elspeth yanked the bedding back up.

Her father rounded, his thick arms seeming to bulge. She noticed the Ross brothers studied him with wariness.

For a long moment, her father was silent. Finally, he turned and glared at Malcolm.

"Ye will marry my daughter. It will happen without haste."

CHAPTER NINE

Alec found himself at the sturdy cottage once again. This time, he and two warriors were there to take the woman, Paige, and her grandfather back to the keep. She'd been reluctant, however now, days later, he was sure she'd reconsidered. He noted that the one chicken they owned and had been in a cage was now gone.

It was sad that his people had been dragged into hard times all because of the rash act of his brother who was too arrogant to see the error of his ways.

Just as he and his men dismounted, Paige appeared. By the reddening and swelling of her eyes, she'd been crying.

"As promised, we have returned for ye and yer grandfather."

She sagged against the doorjamb. "I require assistance. My grandfather died last night in his sleep."

There was a pang in his chest at noting the fact she could barely stand under the weight of her grief. Alec went to her and swooped her up in his arms. "I will send someone to come and see that he is properly buried. Ye need to come with me and be taken care of."

Paige did not protest. Instead, she seemed to melt against him. In that instant, Alec realized he never wished to release her.

"Ye will live at the keep," he repeated, not sure why since it was the sole purpose for his visit.

His men went inside and returned with two small bundles that she'd obviously prepared and they mounted their horses.

"I should go see him," Paige wailed.

"It will do no good. My men will return to take care of yer grandfather. I swear it."

He took her by the waist and lifted her to the horse, aware of how painfully thin she was. It was as if he lifted a child when placing Paige atop his horse. Her gaze met his for a moment and, through the redness, he saw the beautiful blue color he'd first noticed. Her blonde hair was askew and her shawl lopsided, but none of it distracted from how beautiful the woman was.

When Alec mounted and held her against his chest, once again, the strong sense of protectiveness took over. He would fight anyone and anything that dared try to take Paige from him.

When she shivered from the cold, he pulled the heavy tartan around them both, cocooning them in a world they'd share for the short trip to his keep. He wished for the trip to be a longer one. The feeling of her frame against his body made him want to keep her safe for the rest of their lives.

It must have been apparent because both guardsmen occasionally shifted their gazes toward him and frowned.

"Have ye lived here all yer life?" Alec asked the quiet woman, trying to distract her from the grief.

She let out a staggered breath. "Aye. I have never been anywhere else."

"I do not remember seeing ye before."

"There has been no reason for me to come to the keep. My grandfather did on occasion and then my brother went to see yer father for clan business. I didn't ever need to go"

It made sense. There was rarely need for women to come before the laird unless there was some sort of marriage problem or an argument between two of them.

Alec attempted to shift in his seat. Her round bottom tucked against his most sensitive parts was causing a reaction he didn't wish to have at the moment. To distract himself, he decided to continue speaking.

"What of ye? Have ye ever seen me?"

She nodded. "Aye, twice perhaps. At a festival once and another time when ye competed at the games." Thankfully, she seemed to not notice his body's reactions to her body.

"I wish I had seen ye," he said and waited for a reaction.

Once again, she sighed. "When will they return to bury my grandfather? I do not wish for someone to come upon him and get rid of his body to take the cottage."

Alec looked to his men and motioned to one. "Go back to the cottage and remain until men return to bury the dead. Ensure that no one destroys anything."

"Aye, Laird," the guard replied and rode away.

Too soon, they arrived at the McLeod Keep. The imposing, stark grey stone building was high on a hill surrounded by a tall wall for protection.

Paige immediately sat straighter and leaned forward. Although she shivered, he didn't try to keep her in the confines of his tartan. He allowed her to keep some form of decorum. In truth, she should have been riding with one of the guards, not with him, the eldest son of the laird and next in line to earn the title.

The gates were opened as they approached and, soon, Alec and his small party found themselves in the courtyard.

"I will go directly to the kitchens," Paige whispered. "If ye would please lower me."

Alec didn't try to argue with her. His own thoughts were in a jumble. "I will ensure ye are shown to a bedchamber. I do not wish ye to do anything today."

He intended to let the cook know that Paige was in mourning and should be left to her own devices until he instructed otherwise. She would not be made to work or do any chores unless she desired.

Unbeknownst to the slight woman he'd been holding, her future was to be far different than she had ever imagined.

PAIGE'S LEGS THREATENED to give out as she walked in the direction Alec had indicated. She'd barely slept in two days and had no idea what to expect there at the keep. If given the opportunity, she would have remained back in the cottage. However, twice already, robbers had come around. Once they went off with their only goat and the second time with their hen.

With no eggs or goat's milk, she and her grandfather had been on the verge of starvation. The food she'd taken back with her from the keep had lasted them for longer than it was meant for. She'd ensured to only eat once a day so her grandfather would have a bit more.

He'd died in his sleep. Although she mourned, in a way, Paige was relieved he'd not have to see what she'd come to. There was no doubt in her mind what the laird had in mind when it came to her future.

Although a virgin, she knew what happened when a man was aroused and Alec McLeod had definitely become so. The hardening member pressing into her bottom meant he'd had improper thoughts and desired her.

She stumbled forward and held the bundles tighter as she looked from one door to the other attempting to remember where the entrance to the kitchens was.

A young woman rushed past her and although Paige tried to stop her to ask, the woman rushed to the laird. Although Paige was exhausted, she waited for the woman to come back. It was interesting to watch the exchange. The young woman looked toward her and nodded and finally came to Paige.

"My laird's son instructed that ye should be taken to a chamber and a meal brought." The girl grabbed her bundles with surprising strength and marched forward. Paige hurried to catch up.

"I am Paige. What is yer name?"

The maid's warm smile put Paige at ease. "Rhoda. My mam and I work here," she added for some reason. Then she hurried up steps. "Up here, Miss. I will show ye…"

Paige interrupted at the top of the steps. "Ye must have misunderstood. There is no reason for me to be up here."

"What are ye doing, Rhoda?" An older woman stood just past Rhoda and looked to them with curiosity. By the woman's fine attire, she was either Alec's mother or another family member.

Rhoda froze but then quickly recovered. "Yer son instructed me to bring her here to the guest chamber, my lady."

The woman's eyes roved over Paige, making her feel even more inadequate and weak. "I do not wish to be here. Please show me the kitchens, Rhoda." She then looked up to the woman. "I am sure he is mistaken, my lady."

The older woman looked away and down the stairs for a moment then returned her attention to them. "Do as he says," she murmured and swept past them and down the stairs.

"Who is she?" Paige asked the maid as they entered the first chamber on the left.

"Lady McLeod," Rhoda replied. "She is quite a lovely woman."

The woman hadn't seemed unfriendly. Paige would describe her as more stern than anything else. She'd not bother to put anything away or sit on the fine furniture, as she was sure Rhoda would soon be sent back to take her to the servants' quarters.

Rhoda didn't seem to think the same. She hummed as she laid Paige's bundles on the bed. "Should I help ye put things away?"

"Nay, I thank ye, but would prefer to be alone right now," Paige said with a soft smile as to not hurt the girl's feelings.

Offering a bright grin in return, Rhoda shrugged. "I will return shortly with a light meal and leave ye to it then." The girl practically skipped away, obviously a happy spirit.

Unlike the maid, Paige felt adrift, lost amongst what was to be her life. She wandered to the window and peered out. It would be a few moments before someone came to fetch her and take her to the servants' quarters. Nonetheless, she went to the washstand and made quick work of washing her face, arms and hands then dried off with the soft cloths that hung on hooks on the side of the stand.

When no one returned after a few moments, she took out a comb from one of the bundles, returned to the window and loosed her hair. As she watched the comings and goings in the courtyard, she untangled her long tresses.

There seemed to be much activity. A group of men trained with swords on one end of the courtyard. On the other, women hung wet clothes to dry. A group of women were also gathered around a large simmering pot, seeming to chat while watching over children who ran in circles playing.

No doubt these people were displaced because of the clan war. She wondered how many of the women were widowed and children orphaned because of it.

After a discreet knock, Rhoda returned with a tray holding a bowl of steaming food and a cup. She placed the tray on a table. "Mister Alec asked me to tell ye to make yerself comfortable. I'll leave ye to rest."

Before Paige could formulate a sentence, the maid hurried out, closing the door behind her.

"Of all the things," Paige murmured, sniffing the food. It smelled delicious. How had they not realized the mistake by now?

Ignoring her growling stomach, she went to the door and opened it slowly. Peering out and not seeing anyone, she tiptoed to the stairwell and went down a couple steps. From her vantage point, she could see the great room.

Lady McLeod stood facing Alec. "How can ye decide this so suddenly and without taking yer station into consideration? Tis not the way, Son. Think about it. Yer father is right to be furious."

"I have made up my mind," Alec replied, his face as hard as stone. "I am to be laird…"

"And that is why a suitable wife should be found. Not a village girl who we barely know anything about. I am sure she is pleasant, and admittedly quite lovely, but, Son, ye cannot marry her."

Paige turned and hurried back to the room, closing the door softly behind. Were they speaking of her? No. It couldn't be. Why would Alec McLeod, the son of her laird wish to marry her?

Chapter Ten

THE EVENING SHADOWS crossed over the floor of Ian's chamber. Everything hurt, making it impossible to remain comfortable. The travel to Ross Keep had battered his already fragile body.

He lifted his gaze.

Thankfully, the lovely woman pacing back and forth in the room took his mind away from the pain for a moment.

Ceilidh wrung her hands. "How has it come to this? We come to rescue Elspeth only to be found out by her father. And now her father demands the laird marry her."

In truth, he had kept from chuckling at the irony of the situation. Malcolm had just announced no warrior was allowed any kind of emotional entanglement and here he was finding himself in a major one.

If the lass had been found in Malcolm's bed, the father had every right to demand marriage. Whether there was any physical involvement or not, the woman had been found not just in the chamber, but upon the bed and half-dressed at that according to the beauty pacing before him.

"Tis not a dire situation. I am sure all will be well."

She stopped pacing and came closer. "How are ye feeling? I should mix more tincture."

"In truth, I am not well. However, I do not wish more of that vile liquid."

Her pretty face became marred with a frown. "The vile liquid, as ye call it, has kept horrible pain at bay."

She started to head to the door and stopped. "Oh dear, what if Elspeth's father asks about me? If he tells my father…" Ceilidh turned to face him, her face bright red. "Should I remain here until he leaves?"

Ian hadn't considered the fact they'd been cloistered in his bedchamber for a few hours. "I am ill and tis known ye and Elspeth brought me here to heal. The man is aware I could not do ye any harm."

Her teeth bit into the plump bottom lip. "True. Where is Conor? That boy is never about when he is needed." She went to the door, opened it and peered out.

"Why is no one about? I know hundreds of people live here."

Despite the pain, he chuckled. "Not that many."

"If ye would point me in the direction of the kitchen, I shall go see about getting ye some food and…tincture."

He grimaced and motioned with his right hand. "Go to the right and down the second corridor."

"If ye wish to sit for a moment, I would like it." Ian wanted to take the opportunity to ask what he'd been wishing to say.

Of course, she thought something was wrong and she hurried to his bedside. Immediately, she pulled his tunic up and lifted the bandages. He smiled, liking her being close, her hands on his heated skin.

"The wound is healing well. I do not see any oozing. Do not allow the healer to put pumice in it." She replaced the bandage and lowered his shirt.

Then reaching for his face, she cupped it with both hands, her expression grim. "Ye are a bit warm. I will open the window and allow fresh air in. This room is quite stuffy."

Before she could move away, he took her hand. "I remain quite ill, but thanks to ye, I am not going to die." He met her gaze, wishing to convey what he wasn't allowed to.

"Thank ye, Ceilidh."

Her eyes widened just a bit. It was gratifying when she didn't pull her hand away, but instead relaxed just enough to let him know she didn't find his touch unpleasant.

"I am glad to see ye recovering. To be honest, we, Elspeth and I, did not have much hope at first."

He nodded and reluctantly released her hand. "Neither did I."

Clearing her throat, she rushed to the window and made a show of throwing the drapes aside. "Ye have a grand chamber for a warrior. Ye must be held in high esteem."

"All of the laird's personal guards have a chamber like this. There are ten of us."

Ceilidh frowned. "He did not seem overly concerned about yer welfare. I must be bold in telling ye this."

He wasn't surprised. Malcolm had changed drastically since his father's death. Although never quite of an easygoing nature per se, the laird's eldest son had always been kind and levelheaded. Everything became different upon the day the laird had been slain by a McLeod. The laird's death had brought more deaths, along with that, vengeful attacks, burning of villages and destruction of families.

"My laird is a fair man."

Ceilidh sniffed with disdain. "I do not trust a man who cares little for his people."

Ian wasn't about to argue or defend the laird. Most of the warriors and guards were growing weary of the incessant battles, the killing and revenge that would never bring about good cause. Nor would so many dying and suffering bring the laird back.

He'd become so lost in thought that when he looked back from the window, he noticed Ceilidh had left. He let out a breath and considered what he'd do to ensure to see her again. Once healed, he could call upon her. All he had to do was find out her family name and where she lived. From the hours she came and went from the healing room, it was obvious she didn't live far from Elspeth's family.

"Idiot," Ian said out loud when the remainder of his left arm pained him. How stupid was he to think a woman would wish to spend time with him? The only reason Ceilidh visited was because of her caring nature. He was an injured man to her and nothing else.

Frustrated, he attempted to slide up and get comfortable. Somehow, he turned sideways and fell to the floor. He let out a yowl at the searing pain that had him almost blacking out.

Only a few moments later, Ceilidh came through the door and her footsteps faltered.

"Oh my goodness." She hurried to put a tray on a table and then her face appeared over his. "What happened?"

"In an attempt to get comfortable, I ended up quite the opposite," Ian gritted the words out, feeling foolish. He started to try to sit up, but she kept him from it, her hands pushing down on his shoulders.

"Why didn't ye call for help?"

He let out a breath in attempt to keep from moaning. "I was too busy trying not to lose consciousness."

"It is best for ye to remain here for a bit." She reached to the bed and gathered a small blanket that she rolled and placed under Ian's head.

She then inspected the amputated left arm to ensure the stitches had not loosened. Thankfully, he'd not fallen on it, but on the opposite side. Seeming satisfied, she then went to the tray. "Ye will need tincture to keep the pain at bay."

Ian grimaced. It was vile, but it would make him feel better once its effects took over. "Can I have bread to eat after? Maybe a large tankard of ale?"

When Ceilidh smiled at him over her shoulder, Ian realized he would gladly drink a loch full of the vile liquid to see her smile.

CHAPTER ELEVEN

THE DOOR BURST open and Elspeth whirled from the window where she'd been watching the goings-on. She expected to see her father, brother or mother demanding they leave. Instead, Malcolm stood just inside the doorway, a murderous expression on his handsome face.

"Yer da is being unreasonable. Refuses to listen to reason. I am done speaking to him and have had him, along with yer brothers, escorted out of the gates."

Elspeth started for the doorway, but realizing her blouse remained torn exposing half her chest, she pulled the shawl tighter and glared at him. "Ye are an oaf. How am I supposed to return home if ye keep me here and remove them?"

Obviously by his gaze shifting sideways, he'd not considered it. "He said ye would not return with him."

"Of course he did. My da says things he does not mean when he's upset." She huffed and turned back to the window. In truth, her injury was throbbing and with the huge bed in the room, she wished for nothing more than to climb upon it and sleep for hours. "If ye would fetch my wagon and Ceilidh, we will be on our way."

"Very well," he replied. There was a clenching at his jaw and she waited for whatever else he wished to say. Of course he would not marry her. She was nothing more than a mere peasant and far below his standing.

Not only that, but he was laird and, as such, his marriage had probably been arranged a long time earlier.

She let out a breath. "I do not expect anything from ye. In all honesty, I do not think Father did either. He has a temper and often says things without thought. The reputation of someone of my…level does not matter much. Especially during these times."

There was flatness in his expression that made her wonder how someone like him could continue day to day. It was as if he were hollow, without a heart or feelings. She pitied him in a way.

"Why do ye look at me that way?" The question startled Elspeth, but she didn't look away.

"It seems as if ye have everything and yet nothing." She pointedly looked around the room. "While ye send men out to die for ye, there is little care or thought about consequences and that most warriors do not return from battle to be cared for." She looked down at her soiled clothes and shook her head.

"I think that of the two people standing in this room, I am by far the richest. I have hope and care for the men that ye leave behind on the battlefield. Each of them, whether yers or the Ross', they will forever think of me and my family with fondness."

He looked away for a moment and then to her without speaking. The flatness in his expression remained.

Elspeth was not finished. "What do they think of ye? How do they remember yer da? Ye have chosen to mark his death with war, desperation, and despair among the people."

"Ye know nothing of me or my family…" he started, but Elspeth didn't want to hear it. He had no excuse for what she'd seen happen out on the bloody grounds of a battlefield.

"I know everything. I hear everything. The revelations just before death, of men wishing me to inform loved ones last messages as life ebbs from them." By now, she was furious and tears rolled down her cheeks. "I know that none has ever remarked being glad or proud for the cause that is bringing them death. Tis ye and only ye that wish for this war."

His nostrils flared and Elspeth took a step backward. She'd gone too far. Allowed her passion free rein. If he slapped her across the face, it would not dampen her day. On the contrary, she would be even more convinced the man was a despicable overlord to his clan.

He remained calm, speaking as if he were remarking on the weather. "That is enough. Ye can leave, but not until the morrow. Yer friend is caring for Ian and does not wish to leave his side." His gaze swept over her and to the bed. "I will have a change of clothes brought. Ye may remain here. This is a guest chamber, not mine."

To her surprise, he didn't seem affected by her blurted speech. It was as if the dead soul inside him did not absorb insults.

"I should not stay here…"

"Ye will be at last meal. Make sure of it." His gaze met hers for a moment. "And I repeat, ye know nothing of me or my family. Ye are but…"

"A mere village woman. I know." Elspeth held her head high. "And proud of it."

Just for a moment, she thought she noticed a flicker of something akin to respect in his gaze. However, it was gone within a second and he gave a one-shoulder shrug as if not caring what she thought.

"I do not wish to remain here," Elspeth repeated, wishing nothing more than to leave the keep altogether, but thoughts of the injured Ian brought her to reconsider. She'd never forgive herself if he were further injured because she'd been too distracted to pay attention to the man who'd been ravaged by fear and pain out on the battlefield.

Malcolm didn't respond. Instead, he strode past her to the window. "Yer father is gone. I cannot allow ye to travel alone this late in the day. Nor can I spare any guards at this moment."

"Can I see about Ian and my friend then? I must ensure he is not worse because of traveling here."

"Aye," he replied.

She hesitated, turning to look out the window once again.

WHEN MALCOLM LOOKED out from the guest chamber window, he could see Elspeth's father and brothers slowly riding away. It had been hard to convince them to leave in order to not have them thrown in the dungeon. In truth, he'd had to promise to marry Elspeth within seven days. They would return then along with a priest and her mother.

He'd planned to tell Elspeth. But upon entering the room, he'd been struck dumb. Unaware of what a fetching picture she made, Elspeth had faced him without fear. Her eyes ablaze, hair pulled back showcasing her soft jawline and pursed lips. Then his gaze had traveled down and caught a glimpse of the tops of her breasts. Her blouse had been torn and unbeknownst to her, she'd not held the shawl high enough at first.

His mouth had watered at the sight and it took all his strength not to throw her atop the bed and have his way. No, it was best to wait. Once a priest blessed them, he would have to provide proof of her virginity. Not that there weren't ways to fake it.

Malcolm had a feeling Elspeth wouldn't agree to the marriage. She had little regard for him and, truthfully, by the way she exploded, her opinion of him would not change.

Although he'd professed and banned entanglements of any nature with women to his warriors, he now wondered about the effects Elspeth would have on him. Would his mind be left behind with her while he went to battle next?

"Ye may go see about Ian and yer friend, but ye will sleep here." He turned and walked from the room not wanting to hear any protestations. Malcolm always respected women and their opinions. His entire life, in private, his mother and sister often spoke their thoughts and his father had listened and taken their opinions into consideration.

Malcolm made his way down the corridor toward his own chamber only a few feet away. He needed whisky and time alone to think.

Elspeth was quite vocal. Under most circumstances, he welcomed it. But at the moment, with everything that had happened, her words had not been what he wished to hear.

His father had always allowed his mother freedom to speak and to advise on matters. He planned to follow suit, at least after a while. However, Elspeth could not continue to rant on about his shortcomings.

Just as Malcolm was about to enter his chamber, Tristan walked toward him, a grin stretching across his face. "I hear ye are to be married."

As always, Tristan found humor in whatever caused Malcolm discomfort.

"Unless I can find a way to avoid it. The lass detests me, which may help."

This time Tristan chuckled out loud and followed him into the room. "I hear she is the healer that comes to the battlefields. She's quite lovely. Good at what she does. It keeps me at ease that those that need healing will be cared for by her."

Malcolm was astounded as he'd never heard anyone speak of her. "Ye know Elspeth?"

"Aye," Tristan replied. "We all do. She, her friend, Ceilidh, and grandmother are angels in times of darkness. Ye may not have noticed since ye leave as soon as a retreat is called."

Although there didn't seem to be accusation in Tristan's words, they struck. Malcolm studied his brother who poured whisky into two cups and handed him one. "I do what has to be done."

Tristan lifted an eyebrow and nodded. "I know, Brother."

"Where is Kieran?" Malcolm asked, not having seen his youngest brother all day. "I hope he's not up to anything that will put his life in danger."

There was a beat of silence. "I worry about him," Tristan finally said. "He hasn't been eating well and speaks rarely. Tis as if he lost his way since Da died."

"What can we do?" Malcolm wasn't sure he wanted to hear the reply. "Kieran is a grown man and although the youngest of us, he must learn to adjust."

Tristan held up a hand. "Ye have no argument from me. Tis like he has the devil inside. Only exists to fight, to loose those arrows of his."

There was nothing wrong with the need to battle and avenge their father. At least in Malcolm's estimation it was what he expected from both his brothers. That Kieran was consumed sounded reasonable.

"He is well within his rights to be angered."

There was a slight narrowing in Tristan's eyes and his brother drank down the rest of his whisky. "When will it be enough, Brother?"

"When the bastard is dead. Ethan McLeod's head under my boot. Even then, I am not sure it will be enough."

After a long beat of silence, Tristan stood and went to the door. "I hope it comes to be soon because I am not sure how much longer we can continue to put our people's lives in danger to avenge Da."

He'd had enough. The crashing of the cup against the stone hearth didn't surprise Tristan who gave him a bored look over his shoulder. "What say ye now, Brother?" The flat tone made Malcolm angrier.

"Tis not a holiday. Tis not something we do because there is naught else to be done. Our father was killed. The bastard McLeod cut him down without provocation. It is expected that we avenge. Retaliate."

Tristan stood still and it was obvious by the clenching of his jaw that he had more to say. However, he remained silent.

Malcolm was not finished. "I will not cease until justice is done. If ye do not agree, to hell with ye then."

"Tis not that yer intentions are wrong, Brother. However, our people should not suffer because of it. The sooner ye accept that they should be our priority, the better."

The anger turned to fury and Malcolm wished for the cup again to throw. Did no one understand?

Thankfully, Kieran remained loyal. He glared at Tristan. "Ye do not have to accompany us. Remain behind. Tis what ye wish, is it not?"

Instead of arguing further, his brother shook his head and walked out.

Malcolm wanted to feel justified, to be sure of his decisions. The last thing he needed at this point was to hear how wrong he was from not one, but two people, one right after the other.

In the beginning, every Ross warrior thirsted for revenge. They had fought ruthlessly without regard for life or limb. Nothing stood in the way of what they sought and the McLeods had suffered many losses. As time passed, however, he'd noticed a lack of zeal. Barely had battles begun than they ended, a retreat called from one side or the other.

It was best to hear a voice of reason. His father's brother acted as advisor. If anyone would motivate him to continue forward, it would be Gregor Ross.

When Malcolm walked into his father's study, his uncle sat at the desk. He resembled his father so much that Malcolm stopped, having to regain control.

"Uncle, sometimes ye look too much like Da and it astounds me."

Gregor chuckled. "And ye look like a younger version of him. Looking upon ye makes me sometimes think tis he."

The older man looked to a map and motioned him closer. "I have scouts here and here." He pointed to two places on the map.

"What of the McLeod people on the border region?"

"Other than a farmer who refuses to give up his land, everyone is staying inside the keep gates."

"Cowards," Malcolm muttered. "They are scared to leave."

"On the contrary, these are the brave ones."

Ignoring the statement, Malcolm studied the map for a few moments longer and then went to a chair and sat. "What do ye propose?"

His uncle neared and lowered to another chair. "If they do not wish to engage, there is naught we can do but wait."

"What of revenge? I cannot ask my people to remain waiting as well."

When his uncle stroked his chin, Malcolm knew he had a plan. "How about we act as if we're not interested in another battle? They will let their guard down. We keep our scouts in place. When Ethan leaves the confines of the keep, our archers dispose of him."

There was a slight curl on his uncle's upper lip. "Tis the only way to end this."

Malcolm wanted to agree. A part of him hoped it would be Kieran's arrow.

His cousin, Aiden, strolled in without looking at them. He poured a good amount of whisky into his glass and sat in the remaining chair. "I hope there is news. Tis an entire day since Kieran left."

Both turned to him. Aiden drank from the whisky, not seeming one bit perturbed that his cousin was missing.

"What do ye mean?" It was Gregor who spoke. "Was he not gone with ye?"

Aiden rolled his eyes and Malcolm's fingers curled into a fist. The arrogant man was a constant thorn in his side. So unlike his uncle who Malcolm respected and trusted. Aiden had always been jealous and vindictive.

"Where is my brother?"

"We went to the forest. He claimed to want to spy on the McLeods. However, he went east and not west and, soon after, I lost him."

This time it was Gregor who was annoyed. "When was this? Why are ye just now saying something?"

"I told Tristan an hour ago. We went yesterday evening."

Malcolm was not convinced of the true reason for their venture. No doubt, they'd gone to the village to find willing wenches for bedding. If he knew his younger brother, sex was foremost on his mind. Other than being a formidable archer and warrior, Kieran loved to bed women.

"What tavern did ye go to?" he asked and leaned forward, daring Aiden to lie. "Tell me now."

His cousin didn't bother lying. "MacLeary's. I left first thing this morning thinking he'd return later as he didn't answer the door when I knocked."

"Tis a time of war. We have enemies..." his uncle started, but Aiden interrupted.

"If anyone can take care of themselves, tis Kieran. I am not his keeper." With that, he stood and walked to the doorway. Aiden stopped, the dark eyes looking to Malcolm.

"I am sure Kieran is well."

As if beckoned, his younger brother ambled into the office. Like a cat of prey, Malcolm was upon him. With his fingers curled into the rough fabric of Kieran's tunic, he slammed the younger man against the closest wall.

"These are not times to be whoring. Ye know my command."

Kieran was muscular, tall and lithe. He swung an elbow upward dislodging one of Malcolm's hands and shoved him away.

When Malcolm threw a punch into Kieran's gut, the younger man let out an oomph followed by several expletives.

"Would ye have me send guards in search of ye? Put lives in danger because ye needed to fuck?"

Instead of a reply, Kieran whipped around and swung hard, his fist making a crunching sound on the side of Malcolm's face.

Malcolm swayed and refusing to fall, tackled his brother.

"I am not a child to be chastised," Kieran yelled and bucked Malcolm off. Both rolled, still grappling.

Not prepared for the hard punch to his jaw, Malcolm released his brother, falling onto his back.

"Get up," Kieran growled, hands fisted.

The brothers were evenly matched. However, Kieran had the advantage of youth on his side. Malcolm rose and narrowed his eyes. "Ye are not to put our clan in danger again."

Without a response, Kieran rushed at him. Malcolm expected it and evaded. As Kieran came close, he took hold of his brother's tunic and slammed him into the wall.

"What is going on?" Their mother rushed in. "Stop at once."

Kieran shook his head in an attempt to clear it and Malcolm took the opportunity to punch him in the stomach. His brother doubled over and threw up.

"Idiot," Malcolm swore as his mother approached. She looked up at him, her face twisted in fury. "Ye both are." She slapped him across the face. "I'm tired of this life ye have created."

"I did not create it, Mother. Tis the man who killed…"

"Enough," she screamed and looked down at Kieran who'd given up trying to stand and remained on all fours. "Both of ye are a disgrace to yer father."

Malcolm started to say something but his uncle held up a hand, signaling for him to remain silent. "Come, allow me to escort ye to get something to settle yer nerves."

Two guards who must have been instructed by his uncle rushed to help Kieran to stand.

Of course, his brother shook them off once on his feet. "Leave me be." He glared at Malcolm. "Tis only because I drank that ye can best me. It won't happen again."

"Drink? Or yer disregard?"

Without replying, Kieran stalked from the room.

CHAPTER TWELVE

PAIGE COULDN'T DECIDE whether to sit or stand. Surely this nightmare would end. Deciding it was best to just do what was proper, she grabbed her bundles and went to the door. It was hard to hold her parcels and open the door, but she did and peeked out. There was a guard on one end of the corridor. Thankfully, he stood by the window and peered down. Obviously the man was too bored to bother with keeping an eye on her. She didn't blame him. It was a mild evening and there were probably many things he'd rather be doing.

She took a step to rush down the stairs and then thought better of it. The guard would be punished for letting her get away. Clearing her throat, she pretended to be confused as to which way to go.

The guard immediately rushed to her. "Ye are to stay in the bedchamber, lass," he told her. He seemed to recognize her, his gaze friendly. "Are ye bored as well?"

"Aye. I prefer to be outdoors. Would ye walk with me? I would like to deposit my things downstairs in the servants' quarters first."

He frowned for a moment. "I was told ye would be staying up here. And to keep ye safe."

Of course he would not agree so easily. Paige decided to appeal to the fact that he and she were on the same social level. "As ye may understand, tis not my place. I know Alec McLeod means well, but his mother is upset and so is yer laird. I would appreciate it if ye would walk with me."

He considered her words for a moment. "I will take ye for a walk. We shall go through the kitchens. What ye do with yer belongings is not up to me."

When he took the bundles and motioned for her to walk ahead, relief filled her. Her legs were heavy, steps stilted. It was as if there were two boulders, one on each shoulder as she made her way down the stairwell. If only she could turn time back to the day her brother spoke of coming here. She would have argued harder and convinced him to seek another way to feed them.

They passed along the side of the great room. Thankfully, it was empty and then they walked down a second corridor to the kitchens. Paige peeked in to see two women. The older one, a red-faced, plump woman hurried to and fro from a sideboard to a large wooden table. She turned to the other. "Stir the pot. It will burn if ye do not continue."

The guard pushed Paige in through the doorway. All the foodstuffs, pots, pans and dishes took her aback.

Paige had been in shock; racked by grief the last time she'd been there, it was as if stepping into a place she'd not been before. Along one wall there were shelves laden with cups and tankards. On a lower shelf, plates and bowls were stacked.

She turned to look to a wall with a window where bundles of herbs dried in the sunlight. This was truly a place she'd only dared to dream about.

"What is this?" the red-faced woman asked with a broad smile directed at the guard. "My son comes for a visit?"

The guard blushed and shook his head. "I am escorting the lass for a walk, Mother."

Nonetheless, he neared and kissed the woman's cheek.

The cook studied Paige, her keen eyes taking in the bundles in her son's arms. "Ye have to accept what is decided. Sit down." She motioned to a chair, not leaving any room for argument. "I will make ye a warm cider."

When a plate with bread and cheese was slid in front of her, Paige took a chunk of each and ate. The guard did the same while standing by the doorway, her bundles at his feet.

"My name is Rose and I have been serving the McLeods my entire life. They are a good people. Ye will see."

Paige bit her tongue to keep from stating how they'd sent her brother to his death. "Tis not that I am ungrateful, but I know my place and I should be here, in the servants' quarters."

Rose looked to her son and then to her. "Where are ye staying now?"

The guard replied for her. "On the second level, the chamber next to Alec's."

"Oh!" Rose's mouth formed an "O" and the girl who was stirring the pot turned to look at her with the same expression.

Paige swallowed the sweet cider. "Ye see, both the laird and lady are cross with him and I do not blame them. Tis best I either come downstairs or leave."

They remained in companionable silence for a few minutes and then Rose stood. "I have much to do. Best get to work. Several girls will be here shortly from their other chores to prepare for the evening meal."

The guard motioned to the outdoors. "Lass, we can go for a walk this way."

Once outside, once again the vast difference from the life she was accustomed took Paige by surprise. The amount of activity and discussions along with the clanging of metal from swordplay was a cacophony almost too much to handle. A group of men with swords strapped to their backs guided horses to corrals.

Pots were suspended over fire in another area and women hovered over them while others scurried to long tables with bowls, serving people who sat.

The guard turned to her. "Those that are being harbored eat earlier so that the laird, his family, guests and guards can be served last meal without being disturbed. There is only room for some inside, so these eating areas were set up."

She nodded in understanding. Just then, the gates opened and four men on horseback rode through. One of the warriors atop the enormous warhorses was Alec. His gaze flew to her and the guard and Paige saw her companion stiffen.

"Remain here," he instructed and went forward without being beckoned.

It was curious to see Alec speak to the guard. The sun shining down on his hair brought out reddish highlights in his brown hair. It seemed not to be an unpleasant exchange, she noted, and relaxed.

Finally, he dismounted and the guard who'd just been with her guided the steed away.

Alec neared, his dark gaze roaming over her as if to ascertain if she was under any duress. "I am told ye do not find the accommodations suitable."

Heat rushed to her cheeks, especially upon noting several people had stopped what they were doing and now watched them.

"Tis not that. I should not be upstairs. I know my place." Paige pointed to the keep. "Yer parents agree with me."

His brow furrowed. "Ye spoke to them?"

"What? No, I did not. But I overheard yer conversation earlier."

"I am in need of a wife. The people would benefit from something to celebrate."

She looked across the courtyard. "They are aware of yer father's generosity by how well they are treated. Although I detest what my brother went through, I find yer family's kindness admirable."

"Tis not just kindness, but duty. The people are not at fault for what is happening."

"My brother would tell ye tis my fault. I am the reason for the clan war." A warrior approached. He was a younger version of Alec, but with a certain demeanor that made Paige instantly dislike him. Arrogance dripped from him like sweat on a summer day.

"Ye would think I would be hailed a hero for what I did. I defended myself and those with me."

Alec's jaw tightened and his nostrils flared. "Ethan, ye provoked it all. Everyone knows better than to believe what ye spew."

The last thing Paige wanted was to be caught between two warriors battling. So she took a step forward and placed a hand on Alec's arm. "Would ye accompany me on a walk?"

She looked to Ethan. "If ye are proud of yer accomplishment, that should be reward enough."

Ethan's eyes widened and then he turned on his heel and stalked off.

"I must admit, ye are a very good peacemaker," Alec said, guiding her away from all the activity before them.

As soon as they were alone, Paige looked up to him. "Please allow me to remain downstairs. I beg of ye. There is nothing to be gained by any kind of assignation with a woman of my low status."

"Do ye not see," he replied, his gaze roving over her. "Ye are who I want as a wife. I am tired. I do not wish to worry that the woman I marry will bring any kind of additional burden to my clan. True, most first-born sons marry for gain, but my clan does not need to be united with another. Right now, what we need is peace."

Paige understood and although she had to admit to being very attracted to the handsome man, she couldn't see how a marriage would help anything. If nothing else, there was the possibility of strife between the son and his parents.

"Ye should think about it more. While ye do, why don't I move downstairs?"

He didn't respond. Instead, he guided her to an area beside the keep. There was nothing but grass and shorter solid walls. A very private area that was no doubt reserved for the laird's family.

"Look at me, Paige."

She had to tilt her head back because he was so much taller. When their gazes met, she saw warmth and something else. His green eyes darkened and her breathing hitched. He was going to kiss her.

The moment his mouth crashed atop hers, Paige was lost. Everything disappeared except for the hard body holding her against it. The taste of him was like nothing she'd ever experienced. As were the hard beats of her heart and the heat that traveled from every extremity to pool in the center of her core.

He pushed past her lips with his tongue and she parted them to allow it. If he were not holding her up, the sensations from their tongues intertwining would have sent her to fall.

Not wanting the wonder to stop, Paige wrapped her arms around his neck and when that wasn't enough, threaded her fingers through his hair. All the while, he continued to plunder her mouth, nipping, licking and suckling every single portion. If kissing brought so much pleasure, Paige was sure not to survive further intimacy with him.

There was a hunger in Alec by the sounds he made, a deep rumble that rose from deep in his chest as his hands traveled down Paige's back, cupping her bottom and pulling her tighter against him. If not for social propriety, she would have jumped up and wrapped her legs about his waist.

If only the kiss would continue forever. Reality was pushed away and Paige prayed for it to remain so.

She moaned softly when his lips left her mouth, not wanting the kiss to end. However, when he trailed his tongue down from the corner of her lips to her jawline, she let out a long sigh of relief.

The warmth of his mouth followed by the coolness of the breeze multiplied every sensation. She raked her fingers across his wide back, wanting to touch and feel more of him and not caring at this point how far things went. She wanted more…no, she needed more. It was as if her life depended on his touches, kisses and caresses.

"Paige," Alec murmured in her ear, the deep rasp of his voice sending currents down her entire body. His tongue traced the rim of her ear and he nibbled at the lobe until she shook with need.

"Please," she begged, not sure what it was she needed. It had to be him, all of him. "Please," Paige repeated.

He bent and pulled her up to sit on a short wall, and then took her mouth again as his hand slid up her leg to the inside of her thigh. "I know, sweet lass. Ye need release."

Licking his way down her throat, his fingers found her core and Paige bit her bottom lip to keep from crying out. Her sex throbbed, demanding attention, begged for more.

Delight was followed by a feverish need for him to continue to stroke the special spot he'd found at the very center of her. Paige writhed and lifted her hips into his hand until losing control. Heat surged down both legs and her eyes closed as the most overwhelming explosion of sensations overtook her.

Her body shattered.

"Ye see, Paige, we are meant to be." Alec pulled her against his chest, allowing for her to regain composure. "Marry me."

"Mmmm?" Paige managed to look up at him. "I cannot." She wanted to hide from him as the realization of the freedom she'd allowed crashed down. "I…I should go."

"Brother?" A pretty woman, who by her resemblance to Alec was obviously related, strolled toward them.

Alec cleared his throat and placed both hands in front of himself to hide his arousal. Mortified, Paige wasn't sure what to do. Here she was perched atop a wall and jumping down would only make the situation worse.

"My sister, Merida." Alec smiled at his sister. "This is Paige, who I am trying to convince to marry me."

Merida laughed, her friendly gaze meeting Paige. "Ye are smart to not agree right away. However, I must tell ye, my brother is a good man. Ye cannot possibly find a better one in all the region."

"What do ye want?" Alec asked, shaking his head.

"Nothing at all," Merida replied, twirling hair around her finger. "Can ye take me to the see Freya tomorrow?"

"No, Merida."

"I need to ensure she and her family are well."

Alec sighed. "We can send guards to check."

His sister blew out a breath and looked to Paige. "Perhaps I spoke too soon. Do not marry him, he is an oaf."

Chapter Thirteen

Murmuring ceased when Elspeth entered the great room and upon Malcolm coming to her side, the silence continued. Every eye in the room followed them as they made their way to the high board.

She did her best to keep from looking directly at anyone, her heart pounding with every step. Finally when seated, she was forced to greet those beside her.

On her left was Malcolm's mother, sitting as still as a stone.

"Lady Ross," Elspeth said by way of greeting and bowed her head.

The woman's mouth thinned into a tight line, her gaze moving down from Elspeth's face to her simple dress. She didn't acknowledge the greeting, turning instead to Malcolm's sister and murmuring, "I am feeling ill."

Elspeth looked down at her empty plate, her stomach lurching at the thought of eating anything.

When Malcolm's shoulder touched hers, she turned to him. "I should go."

"Nay. Ye will remain." He looked past her to an older man on her left side.

"Elspeth, this is my Uncle Gregor."

The older man seemed to be the only one who didn't find any fault with her. He leaned forward so he could look at her, his kind eyes meeting hers for a moment. "How fare ye, lass?"

It was an odd question. Did he wish to know the truth or was he simply being kind?

"As well as can be expected. My injury still a hurts," she said, deciding it was best to be honest. "And ye?"

The man smiled. "I find this to be a most interesting evening and, therefore, I am in good spirits."

Of course, he meant because of her presence. Just then, servants entered and began serving.

When Malcolm turned to her, her eyes rounded. There was purpling beneath his left eye and his bottom lip had been split. Had there been a battle?

"I can treat yer wounds after the meal."

His gaze locked with hers, the darkening of them making her swallow with awareness. "I thank ye. Tis ye who needs tending."

"What happened?"

He shrugged. "Nothing of importance."

Annoyed at his lack of reply, Elspeth wanted to shove him. But then he shocked her by touching the top of her right hand. "Ye think too much."

Hiding a sharp intake of breath, she pretended interest in the room and scanned it.

She looked around hoping to spot Ceilidh, but her friend was nowhere to be seen.

"Yer friend is taking her meal with Ian." Malcolm seemed to have read her thoughts. "Perhaps ye would like to visit her once we finish?"

"I would like that," Elspeth replied, her gaze colliding with his. "Also, I have so many questions to ask ye."

Up close, Elspeth could see every detail of his handsome face. From the light freckling across his nose to the slight crinkles at the corners of his eyes. Malcolm was a handsome man, muscular with wide shoulders, rich brown eyes that changed from greenish to golden brown. Although he didn't seem particularly arrogant, there was a commanding presence about him.

When his gaze fell to her lips, they parted of their own volition and she inhaled sharply, looking away. A tingle of awareness settled in the center of her chest as she did her best to keep from looking to his mother who'd suddenly found her interesting.

Malcolm ran a finger down her forearm. "After ye see yer friend, we will go for a walk and ye can ask me any question ye wish."

Did that mean he planned to go with her to Ian's chamber? Elspeth eyed the large entryway and itched to dash from the room and back to her simple life. How had things changed so much so quickly?

Never in her wildest dreams did she picture herself at last meal there at the Ross Keep and much less at the high board sitting next to the laird.

Thankfully, the people gathered had stopped paying them attention, their new focus being the platters of food placed in front of them. For a moment, Elspeth wondered how it could be that so many were fed daily. There were trays with meats, root vegetables, breads and cheeses.

Enough was served that everyone could eat his or her fill. In addition to that, those that sought refuge outside had also been fed.

The noise of the room was interrupted when the doors opened and six large warriors entered. Amongst them Kieran Ross. There wasn't any mistaking the man. Taller than the other men with thick arms and a broad chest, he towered over the others. Wearing a breastplate and archer's gloves, he looked ready for battle. Across his wide back a sword and bow were strapped. On his side, a pouch with arrows.

The angelic face did little to hide the darkness within him. Everything about him made one want to move away. Malcolm stiffened next to her and it was then she noticed that Kieran's jaw was swollen and he had a reddish mark beneath his left eye.

The reaction of those around was very different than when she'd walked in. The women did not hide their admiration, which Kieran didn't seem to notice. Probably used to it, Elspeth gathered.

"Brother, ye bring news?" Malcolm said by way of greeting when Kieran neared. "Are ye just now returned?"

Kieran's hazel gaze moved to her for a second and then he nodded. "Aye. We can speak after the meal. Right now, I wish to eat."

"First, go to the kitchen and wash up. Ye smell horrible." His mother sniffed and waved him away.

Despite the man's sternness, Elspeth wanted to chuckle at the crestfallen expression as Kieran looked to their plates. However, he did as instructed and hurried toward the kitchen.

"People wash in the kitchen?" Elspeth asked Malcolm.

He shook his head. "Nay, just outside there is a trough that is always filled with water and drying cloths are kept on hooks. Mother cannot abide anyone eating who has not washed up."

Well, it was at least one thing Elspeth had in common with the woman. Her father and brothers had learned to wash before entering the house. Her mother could not stand the sight of grimy hands reaching for bread.

Elspeth picked up a piece of bread and cheese to nibble on. Anything else she was sure would make her ill. She was much too nervous and overwhelmed to eat a full meal.

As she ate, she studied the room. It was quite large, double the size of her entire home.

There were six long tables lined up sideways so that everyone could see the high board if Malcolm were to address to them. Atop the tables were evenly spaced candelabras with lit candles that gave the room a warm glow.

Across from where she sat was a huge hearth with a bright fire burning within. There was another hearth to the right that also housed a fireplace. Two hounds weaved between the tables, gobbling up anything dropped or given to them.

Elspeth wondered how anyone could function with so much activity. However, upon further study, she realized that although it seemed to be chaotic, there was an order to things.

The servants walked up and down between the six long tables, their footsteps sure, as they carried huge heavy trays.

Guardsmen were seated at tables near the doorway. Families and women occupied the center two tables. Warriors again occupied the tables on the far left. Her gaze continued to travel to the back corridor where the serving maids and lads emerged. It surprised her to see most seemed content and not at all bothered by the work.

Everyone needs a purpose, her father always said, and Elspeth supposed the task of serving gave people a sense of purpose.

Abruptly, Lady Ross stood and walked away from the table and hurried down a corridor. The woman's strange actions were no doubt due to Elspeth's presence. If allowed, she would have done the same and left the room.

Already her food had grown cold. The only things consumed were the bread and cheese.

To distract herself when her injury throbbed, a reminder of why she was there, Elspeth studied Malcolm. He'd eaten everything on his plate, and now drank deeply.

"I will wait until the morrow to see Ceilidh, I am not feeling well."

Immediately, he stood and took her elbow. "I will see ye to yer chamber."

Although she wanted to protest, at the same time there was a security that came with walking beside him. No one dared make a disparaging remark when their laird accompanied her.

Once at the top of the stairs, Elspeth hesitated at the doorway and looked up to him. "Can ye tell me in truth why ye wish me to stay here?"

He pushed the door open and guided her inside. "Yer father returns in the morning. He wishes to be present for our marriage ceremony. He did not relent in his demands that ye not be ruined."

"I am but a village girl. No one would give much credence to my word over yers even if I were to accuse ye of making advances."

Malcolm nodded, his gaze darkened. "Tis not much of a sacrifice. I am in need of a wife. As laird, I'm expected to marry."

"To someone who will bring honor and power to yer clan. I bring nothing."

He neared. "Ye captured my interest. Make me curious about what will happen next."

The thought she'd almost drowned because of him made her frown. "Ye tried to kill me."

"I did not think ye would sink." There was a quirk to the corner of his lips. "I saved ye."

She glowered. "Release me to go home. I will convince my da that nothing happened. Ceilidh and I can return at first light and arrive home before they depart."

"Ye do not wish to marry me then?"

There was a strange vulnerability in his gaze that took her aback. The man was arrogant, heartless and didn't show emotion. At least that was the Malcolm Ross she was accustomed to.

Elspeth hitched her chin. "I do not know ye."

Her breath caught when his mouth covered hers and she had to clutch his tunic to keep from falling backward. When his strong arms surrounded her body and pulled her closer, Elspeth wasn't sure what to do. She'd never been kissed before.

Malcolm didn't seem to mind the lack of activity on her part and softly suckled at her lips.

When a sigh sounded, Elspeth was mortified that it came from her. A kiss should have been simple. A pressing of lips and separating. But he continued in the endeavor and, much to her surprise, she didn't wish him to stop.

He glided his tongue between her lips, sending strange sensations through her entire body. At the same time, her curiosity piqued and she parted her lips just a bit to see what he'd do.

Malcolm thrust his tongue into her mouth and withdrew it, while moving it side to side. The strange action became quite enjoyable. Elspeth pursed her lips, teasing his tongue, enjoying the interaction.

When a bolt of heat traveled down from her chest to the area between her legs, she gasped and shoved him away.

The rising and lowering of his chest was exactly what hers did. Both looked at each other although Elspeth was sure her eyes were wider.

"Ye should leave. Please allow me to go."

He took a step closer and Elspeth put both hands up. "Do not come closer. I find myself quite…unlevel."

"Unlevel?" he asked. "What does that mean?"

"Unable to think clearly," she snapped. "Ye must go."

"We will talk in the morning," he said, taking her chin between his fingers. "Ye will marry me, Elspeth Muir." He leaned forward and pressed a lingering kiss on her lips and then broke it off abruptly.

Elspeth stood still, not moving after the door closed behind her. How could a man who cared so little kiss so well?

It felt as if her feet barely touched the ground as she made her way to the washbasin. She removed her dress, leaving only a chemise on, and rinsed her face before climbing into the large bed. Elspeth lay on her back and looked up to the ceiling. She'd never sleep, not with so many conflicting thoughts going through her mind.

Malcolm Ross wished to marry her. It was either a cruel joke or the man planned to use her as a means to an end. She needed to find out the real reason he'd agreed to the marriage.

A few moments later, she could barely keep her eyes open.

ROUGH HANDS TOOK hold of Elspeth and jarred her awake. It was too dark to see, but whoever it was yanked her from the bed and shoved a cloth into her mouth. She was wrapped up in a large sheet and thrown over a man's shoulder.

The men spoke in whispers.

"Let's go down the back way. Hurry."

Elspeth couldn't move enough to struggle. It was impossible to see anything except bits of light from the torches down the corridor.

The bouncing as the man hurried down stairs made her grunt in pain. Not only did her chest hurt from being jostled, but the pressure on her stomach made her want to relieve herself.

Her protests sounded like mumbles, but the men paid no heed and continued out into the night to an area she'd not seen.

The air smelled of damp earth as they made their way past the keep walls to the loch's edge.

"Take her faraway so that she cannot find her way back. Try not to harm her over much," a woman instructed. "Ensure they know to keep her there."

It was Malcolm's mother. Elspeth tried to scream, but the damned gag barely allowed for any sound to escape.

"Yes, my lady," a rough voice replied.

The man who'd been carrying her tossed her onto a hard surface and Elspeth groaned in pain. Why was this happening to her? Hot tears spilled down her cheeks. It was a wagon filled with hay.

Other than the sheet she was wrapped in, there was little to keep the cold at bay. Immediately, she began shivering, not only from the cold but also the terror that seized her.

She fell back, unable to keep her head up and stared up at the night sky. There had to be a way to escape. Hopefully, the men would sit up front in the bench and leave her alone so that she could figure out a way to get untangled and escape.

Unfortunately, one of the men lumbered onto the back of the wagon as the other remained speaking with Lady Ross. They seemed to be haggling over payment until, finally, the man reluctantly accepted what the woman offered.

The second man then climbed onto the bench where he snapped the reins to get the horse to move forward.

"Twas less than ye promised," the man beside her complained. "Ye must give me more than half."

The man on the bench didn't reply for a long moment. They rode in silence for what seemed hours before the man finally stopped the wagon and climbed down.

"We can sell her for more. Lady Ross will not know if we were held up or attacked along the way."

Both men looked to her and Elspeth shook her head. Perhaps she could convince them that Malcolm would pay more for her return.

"Nay," the man who'd been in the back of the wagon retorted. "I do not wish to have the Ross as enemy."

The other man grunted. "What makes ye think he knows? Twas his mother who gave the lass to us."

Back and forth they continued. The entire time, Elspeth grunted, hoping they'd remove the gag and allow her to speak.

Finally, once again the men went back to the same places and the cart jerked forward.

Elspeth must have fallen asleep because she woke to being groped. The man who'd been in the back now lay beside her, his massive hand squeezing her breast. She tried to wiggle free, but he was too strong.

It was then she noticed he'd unwrapped the covering from her body. He planned to take her. Her mind whirled as she remained frozen, partly from fear and also because she needed time to think.

Perhaps she could use his distraction to her advantage.

He took the lack of fight as incentive and pulled her closer, his rank breath fanning over her face.

When he pulled her chemise down to free her breasts, rage surged through her and she raised her free hand and yanked the gag out of her mouth. The man was so intent on her nudeness, he didn't notice what she'd done.

Ever so slowly, she reached up with both hands. When he lifted, she swung upward with her fist, ignoring the crunching of bones and blood spewing.

The man groaned and she peered up to the driver. He kept his back to them.

"Do not take her more than once. I want a turn," he called out over his shoulder.

Her assailant was on his back, both hands covering his nose. "Little bitch," he hissed.

Elspeth grabbed the dirk from his side and swiftly sliced across the neck from one side to the other as her father had taught her.

There was a sickening gurgling sound and she pushed the sheet into his gaping mouth.

The man who drove chuckled and Elspeth scurried behind him.

When he turned, she thrust the knife at him and it sunk into him. Unfortunately, he was quick and shifted so that her thrust was not as effective as she'd hoped. Using his free arm, he backhanded her across the face and she fell back onto the wagon.

Elspeth's head spun and she could barely stay on all fours while scrambling to the back of the wagon. When it came to an abrupt halt, she fell sideways.

The man rounded the wagon, the front of his shirt stained with blood, but the dirk was no longer impaled. Obviously, he'd pulled it out.

"Little bitch," he spat and yanked her off the back of the wagon by the hair. Elspeth screamed, but was silenced when, once again, he slapped her across the face.

When she hit the ground, this time she could barely move. This could not be the way she would die. It wasn't how her life was supposed to end.

She'd spent so much time saving lives, helping those who were left behind on battlefields. And now it would be her who would be left out dying. How ironic was fate?

Light sunrays came up across the horizon and Elspeth tried to gather where she was. She cried out when, once again, the man grabbed her feet and dragged her to the woods' edge.

"First I will fuck ye and then kill ye. Tis only fair."

"Never. Let me go."

Her jaw and shoulder sent piercing pain down through the rest of Elspeth's body and she whimpered. Setting her jaw, she kicked but it was of no use. Her feeble attempts to escape would be no match for an angry man of his size.

The best she could hope for was to find a way to remain alive. Perhaps he'd just leave her behind, if he thought she would die.

Exposed from the waist down as he finally stopped yanking her, his narrowed eyes took her in. Elspeth tugged at the torn chemise and pushed away.

After yanking a short knife from his tunic belt, he loosened his pants, freeing himself.

"Lay back and spread yer legs." He went to his knees in front of her. "Do as ye're told or I will back hand ye again. Makes no matter to me if ye're awake for this or not."

Elspeth shook her head. "Damn ye to hell."

He grunted and yanked her foot so hard she fell on her back. At this point, her wound bled profusely, the blood from her split lip dripped down to join in making the top of her chemise redder.

"Leave me. I won't return to the keep. I swear it." She tried pleading although she was sure he didn't hear her. The hardening of his member told her that he'd do what he intended.

Suddenly, a strange expression came over his face, one of disbelief. For a moment, his reddened eyes rounded and then the man fell face forward onto the ground beside her.

It was then Elspeth saw the arrow impaled in his back.

A few moments later, Kieran Ross materialized like an angelic apparition. If he said anything or also planned to do Elspeth harm, she wouldn't know because she passed out.

Chapter Fourteen

Malcolm paced up and down the corridor as the healer tended to Elspeth. Why had the strong-willed girl run away? It made no sense being that her friend remained behind.

According to Kieran, there had been two men present. Kieran and other archers had caught up to a wagon. In the back was a dead man and there was also another who was in the process of attacking her. It seemed his brother had arrived just in time to stop her from being raped. Of course, he had no way of knowing if either man had succeeded prior to Kieran's arrival.

She was in a bad way. The chest injury was torn open and bleeding and her left eye was swollen shut. There were other scrapes and bruises not to mention her split lip. She barely resembled the woman he'd kissed earlier.

The healer walked out of the chamber and looked to him. "She is resting. It will take several days for the pain to go away. Her wound has been cleaned and sewn shut again. Poor lass."

"Was she…" he couldn't finish the sentence, not wishing to sound shallow.

"Nay, she is intact. A virgin." The healer seemed to instinctively know what he was about to ask.

"I thank ye." He waited for the man to walk away before entering the bedchamber. In the center of the bed, Elspeth was very still but awake. She tracked him with her one open eye.

He leaned forward. "Ye must tell me who did this. Did ye wish to get away so badly that ye would leave with those types of men?"

Just then, the door opened and his mother and sister walked in. "What is this I hear? She tried to run away and was attacked?" His mother neared the bed and gasped. "Goodness, what happened to her?"

"She was attacked," Malcolm replied the obvious. "We do not know if she left or was taken by force."

His mother huffed. "Why would anyone take a village girl by force? Her parents' mouths are watering at the idea ye will marry her."

"She is bleeding all over yer bed," Verity added and sniffed. "Smells horrible in here."

"Then leave," he snapped. "Ye could show some compassion." At the lack of emotion, he wondered if perhaps, like him, they were hollow, too.

Verity walked to the door, but his mother lingered. "Perhaps she has a better sense about things than ye," she said in a soothing voice. "It could be a jealous lover of hers tried to take her to keep ye from marrying."

"Mother, please see about breaking yer fast."

"Or," his mother continued, "someone, a member of the clan, wishes to save ye from yerself." Her cool gaze moved to Elspeth's face. "No one knows with her kind of people."

She swept from the room, leaving behind a trail of a floral fragrance.

Malcolm studied Elspeth.

For a moment, she met his gaze and then focused toward the window. He didn't truly know her. It could be that, in part, his mother was right. By insisting on the marriage, maybe he was doing more harm than good.

ELSPETH WANTED TO sleep and forget all about the night before while, at the same time, she wanted to flee, get away from Malcolm and what he represented. The Ross' were cold and heartless. Even his mother and sister seemed to not waver in the presence of someone suffering.

She tried to move, but every part of her body protested.

"I wish to leave with my father," she slurred. "Please."

"He did not come. They sent a message asking that we postpone the marriage for a few days. It seems yer grandmother is ill."

Her grandmother had always been sturdy, a healthy sort. "I should go help."

"I believe it would cause her undue worry to see ye right now."

Her head throbbed and she could only open one eye. Elspeth imagined her appearance would, indeed, shock her family.

Malcolm took her hand. "What happened?"

What should she say? That his mother had hired ruffians to take her away, gave her to them to do as they pleased? Did the woman really think they'd not harm her?

"I do not know the men. They took me from here. I was asleep and woke upon being taken."

"Where were they heading with ye? Ye traveled north."

She racked her brain, trying to remember where exactly they'd been headed. But all she recalled was something about selling her. "They did not speak much other than to say they were not paid as promised."

His eyes narrowed. "Very well," he patted her hand. "Get some rest. Be calm, a guard is posted outside the door."

Just then Ceilidh entered, her face red and eyes swollen. "Tis just now I was allowed to come see about ye," she explained, rushing to the bed only to stop when Malcolm looked to her.

He stood and nodded. After one last look at Elspeth, a hard expression on his face, he walked out.

By the way Ceilidh's face transformed at taking her in, she must have looked a fright. Her friend's eyes widened and her mouth opened and closed. "Poor dear, what did they do to ye?"

Tears spilled down Ceilidh's cheeks. "Ye must have been scared to death."

"Aye," Elspeth agreed and sniffed. "I didn't expect to live to see morning."

Ceilidh looked over her shoulder to the door, which remained opened just a bit. "Who did this?" she whispered.

Elspeth motioned for her to come closer until the woman was merely inches away. "Lady Ross paid two men to take me and leave me somewhere. She did tell them not to harm me, but I think she cared little what happened to me."

When Ceilidh gasped, Elspeth motioned for her to quiet. "I cannot go home like this. Not only will Father do something irrational, but grandmother is very ill."

"My mother came this morning for me," Ceilidh said. "Fortunately, she knows several of the guards' wives and they've convinced her to remain a few days. I will tell her she cannot come up here because the Ross' won't allow it."

Elspeth nodded. "They barely tolerate me. So that is not a stretch of the truth."

A maid entered with a tray, upon it a bowl of steaming stew and a cup. "Lady Ross instructed a meal be brought to ye, Miss."

"Is it poisoned?" Ceilidh blurted.

"Thank ye," Elspeth replied to the girl who looked at her with mouth agape. "Would ye like me to fetch the healer, Miss?"

Elspeth shook her head. "He has already been here."

The girl hurried out of the room.

"Does she think Malcolm beat me?" Elspeth asked her friend. "The servants will all know about this momentarily."

Murmurs sounded from the hallway; the guard had stopped the girl. "No word of what ye have seen, or else I will beat ye myself." The guard's deep voice left no doubt he meant every word.

"Yes, of course," the maid replied in a trembling voice.

Ceilidh shook her head. "Seems not right away, although this kind of thing does not stay quiet long."

"What should I do?" Elspeth asked her friend. "Malcolm is speaking about marriage. How can I marry him? It will be a huge disaster."

By the way Ceilidh scrunched her face in confusion, the answer was not clear to her either. "Everyone is talking about the marriage. They think ye have done something to force him into it."

"Would anyone truly believe Malcolm can be made to do anything against his will?"

"That is what Moira said this morning," Ceilidh giggled and took Elspeth's hand in both of her own. "All will be well. I am thankful ye were rescued. If ye'd been lost, I would have died."

Elspeth shook her head. "There has to be a way to convince Malcolm to return me home."

"Ye dislike him?"

It was hard to put how she felt into words. "Malcolm is quite different than I thought. Tis like when we are alone, he is a different person."

Ceilidh's eyebrows lifted.

"I do like him and, given time, I could grow to care for him. However, a marriage between a laird and a simple village girl can only make for trouble.

CHAPTER FIFTEEN

P AIGE SNUCK THROUGH the side door of the keep and ended up in the corridor just outside the kitchens. She listened for anyone about, but could barely hear over the thudding of her own heartbeats.

What was Alec thinking by bringing her here and announcing he would marry her? If he persisted on the idea of marriage, she'd have to find a way to dissuade him.

Her bundles had been left just inside the door, she hoped they remained. Of course, it would be impossible to get away, but she could hide. After all, the keep was huge and there had to be plenty of places to squirrel away.

With a sigh of relief, she found her bundles, hoisted the humble parcels and tiptoed to where she hoped were the servants' quarters. People she'd met who worked at a keep always referred to their quarters being "downstairs".

"What are ye doing?" The familiar voice startled Paige so badly she dropped one of the bundles. Paige whirled.

Just behind her, Lady McLeod studied her with curiosity. "Who are ye hiding from?" The woman was slight, with a welcoming softness in her expression and kind eyes. Although she'd only spoken to Lady McLeod once, it seemed the woman could be quite stern and to the point.

Best to tell the truth. After all, if anyone would help, it would be Alec's parents. "I hide from yer son, Lady McLeod. I do not wish to be the cause of any problems in yer family, Lady McLeod."

The woman's face softened. "Tis nothing against ye personally. My son is impulsive." She waved her hand as if it explained away any further speaking.

"I was thinking," Paige began. "I could perhaps hide in the servants' quarters. At least until tis safe to go."

Lady McLeod considered her for a long moment. "That is the first place my son would search." She let out a breath. "He will not change his mind. The McLeods come from a long line of stubborn men."

"And yet ye tried to make him reconsider," Paige blurted, instantly regretting it. "I overheard," she finished weakly.

The woman shrugged. "His father asked me to." Her lips curved. "Come along, ye may stay in my drawing room. He will not think to look for ye there."

They walked side-by-side. All the time, Paige wondered why the woman didn't just make her stay in the stables or perhaps with some of the refugees. Then again, it was probably to keep Alec from becoming angry with anyone.

"Why are ye helping me?" Paige asked Lady McLeod.

The woman chuckled softly. "Tis better than allowing ye to run off or be harmed in some way. My son cares for ye, so I will ensure yer safety."

The arrived at Lady McLeod's drawing room. It was small, but nicely furnished. There was a writing table and chaise. Thick rugs under her feet were like walking on plush grass. From the window hung plush curtains that kept the chill out.

"Ye can start a fire in the hearth. There are blankets and a washbasin," Lady McLeod pointed out.

Paige looked around the room. It was much too grand a chamber for her to be in. "Why does yer son want me?"

The woman paused and considered. Her gaze took Paige in. "Ye are a lovely lass and from the way ye are acting, a sensible one. My Alec, although impulsive, is not daft."

Lady McLeod looked to the door to the drawing room. "Remain here, ye will be safe, warm and well hidden."

"What about Al…yer son?"

"Leave him to me. I shall inform him that ye are safe and in my care. Once he decides to act responsibly, he and I will discuss further what should be done."

Lady McLeod swept from the room, not seeming to have a care in the world. Paige couldn't help but frown at the doorway. This had been much easier than she expected.

What would Alec do? Although she had to agree that he did seem impulsive, the thought of hurting him in any way was not her intention.

ALEC HAD GIVEN up trying to find Paige. His horse was now returned to the stables and he sat in the great room at one of the long trestle tables across from his mother. For what seemed like hours, she'd explained to him the error of his ways and how Paige had asked for help in hiding her.

He had an idea now where she was and as soon as his mother went to bed, he'd go in search of the girl and ensure she was well and that, indeed, it was her idea to hide. Other than that, he wondered if perhaps he had been impulsive.

Amidst war, a man could become confused. However, in his case, the possible lack of a future made him ponder more about what he might never have or experience.

A wife, children and one day becoming laird of his clan was not guaranteed when he was faced with constant battles and possible death.

He studied his mother for a moment, not hearing what she said. Although seeming calm, he knew she constantly worried. Not just about him and Ethan, but about their people. The many who now sought refuge within the keep's walls. There were also the farmers and surrounding villagers who remained steadfast trying their best to defend against the Ross warriors.

"Mother, it is not that I do not agree with ye, but I wish to be married. What would ye have me do?"

She leaned forward. "Do as yer father asks. Travel east, ask to speak to the Campbell and ask for one of his daughters' hands to marry."

"Why would they agree? They are powerful and have nothing to gain from joining with us. We are not only smaller, but are embroiled in this clash with the Ross'." Alec shook his head. "The Campbell will see right through it."

"Of course he will. He is an astute man. However, he and yer father are friends. The Campbell respects yer da."

He bowed his head and considered what she said. The Campbells would not just even the field between them and Ross Clan. With their huge army, they would bring the war to an immediate end. That was if the Campbell agreed, which Alec had major doubts.

"What if Da meets with him and asks for his help? Or perhaps marry Merida to his younger son. He seemed interested the last time we visited," Alec pointed out.

Merida, his sister, looked up from where she'd been sewing with two servants, her mouth wide open.

There would be a much more spirited conversation now, as his feisty sister rarely kept her opinions to herself. The garment she worked on dropped to the floor as she stormed to where he sat.

"I will marry whom I please. I refused to be yer pawn, Brother," she said, her eyes like arrows into his. "Tis yer duty to marry for the clan's sake."

His mother motioned to Merida. "Tis each of yer duties. I have to agree that the idea has merit. The Campbell's daughters are not quite of age yet."

"I refuse. Roald Campbell is a toad."

Their mother laughed. "Oh, Merida. Roald is fair of face and has always paid ye attention."

Merida whirled and stormed toward their father's study. "I will tell Da I would rather toss myself from the parapets than marry a Campbell."

"I am ready for this to end." Alec's chest constricted. "Very well, Mother. I will not seek marriage to the lass."

"She is a kind and lovely girl," his mother replied. "I can see why she appeals to ye. Her thoughts are level and there is a certain calmness about her. Perhaps Ethan…"

"No!" Alec growled. "My brother would not treat her well."

"He needs something! I am only suggesting she could perhaps bring peace to his troubled heart."

It was as if cold loch water were poured over him. A chill filled his entire being and Alec fought not to shiver in front of his mother. As first-born, it was true that his first duty was to the clan. If there were a chance to bring peace to this clan, then it would be well worth it.

His father had brought up the idea of marrying him to a larger clan as an alternative if the request for a truce was not received well. When Paige's brother's body appeared, it didn't leave them any other option, but to ask for help.

Every part of him rebelled against the idea of Ethan taking Paige for a wife. Although not cruel to women, his younger brother was restless and without patience. Ethan lived for battle, seeming to relish bloodshed and violence. It was troubling.

"I will go speak to Father. If not Clan Campbell, perhaps the Murrays. Their daughters are of marriageable age."

Lady McLeod let out a long sigh and reached for his hand and took it in both of hers. "This is for the best, Son."

When he walked up the stairs much later, he looked in the direction of his mother's drawing room. Paige was there, he sensed it. The beautiful woman who'd come undone in his arms was probably fast asleep. Her arousal had overcome his senses and every inch of him now demanded to take her.

It would never be. Of course, he could. Alec was sure that if he went to her, it would not be hard to seduce the beauty. However, what good would that bring? It would be a constant torture upon seeing her daily if she married Ethan and knowing his brother had every right over her body.

As hard as he tried, Alec could not picture the Murrays' daughters. There were three, or was it four? All blonde and, from what he remembered, very attractive.

His manservant stood from a chair when he entered the room. "Would ye like something to eat or drink?"

"No, thank ye, Liam. I will wash up and go to bed. Please do the same. I have told ye not to wait up if I linger." He placed a hand on the young man's shoulder. "Tomorrow or the next day, we will travel north. Would ye like to come with me?"

Liam nodded. "I would." The young man hobbled away, his body swaying side to side as he forced the uncooperative right leg forward with each step.

Alec focused on the injured leg. Liam had been much too young to go to battle and, because of it, he'd been immediately overtaken. Although barely escaping with his life, the younger man would never walk without a horrible limp.

This was the reason the war between them and the Ross' had to end.

Ethan's lack of control and killing Laird Ross was, indeed, reason for revenge. However, it did not justify the continuous maiming and killing of innocent people who had nothing to do with it.

In a way, Alec had considered asking Ethan to give himself up, to accept the consequences of his actions. As much as he loved his brother, there was a time when one should realize how much damage he had caused and want to stop it. On the contrary, Ethan continued on as if enjoying the consequences and not one bit repentant.

"I almost forgot," Liam said, bringing Alec out of his musings. "The woman, Paige, asked me to tell ye she was sorry for causing ye any hurt. And to thank ye for the protection offered."

Alec nodded. "Sleep well, Liam."

PAIGE WOKE WITH a start, not quite sure where she was. Taking in the luxurious surroundings, the fog subsided and what had occurred the night before came to mind. It had been a long time since she'd slept so soundly. It didn't hurt that the chaise she laid upon was soft, enveloping her like a warm hug.

Shivering, she went to the corner behind the screen and relieved herself. After, she quickly went about rinsing her hands, arms and face. Feeling self-conscious, she dipped a cloth in the chilly water, lifted her chemise and washed her body. She kept an eye on the doorway, hoping no one would enter and find her exposed. And yet, she needed to clean. So she did quick work of washing between her legs and once that was completed, she rinsed the cloth and wiped down each calf and foot.

Feeling refreshed, she untied a bundle, pulled out a clean frock and donned it. Then she brushed out her hair, braided it and allowed it to hang down her back.

Her stomach growled and she let out a sigh. With only having had a small meal the night before, she was ravenous. Perhaps she could offer to help in the kitchen in exchange for a meal.

With that thought in mind, she grabbed her soiled clothing to wash later and headed down the stairs.

"Tis something that must be done, Son. We must have peace. Our people are dying and there isn't anything else to be done."

There wasn't a way not to overhear the laird's deep voice and Paige worried about walking past the doorway of what was obviously Alec's chambers and being seen. She hesitated upon seeing a guard's back. The man stood in the doorway facing in and blocking some of the view. It was possible she could scurry by and not be considered as spying.

"It may be a sacrifice, Son, but ye must go. Tis the only way I can see our clan ever having peace. Tis not possible to leave until later this day. The scouts will return then. I must hear what is happening. We do not want to be attacked while we are away."

Her heart sank. Was Alec going to attempt to speak to the Ross'? Surely they'd kill him just as they had her brother.

When would the madness stop? Did men not think before formulating such idiotic plans?

When several men began speaking, Paige took advantage and hurried past the doorway.

The kitchen was bustling with activity. She went to Rhona, who smiled at her. "I am hungry. May I eat and then offer to help in some way?"

The cook pushed her into a chair. "No, ye cannot help. Alec will have my hide."

A bowl of boiled grains and bread were shoved in front of her and she ate without tasting any of it. It was best to have a full stomach for what she was about to do.

Chapter Sixteen

Another day passed and Elspeth felt minimally better. Fortunately, she could open both eyes now. Malcolm stood at the window, peering out. He probably thought her to be asleep which gave her an opportunity to study him.

With a proud stance, wearing the Ross colors, he was every bit a laird. The stern set of his jaw and blank expression told of a lack of emotion. The man was both handsome and terrifying. How many men had he slaughtered in battle? How was it possible for someone to live with the fact they'd taken a life?

And yet he stood there, seeming to consider the day ahead, plans for another battle or confrontation that would lead to more death and violence.

He leaned forward, seeming to find something interesting in the distance and she wondered if scouts returned with reports. An excuse for them to fight again.

The sunlight made the strands of his hair a reddish tone and his long eyelashes fell and lifted as he studied the landscape before him.

She let out a long sigh and he turned to her. For an instant, his face softened, but it was gone before she could be sure it wasn't a figment of her imagination.

"How do ye feel?"

Pushing up, she sat and raked the tangles back from her face. "Like I was slapped multiple times."

Malcolm scowled. "If they were not already dead, I would hunt them down and ensure it."

Violence. It seemed the man did not think of much else.

"I do feel better. Would ye mind giving me privacy? I need to get out of bed."

He nodded, and went to the door. "I will be right outside."

Why didn't he leave? Not that she should care, but surely the sight of her had to be frightening. By the aching of her face, she was sure there was still much bruising and swelling. Also, she'd not had a chance to even run a comb through her hair.

Having spent most of the last day sleeping from whatever it was the healer poured down her throat, she felt dirty and smelly.

At the washbasin, she dared to look into the mirror and winced. A lump had formed on the right side of her face and dark purpling marked the same side. There was a bright red mark where she'd been slapped. The man must have been wearing a ring because there was a lesion on her chin. Although her left eye remained swollen, at least she could open it now.

Still, beauty she was not at the moment.

The same servant girl entered and placed a tray on a small table. The girl kept her gaze averted.

"Can ye help me with my hair please?" Elspeth asked. She wanted to comb her own hair, but with her chest injury, she could only lift one hand.

"Of course, Miss." The girl seemed relieved to have something to do and hurried over to a chair that Elspeth lowered to. "Just untangle it and braid it please. Being in bed makes it hard to keep it in order."

"What is yer name?" Elspeth asked the young maid.

"I am Maggie, Miss."

The girl chatted about the plans for a meal and her friend's predicament at needing to see her family due to a relative's illness, but not allowed to go. It was obvious everyone was paying a price because it wasn't safe to travel. And yet the battles would continue unless something drastic happened.

"There now, perfect." The maid studied her. "Ye look much better today, Miss."

"If this is better, I cannot imagine what I must have looked like before," Elspeth admitted.

"Ye are healing." Malcolm stood at the doorway and Elspeth wondered how long he'd been there. She refrained from saying anything.

The maid gave Elspeth one last smile and left.

"I sent a messenger to let yer family know ye are well. They responded with news that yer grandmother fares better."

Elspeth blinked back tears. "I am pleased to hear it."

He didn't sit. Instead, he motioned to the tray. "Ye should eat." Then he walked back to the window and paced back.

"Why do ye not accept a truce?" Elspeth asked between bites. "No one will truly win. Ye must be aware of it."

"Tis a matter of revenge, Elspeth. Unless ye have lost someone in that manner, I do not expect ye would understand."

It was the first time he'd said her name. It sounded different, felt intimate. She couldn't formulate a response when considering that it was true, she'd not lost someone in the battles. However, the thought of her father or brothers dying would make her angry.

"And yet ye expect yer people to accept the deaths of their loved ones without resentment?"

His eyes widened and, for a moment, she considered that perhaps it was not wise to overstep with a man who had no heart nor did he care for others.

"I wanted to inform ye that once ye have recovered, we will continue forward with the handfasting."

"Why? It makes little sense. My father will accept me back home. He will believe me when I say nothing happened."

He came to where she sat and bent at the waist. They were close, their faces but inches apart. "Tis like I said. A matter of principle." His gaze moved to her lips and Elspeth was sure he would not kiss her. Perhaps a droplet of blood or cut caught his attention. Surely he wouldn't wish to kiss in her current state.

Ever so softly, his lips brushed over hers. And even though he didn't press in, the gentleness of the kiss made her eyes fall closed. He continued the light butterfly-gentle kisses across her lips and to the sides of her mouth.

Elspeth could barely breathe, unsure she could ever take a full breath again. The strong pull between them had to be because of everything that happened. Her thinking was not right. The chaos of their lives and surroundings. This was not a time for sentimentalism.

Malcolm Ross was not a man who would take time for pleasures like this. Why did he kiss her and why did she feel such strong reactions to his presence and touch?

Cupping her jaw again as gentle as a feather's touch, he pressed a kiss at her ear. There, he dared to press a bit harder, the warmth of his mouth sending tendrils of awareness down her spine.

She reached up and with trembling fingers, touched his face.

Malcolm lifted just a bit and looked into her eyes. "I find it impossible to remain away from ye. It is not a sacrifice on my part to marry ye, Elspeth. I wish to have ye as a wife. It feels right."

A shaky breath left her and realizing she was still touching his face, she withdrew her hand. "I do not understand. I am but a village girl, not trained or able to sit to yer right as lady."

"My mother will teach ye..."

She couldn't hear the rest of what he said, knowing the woman would never accept her and would probably try again to get rid of her. There wasn't time for illusions. It was best not to allow her heart free rein only to suffer when being torn from him would break her heart.

"...once yer parents arrive, ye and I will marry here in the chapel. Mother will insist a wedding festival take place after..."

"The clashes between ye and the McLeods end? How long will that be?" Elspeth could not keep the bitterness from her voice.

His face hardened, the same lips that had been so gentle on hers pressed into a tight line.

"Malcolm," Tristan said, entering the room. "Someone is at the gate. A woman. She demands to speak to ye."

Malcolm rushed to the window and Elspeth looked between the two men, hoping to find out more about what was going on.

"Could it be a trap of some kind?" Malcolm asked.

His brother shook his head. "Nay, Kieran and two of his archers are escorting her."

"Allow her in. Tell Kieran to bring her to the great room. I will go find Uncle Gregor."

Both hurried out of the room without even a glance in her direction. Malcolm was bent on this revenge plan of his and would not stop. She wanted to scream in frustration when the door opened and he walked back in.

"I will speak with ye later. Do not worry. I am sure this is more about the woman's family or a need than anything to do with the McLeods."

He pressed a kiss to the top of her head and walked out. Elspeth closed her eyes and sat back.

What was she going to do?

How strange that a woman had come demanding to speak to Malcolm. Despite knowing it wasn't any of her business, Elspeth couldn't help but wonder what was happening. Perhaps the young maid, Maggie, would know. Servants were rarely paid any attention to and knew the entire goings-on in the keep. Not one to spend the days idle, she went to the doorway, cracked it open and was startled by the huge warrior standing outside.

He looked at her without expression. "Is there something ye need?"

Elspeth cleared her throat. "Could someone fetch Maggie?" She pulled the robe she wore closed at the neck. "I need a dress."

"My laird said ye will remain abed and not be allowed to leave the room." His gaze moved over her in a perfunctory manner. "Ye are dressed well enough for remaining in bed."

Heaving a sigh, she closed the door in his face. "Abed. No one remains in bed all day. If anything, I should be dressed in case someone comes and tries to take me again." She continued mumbling while pulling a trunk open. It was all men's clothing. Several tunics and breeches as well as neatly folded tartans.

Apparently, Malcolm was a neat person. Or his manservant was anyway. She'd not considered where he had been sleeping and instantly looked to a door on the opposite side of the bed. She went to it and gently opened it.

It was a simple chamber. There was a slender bed and what looked to be a pallet on the floor. Atop the bed, a tunic had been thrown over it. The room had to be his manservant's. However, by the fine fabric of the tunic, that did not belong to any servant. It had to be Malcolm's.

Why would he sleep there and not in one of the finer bedrooms?

The door to the small room opened and a male servant walked in. He stopped in his tracks at seeing her.

"Is there something ye require, Mistress?"

Elspeth almost looked behind herself to see if someone else stood there before realizing he was speaking to her. "I am not yer mistress. Is Mal… yer laird sleeping here?"

The young man blushed and looked to the tunic upon the narrow bed. "He did."

"And ye here?" Elspeth asked, pointing to the pallet on the floor.

The young man swallowed visibly. "Nay. He sleeps there."

When her eyes rounded and her mouth fell open, he explained

quickly. "My laird wishes to be nearby to hear if something happens to ye. He only slept here last night. He will no doubt relocate to another room tonight…"

She nodded. "I will ensure that is true. Perhaps ye and he can sleep in the room I am in and I in here." Elspeth was satisfied with the idea and gave him a firm nod. "I will speak to him about it."

The young man didn't seem convinced in the least. "Aye, perhaps."

She walked out of the room, her mind awhirl. For a heartless man, Malcolm seemed to take much care with her. Whatever the reason, she couldn't fathom. Yes, perhaps there was sexual desire between them. She wouldn't deny it, but that was not reason enough. A man such as Malcolm always had an underlying reason for his actions. What she needed to find out was what role she played in his plans.

Maggie entered the bedchamber just moments after Elspeth returned.

"What is happening? Is there something amiss? I heard a woman arrived to speak to the laird," Elspeth asked her without hesitation.

"The servants are all doing their best to find out what it is all about. The woman came demanding to speak to the laird. She is angry about something." Maggie seemed free with information.

"A spurned lover perhaps?" Elspeth mused, not liking the idea at all.

"Nay, she is a villager from McLeod lands."

"I suppose I will hear about it soon enough," Elspeth said, pretending nonchalance. "Why aren't I allowed to dress and leave the chamber?"

The maid went to a wardrobe and opened it. Inside was the dress she'd worn upon arriving. It had been washed and pressed. "He is afraid ye will come into harm. But if ye wish to dress, I cannot possibly stop ye."

Despite the maddening situation, Elspeth giggled. "I like ye, Maggie."

CHAPTER SEVENTEEN

IN THE GREAT room stood one of his scouts. He was a bloody mess and barely able to stand. Several guards were helping him to lie upon a table so that the healer could care for him.

"What happened?" Malcolm asked, helping them with the large man.

"They were ambushed. It was as if they knew where to hide in wait." The guard speaking shook his head. "The other three are dead."

Once the man lay upon the table, Malcolm went to go see about the unexpected visitor.

Mind awhirl, Malcolm stalked to the courtyard where the woman stood next to Kieran. His brother's size made her seem especially frail. However, there was pure determination in the gaze that met his.

He had to admit she was beautiful. With golden hair that had escaped its trappings surrounding her face, she reminded him of a woodland Fae.

"Ye are brave to come without escort," he informed her, looking her up and down in an effort to intimidate her.

It worked and she swallowed visibly. "I am not afraid of ye," she lied and looked to Kieran and the other archer who stood to her opposite side. "As far as escorts, I have more than I need it seems."

When she lifted an eyebrow in challenge, he had to admire her bravery.

Noting the craning of necks and obvious observers who had begun to gather, he took her elbow. "We will speak inside."

He guided her into the keep, through the great room, which was curiously full of servants pretending to clean, and down a short corridor to his study.

Once inside, he motioned for someone to bring her a drink. Hospitality did not wane even during times of war. Once she was seated, he moved to stand next to the chair opposite her.

"What is yer name?"

"I am Paige O'Leary. Clan McLeod." She hitched her chin proudly. "I demand a truce."

There were chuckles from the men who'd entered with them. Just then, his uncle and Aiden entered. Aiden eyed the woman with interest and Malcolm got the distinct impression he'd come upon her before. In contrast, the woman didn't seem to notice Aiden at all.

"Is that what the McLeod has come to? Sending women as messengers? What makes ye think I won't kill ye and send yer body back like the last one?"

The woman flinched and let out a sharp breath. She stood slowly and approached him. "That messenger ye sent back dead was my brother. He'd gone to work for Laird McLeod so that he could feed me and our grandfather." A single tear trickled down her cheek and he followed its progress. "Ye had no mercy for him, I do not expect less. However, I came without anyone knowing because I have nothing to lose."

"Tis the way of war."

"No, this is not a war. This is a vendetta. One that is affecting women, who ye seem to think do not count. We are the ones losing our husbands, sons, fathers and brothers. While ye continue on this quest for whatever it is."

"A McLeod killed my father."

"A Ross killed my brother," she retorted, not backing down. "My grandfather as a result as well."

Malcolm could feel fury coiling in his chest. "I will not justify myself to a…"

"Woman? A McLeod?" The woman was relentless, braver than some of the men in the room. "If ye truly wished to avenge yer father, why not seek justice by slaying the one who killed him? Not making us all pay for his actions?"

The starkness and truth of the statement made his heart plummet. It was true. All the deaths so far had been men who'd had nothing to do with the one bastard who'd killed his father.

The guards who'd been there had informed him that it was Ethan McLeod who'd struck out when his father had confronted him about being on Ross lands. Then like a coward, he had raced away with two men while the four that remained had been cut down by Ross guards.

He looked around the room and saw that everyone present looked anywhere but at him. His own men agreed with the woman.

"Take her away. Put her in a chamber and lock the door." He was not about to continue to argue with her.

"Tis the truth and ye know it," she cried out as two men took her by the arms. "Ye killed my brother and yet I forgive ye and ask for peace." Her hurt-filled eyes bore into his as tears poured down her face.

Malcolm looked to one of the guards. "See that no harm comes to her. Ensure she is brought food and drink."

The woman's sobs echoed as she was taken away. Malcolm whirled away from the door and poured a drink.

"Tis nothing but drivel," Aiden said, coming to his side. "A woman bent on revenge. I am willing to bet if ye were left with her and a dagger, she would not hesitate to plunge it into yer heart."

He didn't want to hear his cousin at the moment and looked at him. "Ye recognized her."

The statement made Aiden's eyebrows rise. "Nay. Why would I?"

"It was yer expression when ye entered."

He looked to his uncle who studied them and then shrugged. "I do not think she was sent by the McLeods."

Malcolm moved away from his irksome cousin. "What makes ye say that?"

"For one, she walked. Secondly, she didn't state anything based on speaking to a McLeod. Her plea was about the people and the impact on her family alone."

His uncle was the one person Malcolm respected as much as his own now-departed father. The man never argued with him, nor did he try to change Malcolm's mind even if he disagreed.

"Now we must ask ourselves how to return her without harm."

"Why should we?" Kieran spoke. "Give her to a man here."

"Are ye volunteering?" Tristan, who sat in a chair, asked with a smirk. "Marriage may settle ye."

The younger brother ignored Tristan. "I think she was sent by the McLeods to spy."

Malcolm swallowed his drink and paced. "It could be anything. For now, she will remain locked in a chamber. I will decide on it later. I must speak to the injured guard and find out what he saw."

"I can do that if ye wish," Aiden said, making for the door. "Ye have much to do."

He wasn't sure exactly what to do at the moment. There was the fact they could retaliate for the killing of his scouts. It would mean more bloodshed.

"If ye truly wished to avenge yer father, why not seek justice by finding the one who killed him? Not making us all pay for his actions?"

The words repeated in his mind and he rounded his father's desk and sunk into the chair behind it.

His uncle let out a sigh. "Tis tiring and eventually a decision must be made. This cannot continue forever."

Kieran growled under his breath. "No. We must continue until our father's killer pays. The rest of the damned McLeods with him."

Men rushed in and Malcolm jumped to his feet. "What now?"

"Tis Alec McLeod. He is here."

As one, they hurried out and down the corridor. "How many men did he bring?"

"None."

Malcolm froze as realization filled him.

"Why would he do it? He was not the one who killed Father?" Kieran said. "Killing him will be satisfying, I must admit, but not as much as…"

"He comes because he is in love."

The words made everyone stop and stare at him.

"Have ye gone daft?" Tristan asked, shaking his head. "No one is that foolish."

"Mark my words." Malcolm continued toward the courtyard.

Unlike the woman, Alec's face was bruised and bloody. He struggled against the warriors who held him in place.

People in the courtyard surrounded the small group, mostly his warriors and a few nosy clansfolk.

"An unexpected surprise," Malcolm said, taking one slow step at a time down to where Alec stood. "Two surprises in fact."

"Release her. I offer myself in her stead."

Malcolm turned to meet Tristan's gaze and lifted an eyebrow.

"I do not take direction from a McLeod," he responded and then looked to the guards. "Bring him inside."

Instead of going into his study, they stopped in the great room. Alec looked to where the injured guard was now moaning in pain as the healer did what he could to help.

Malcolm walked to a table near it and ordered the servants who remained to leave. "Ensure ye are out of earshot or ye will be whipped."

The servants' eyes popped wide. Some looked to each other and shrugged. Damn them, they knew he would not follow through with the threat. Hopefully, Alec hadn't noticed their lack of concern.

He didn't care if the man stood or sat. He wasn't injured enough to need the latter. "Release him. He will not go anywhere. Remain at the doorways."

The guards released their holds on Alec and went to the designated exits.

"Now, explain to me why ye are really here," Malcolm demanded in a bored tone. He knew exactly why at noting the man searching the room. No doubt looking for the fair Paige.

Alec's upper lip curved in anger. "If ye hurt her, I will…"

"Do nothing. Ye are only one man and without a weapon."

"I demand ye release her. I am freely giving myself. What more would ye want?"

Malcolm chuckled without mirth and shook his head. "Do ye really need to ask? I want yer brother's head."

To his credit, the man looked down and nodded. "I understand."

"Then bring him here and we will exchange the lass for him," Kieran said with a smirk. "Would ye do that?"

"He is my blood," Alec replied. "I cannot."

Kieran shrugged. "Then she remains."

Malcolm noticed movement at the top of the stairs. No doubt a nosy servant. He walked closer to see who it was, but the person scurried away. "I do not agree to yer terms. Perhaps if we keep ye here, yer brother will come for ye."

When Alec met his gaze, Malcolm knew the younger brother would do no such thing. He looked to his two brothers and had no doubt neither would hesitate to come for him.

"Love makes ye do stupid things, McLeod," Malcolm said and then motioned to the guards. "Take him to the dungeon."

>>><<<

Elspeth hurried back into the bedchamber, her heart pounding. Had Malcolm caught her spying? He had seen the bottom of her skirts, which unfortunately were a distinct blue.

Struggling with her uninjured arm, she unfastened the ribbon in the front of the bodice and managed to wiggle out of the overdress. The removal of the shift underneath was simpler.

In a clean chemise Molly had brought, she hung up the dress and returned it to the wardrobe. After, she grabbed the discarded shawl and wrapped it about her. If he came, he would not know she'd dressed.

Thankfully, the guard at the door had gone down to help with whatever was happening after instructing her to remain in the chamber. He'd not seemed to notice she'd dressed when she'd opened the door to his knocks.

Just as she went to the window, the door opened and Malcolm entered. He looked to her and frowned. "Ye should not be out of bed."

"I need to stretch my legs," she replied. "Just for a moment."

He nodded and opened the trunk at the foot of the bed and then spread a tartan on the floor. Down on his knees, he pleated it and then stood when he was satisfied. He removed the breeches he wore and stood in only a tunic that came to his upper thighs.

"Can ye not dress somewhere else?"

He gave her a bland look. "Ye have seen me fully bare, do ye not remember?"

Heat rose to her cheeks and she turned away. "Not on purpose."

"Hmm." He gave a noncommittal reply.

Once again, he straightened the tartan and lay upon it. Elspeth couldn't help but watch as he expertly tied it about his waist and then got to his feet.

Pulling one end, he brought the loose fabric up over his shoulder and then joined it with one from the front. He walked to a side table and used a broach upon it to secure it in place.

Once done, he looked every bit the Laird of Clan Ross.

"What is happening?" she asked.

He looked directly at her. "Much. I must address the clan."

"May I attend?"

For a long moment, he seemed to consider it, and then shook his head. "Nay, I will return and inform ye what is said." He came to her and, once again, as if they were lovers, kissed her on the mouth lightly. "Get rest."

Elspeth wasn't sure what could be done. She knew now that not only a woman named Paige had come, but also Alec McLeod, Laird McLeod's oldest son and next to be laird.

There had to be a way she could help. Her mind raced. She would not allow these people to die. She would speak to Malcolm and convince him to allow them to go.

Chapter Eighteen

Malcolm looked over the gathered people in the inner courtyard. At the top of the steps, he stood at the keep entrance, his brother, Tristan, to his right and Uncle Gregor on the left. Kieran stood beside Tristan, his mother and sister behind him.

There was whispering between his mother and Verity and he overheard them mentioning the upcoming preparations for the evening meal. How different these women were than the two women there against their will.

Elspeth fought to heal people and even while injured, she had asked for action from him. The other woman, Paige, had risked her life in an effort to bargain for peace between two warring clans.

His mother and sister worried about mundane matters and, in a way, he was glad for it. They'd not had to suffer a day in their lives. The worst pain they'd experienced was the loss of a husband and father. As far as he was concerned, that would be the way it would remain.

The gathered people quieted when he lifted a hand to get their attention.

First, he scanned the faces ensuring everyone knew he was aware of their presence.

"Tis time to consider what Clan Ross will stand for in the future," he began. "We must not relent in our pursuit to avenge not just my father's death, but so many others who have died since."

People looked to one another when he paused, remaining silent, not wishing to miss a word he spoke.

"However, the ongoing battles have cost us all much." There was a collective inhalation and, as one, the people leaned forward in anticipation of what he would say.

"Laird McLeod's eldest son is our prisoner now. Turned himself over to us and I accept this as a reason to call a truce for now."

The only sounds were of birds in the distance and a child crying. The babe was quickly quieted.

Malcolm could not tear his gaze from one young lad, his dirty face drawn in expectation. He was orphaned, losing his parents to illness and then his older brother in battle. The boy had to fend for himself now and it showed in the bare feet and torn, stained tunic he wore. These were the true victims of war.

"We shall send a messenger to the McLeods agreeing to peace. Once they accept, ye can all return to yer homes and land."

There was crying and cheering. People hugged one another as Malcolm and his family watched.

Several farmers and village men walked up to him and shook Malcolm's hand, swearing fealty on behalf of themselves, their sons and their families.

In exchange, they were promised food and any help needed for livestock and farms.

As the people dispersed, a heavy weariness fell over Malcolm. The weight that had pressed down on his shoulders since the battles began may have lifted, but he was left with the burden of so much to be done and a decision of what to do with the two people who'd come of their own volition.

"Tis stupid," Kieran muttered. "Tis Ethan who should be in our dungeon."

Malcolm followed his younger brother inside the doorway of the keep. "We will continue in our quest to find him. Ye can have the honor of killing him. But our people cannot stand for us to remain at war any longer. Winter comes."

"Once this is done," Kieran motioned toward the courtyard, "my men and I go to hunt."

"No." Malcolm grabbed him by the tunic and held him in place. His brother was broader and taller, but Kieran respected him and didn't struggle. His hazel eyes narrowed as they stood nose to nose.

"Ye will wait until the truce is in place. Until we are sure they are not going to retaliate immediately for Alec being here. A battle right now will throw us back into war right as winter sets. It would not be fair to the people. Our father would never allow any kind of battle to cause families to be hungry through the harsh season."

Kieran's shoulders lowered. "Ye are right." Although his brother seemed to agree, Malcolm knew him well. There was a restlessness in his brother that rarely settled.

"I need ye to escort the next group of men who guard the northern post. It will be good for ye to ensure all is well there."

Of course, it was an excuse for Kieran to be gone for at least three days, but it would be good for his brother. Being he was in charge of the guards there, it was not an odd request.

"Aye, my men have been there overlong," Kieran finally agreed.

Their uncle walked in. "I will be traveling with the messenger who goes to see Laird McLeod. Tis best one of our family goes."

The brothers frowned at their uncle. Malcolm wasn't keen on losing his uncle if the McLeods decided to kill the messenger. "Why doesn't Aiden go?"

"I will go," Gregor insisted. "Tis my job as my brother would always send me for such matters."

It was true. Their uncle had always been the intermediary when it came to discussions between clans. He was gifted in such a way.

"Very well, but there will be twenty men with ye," Malcolm said, not allowing for argument.

"They will think we come to fight," his uncle said with a chuckle, "not to barter peace. Let it be ten."

"I think that's too few, but ten it is," Malcolm replied. "No less."

"Very well," his uncle said. "I depart at first light."

MALCOLM TRUDGED THE rest of the way inside. So much had happened and there was still much to be done. From providing foodstuffs to the people, assigning escorts and ensuring that he made the correct decision when it came to both Alec McLeod and the woman, Paige.

Perhaps he'd send the woman to the McLeods with his uncle. She could be turned over to them and they would keep her safe.

The thing that had to be decided was what to do about Alec. If they bartered for peace, Laird McLeod would demand the return of his son.

He placed a hand on his uncle's shoulder. "There is something more we need to discuss, Uncle." They made their way to the study. Soon Tristan, Kieran and Aiden joined them.

Malcolm narrowed his eyes at his cousin who didn't seem the least bit perturbed that his father would be heading into the lion's den in a manner of speaking.

"Do ye plan to accompany yer father?" he asked his cousin, who'd obviously not thought of it.

"Father asked me not to." Aiden shrugged. "He is overly protective," he added when Tristan cleared his throat.

Gregor Ross looked to his son without expression. "I simply asked that ye help with so much that has to be done with the farmers on the eastern lands. Those people have always been our responsibility."

Malcolm decided it wasn't his place to intercede, so instead he decided it was best to keep Aiden occupied with a task that would keep the man out of his hair.

"Aiden, speak to Ruari about such things. I'm sure our cousin will need help."

Son to Malcolm's father's cousin, Ruari Ross had come to live at the keep as a child. The man was a loner who spent his time at the stables when not battling. He had a gift for horses and seemed to prefer their company to that of humans.

It was Ruari who also kept watch over the inventories of grains, livestock and such. He'd be the one to organize the handing out of food to the clan's people.

Both Aiden and Kieran walked out, leaving Tristan, Malcolm and Gregor. His uncle spoke next. "What will be done with our prisoner? I am assuming ye are having trouble deciding."

"Laird McLeod will demand his return," Tristan said. "Then again, what will that say of us if we return him so easily?"

"He should remain here," Gregor said. "I will inform Laird McLeod he remains alive and will be safe, but that we won't release him for the time being."

"They may not agree to a truce then." Malcolm rolled his shoulders in an attempt to relieve the tightness.

They were silent for a long moment, each in their own thoughts.

"Supper will be served shortly." Verity entered, seeming to be in good spirits. Her face was alight with a soft smile. "How long before I can travel?"

"A few days yet," Malcolm replied. "Anxious, Sister?"

Verity nodded with enthusiasm. "I grow tired of remaining within the walls. Mother wishes to visit friends and I wish to go with her."

"We shall discuss it later," Malcolm said. "Go now."

"Mother insists ye come for last meal. We celebrate the coming end to the clashes."

Tristan took their sister's arm and gently walked her to the door. "Tell her there's not peace yet."

Verity looked at Malcolm. "I thought it was done. Ye said…"

"Not yet. Go now," Malcolm said, becoming annoyed.

His uncle waited for Verity to be out of earshot. "So it is decided. I travel with the girl tomorrow and Alec McLeod remains."

"I will speak to Alec as well," Malcolm replied. "If I had my way, tis on my back that I would spend the rest of the day."

"The yoke is heavy." His uncle placed a hand on his shoulder. "But ye must bear it. Yer father would be very proud."

Heavy, indeed, Malcolm thought. And it seemed to not be at its heaviest yet. He had a feeling the road ahead would not be easy.

Deep in thought, Malcolm hurried past the great room so that his mother would not spot him and then hurried up the stairwell.

In his bedchamber, Elspeth sat in a chair with a book in hand. She looked up and met his gaze. She didn't smile, but he recognized warmth in her gaze.

"How fare ye?" she asked. "Tired?"

"Very much so," he admitted, lowering to a chair opposite her. "It has been a long day."

She stood and pulled the shawl around her to cover the chemise she wore. Then she poured hot water from a kettle that hung over the fire in the hearth into a cup. She added herbs and stirred it.

"Drink this and rest." She held the cup out to him.

When he took it and sipped it, she lowered and leaned forward. "I heard from the window what ye said. I am glad for it."

She paused before adding, "It would be a good gesture to return the laird's son to him."

Malcolm hated to disappoint her as she seemed to finally be comfortable around him. At the same time, he wasn't going to lie. "I am not releasing Alec McLeod."

For a moment, she looked at the fire, her brows drawn in a scowl.

"Ye cannot kill him. It will not bring yer father back."

"I am aware." He didn't want to continue the conversation of what to do. What he wanted was to relax for a few moments before facing more people.

"Would ye like to join me for last meal?"

She seemed shocked and looked down to her chemise. "I do not, not tonight."

Although he wanted to question her, he was too weary. Instead, he changed the conversation. "Ye look better already."

Her keen gaze met his and then she looked away. "I am still a bit sore but better. Yer healer is truly gifted."

It reminded Malcolm to find out about the injured man. He made a mental note to ask how the man fared.

"Do ye read?"

She lifted the book and placed it on her lap. "Very little. Some words I can make out. Most I cannot."

Her hand moved across the book and he followed it.

"I wish for ye to return here to sleep," she said, startling him.

"With ye?"

"Oh, no!" Elspeth blushed. "I will sleep elsewhere. I know ye have been sleeping next door. I happened upon yer manservant."

He smiled and nodded. "I want ye safe. However, I do agree sleeping on the floor is not the same now that I grow older." Malcolm made a show of stretching his back.

Elspeth met his gaze. "Ye are not as heartless as ye portray. I like this side of ye."

"Ye seemed to like my bare rear for a target as well."

The laughter that escaped was like music to his ears. "That was truly unfortunate," she said with a wide smile.

She made the load on his shoulders evaporate.

"Why do ye not wish to eat downstairs?"

With a dramatic exhalation and a roll of her eyes, her lips pursed in thought. "Should I state a list of reasons? Or perhaps show ye?"

Malcolm lifted a brow. "Show me."

She pointed to her still bruised face. "Not a pretty sight. It hurts to chew my food. I am sure my expressions are not at all fit for company." Elspeth then placed her hand over the injury on her chest. "My chest hurts after sitting in one place too long. I have to move about to ensure not to stiffen."

"That is a very short list," Malcolm replied.

"I will be at first meal. Tonight, I will eat here."

"Very well. I will join ye immediately after and we can discuss what happened during the meal."

"Ye are kind." Elspeth frowned. "That's something I'd never thought to say to ye."

"And I find ye…" Malcolm stopped, not sure how to explain the fact that she gave him peace, softened his heart and helped him reason.

"Hard to explain how I affect yer delicate soul?" Elspeth teased.

"Aye, very difficult," he agreed, sure she had no idea how he felt.

CHAPTER NINETEEN

"WHERE IS MY brother?" Ethan McLeod demanded, his entire body strung tight as a bow. "Is he alive?"

Aiden couldn't help but wonder how it came to be that he and the man had become allies of sorts. Yet here he was meeting Ethan under the cover of darkness at a predetermined spot.

"He is not harmed. In the dungeon."

"Release him at once," Ethan said between clenched teeth. "It would be unfortunate if I hunt down yer father next."

Before Aiden could rationalize, he grabbed Ethan's tunic with both hands. "Ye know I do not give a damn, either way. He is but a lap dog to the laird. However, I do not like threats."

The man shook free of his grasp. "Why are ye here if not to tell me ye will help my brother escape?"

"Yer father has finally had enough of ye, has he?" Aiden said with a dry chuckle. "I know he cares little for ye."

"I am not like ye, my family is important…"

"Bah," Aiden interrupted. "Aye, I come to tell ye I will help yer brother escape. In exchange, I require a favor."

Ethan huffed. "What is it?"

"Take with ye a woman. She is important to Malcolm and needs to be done away with."

"I do not mistreat women."

"Since when?"

There was a beat of silence and, finally, Ethan nodded. "I will return and be here at nightfall tomorrow."

THE DAMPNESS OF the cavern walls did not give the opportunity to get warm. Alec shivered as he lay on the ground. He didn't know if it was day or night as the only lighting came from a single torch.

From the looks of the other cells, no one had been hosted there in a long time. Thick spider webs formed a dense canvas in most corners. He couldn't help but wonder what the creatures could possibly catch down there.

Not even mice were there as there were no sources of food. For that, he was a bit grateful, as he didn't relish the idea of the wee creature feasting on him.

The sounds of voices reached him just as the area became brighter. A male servant appeared holding a torch and, behind him, another man with a tray of food.

"Would ye care for anything else?" the man asked, sliding the tray under the bars. "I brought some warm drink." He pushed a cup through the bars swiftly, some of it spilling.

Alec grabbed it and held it between his hands, the warmth of it delightful. "A dry blanket?"

The servants looked to one another, and the one who'd carried the tray hurried away. "He will bring one shortly."

The servant sat in a rickety wooden chair waiting for Alec to eat.

"It is daytime then?" Alec asked as he ate. The food was delicious, a hearty stew with fresh bread.

"Tis almost sundown," the servant replied. "End of the day," he added unnecessarily.

Alec was surprised to find the young man didn't seem discomfited to be speaking to someone in the dungeon. Perhaps he'd been wrong and others had been held there.

"Do ye know what yer laird plans for me?"

The servant shook his head. "Tis not for me to know." He shrugged. "Perhaps ye will be hung in the courtyard."

The statement was not exactly comforting. "That would be a quick end to things," Alec said dryly.

"What of the woman who came here just before me? Is she well?"

"Aye, I suppose so. She remains locked in a chamber." The servant looked to his right and immediately stopped talking.

"Here ye are." The other servant returned with two blankets and pushed them through the bars. Alec stood and removed his damp tartan and wrapped one blanket around his shivering body. The other, he carefully placed atop straw he'd gathered into a makeshift pallet to sleep upon.

He tried to ask more questions but with the appearance of the second servant, the one with the torch stopped replying.

As they left, they replaced the torch and left him to his thoughts.

It was impossible to consider what Malcolm Ross would do with him. They were very different men. However, if his own da had been struck down, Alec would probably change. He had to admit that, like Malcolm, vengeance would be his own immediate reaction.

Hopefully, Paige was safe. He doubted even a Ross would purposely harm a woman. It didn't stop him from wishing to bend the bars with his own bare hands to get to her. If something happened to Paige, he would never forgive himself.

With nothing to do but remain with his thoughts, Alec went to the pallet and sat upon it. The worst torture of all was to be alone in a dank place without any idea of what would happen next. His mind raced in so many directions, he was sure after some time madness would set in.

If ever he had to punish someone for something vile, he would not have him or her hung or executed in any manner. Instead, they would be thrown in a dungeon for the rest of their life. This was a punishment he wouldn't wish on anyone he cared for.

"Alec?" A man's voice permeated through the fog of slumber and Alec realized he'd fallen asleep.

Footsteps sounded just before Aiden Ross appeared. The man's keen gaze met his for a long moment.

"If I release ye, will ye flee into the woods and never tell anyone who did it?"

"What of her?"

"I cannot do anything about that," the man said, waving a hand with indifference. "No harm will come to the woman. I am sure, eventually, my cousin will release her."

Alec wasn't sure he trusted the man. Would Aiden release him only to hunt him down to be considered a hero? No, then Aiden would have to explain how he was able to go free. "I do not wish to leave without her."

"If ye stay, ye will be dead within days. Either way, ye will leave her behind. I assure ye, she will be set free soon."

Reluctantly, he had to agree it would be easier to leave and bargain for Paige's release. "Very well."

The cell door opened. He'd not even heard the man unlock it. "Go up the stairs and to the right. There is a doorway out to the back of the keep." Aiden pointed with his right hand. "Once ye're outside, give me time to go to the roof. I will distract the guards. Wade along the loch toward the trees. Yer brother will meet ye there."

Taking his tartan and wrapping the still damp clothing about his body, Alec hurried out and followed the directions.

Fresh air had never smelled better. Alec gulped in breaths as he hurried to the water's edge. Although the night was frigid, there wasn't time to think about it. He waited until he was sure the man had enough time to get up to the ramparts and then continued to the trees.

The sound of someone else approaching from behind made him run faster, his lungs protesting the sudden burst of movement after so long in the cramped cell.

Just as he was sure he'd become lost in the woods, a familiar voice called out. "Alec, over here." It was Ethan.

"Someone follows," he said, mounting the horse his brother brought along. "Hurry."

"They are of no consequence," Ethan said. "I made a bargain and the one who follows is part of it. Ride home. Stay to the shores of the loch as much as possible. There are archers and scouts to the east of here."

He didn't question whatever bargain his brother had made. He would later. Right now, he needed to return home and begin to plan how to rescue Paige. It had been irrational to come alone to the Ross' keep. There would not be a second try like that.

Although the night air should have chilled him further, Alec was much too glad to be freed from the Ross' dungeon to feel it. He wondered why Aiden Ross had helped.

The man had never been one to stand out, whether in battle or otherwise. As a matter of fact, he didn't recall ever seeing him fight. It was as if he found other places to be.

A coward.

It meant Aiden was also probably the envious type who hated the fact his cousin was laird and not he. He'd known men like him. Aiden would probably revel in the aftermath of Alec's escape and relish any disappointment his cousin would feel.

How interesting that someone like that had been most helpful, but Alec didn't feel any kind of debt owed to Aiden Ross.

Suddenly, the walls of his home came into view and his shoulders fell. He was home.

He thought of Paige and he looked over his shoulder. Was he any better than a coward for having left her behind?

CHAPTER TWENTY

AT FIRST MEAL, the atmosphere was somber despite the fact that there was a possibility of peace coming to the clan.

Malcolm turned to his mother who seemed startled at his attention. "Why is everyone so glum? We are on the brink of peace."

At first, she studied the room as if noticing it for the first time. She cocked her head to the side and then turned to him. "It seems the same as usual. Did ye expect everyone to celebrate? After so long a time of battle, they will not believe it until it happens."

If it were true that the people had lost hope long ago and were an unhappy lot, he supposed he'd never noticed.

Kieran sat at the table closest to the entry with archers and other guardsmen. He and the men spoke in low tones. Every once in a while they were the only ones who seemed at ease.

Next to his mother was Verity and then his uncle and cousin, Aiden, who seemed unusually chipper.

Tristan approached but didn't sit. He bowed at the waist to speak into his ear. "Come away from the table. I have news."

Without looking at the others, Malcolm stood and walked a short distance away with Tristan. He followed Tristan's lead and acted as if nothing was wrong and perhaps Tristan wanted to tell him about some adventure.

His brother met his gaze, the hazel eyes darker than usual. "Our prisoner has escaped. It seems, Brother, we have a traitor among us."

Malcolm nodded, doing his best not to turn to look over his shoulder. "Is anyone at the high board studying us with interest?"

"Aiden did, but now he is talking to Verity. No one else is paying us heed as they are used to me coming to report on the night guard."

"What of the guards at the two tables?"

"All of the guardsmen are accounted for," Tristan said, scanning the room. "There is no one paying us any heed. Seems Kieran is regaling the table with his tales of a kill."

"Very well." Malcolm turned and looked in the direction of where his younger brother sat and motioned him to come. It was only then that most of the guardsmen looked over. Vigilance had become a companion as of late and they made sure not to miss a call to duty.

After motioning to his uncle to also join him, Malcolm walked from the room, both brothers behind.

Once inside the study, Malcolm asked Tristan to repeat what had occurred.

"Who was last to see him?" Gregor asked.

"The servants who took him last meal," Tristan replied. "The same servants found him gone this morning. They wait in the kitchen corridor for further direction. They were instructed not to say anything to anyone as of yet."

"What of the woman? Is she still here?" Malcolm asked next.

"Aye," their uncle responded this time. "I was in the kitchen when her first meal tray was retrieved this morning."

Malcolm looked to Kieran. "See that she remains and then have the two servants come here." He then turned to Tristan. "I want to speak to every guard who was on duty last night."

"They are assembling as we speak," his brother replied.

"Kieran, seek the scouts who patrolled the forest last night. Have them come at once."

Both his brothers left and the male servants appeared. Both were pale and wide-eyed.

Malcolm left it to his uncle to question them. On the brink of losing his temper, he didn't wish to scare them witless.

Neither seemed to see anything unusual the night before. One confessed to providing the man with an extra blanket as he was shivering cold. The other admitted to holding a conversation about the time of day.

Once they were dismissed, his uncle shrugged. "They didn't do it." The older man clenched his jaw.

"Someone did. I will find out who." Malcolm slammed his fist on the tabletop. "Damn them, Uncle. Just as we were going to broker for peace."

His uncle nodded. "Whoever it is does not wish for a truce it seems."

"Or it could be they did not wish Alec McLeod dead."

Tristan returned. "Do ye wish to speak to the men now? They are assembled on the north side."

It was an area that would grant some privacy. Malcolm wasn't sure he wanted the story spread as of yet. Although in a keep so overcrowded at the moment, the information would soon make its way around the keep regardless of how much he threatened.

"Let us go then."

The night guards were lined up with expectant expressions. It was immediately obvious most were totally unaware of what happened. Malcolm stood before them. "Someone has released the prisoner. Alec McLeod is gone."

The men looked to one another, but remained silent.

"I will find out who is responsible."

He questioned each man thoroughly. It was late morning and it seemed none had any idea of what had happened.

Finally, they were left with only the archers who patrolled atop the keep's walls. Four men who Malcolm considered his best guardsmen.

The first, an older man, shook his head. "I swear to ye, Laird, we didn't see anything. It was a dark night, indeed, but we stay vigilant."

"Did anything out of the ordinary happen?" Tristan asked. "Any noise or strange animal sounds?"

"Nay," another answer. "It was only when Aiden came up that we talked for a bit and that was only for a few minutes."

Tristan and Malcolm exchanged looks. Malcolm moved closer to the man. "Is it often that he comes up to the ramparts?"

"Nay," the older man replied. "His visits are rare."

Tristan took pity on the sleepy men. "Go, eat and rest, night will come soon. I remind ye to speak to no one about this."

After everyone walked away, the brothers remained standing together. "Seems we may have our answer," Tristan said.

"Why?" Malcolm scowled. "He has it all, and rarely deems it necessary to go to battle." He clenched his jaw as his fingers curled. "How do we approach him? Perhaps I should speak to our uncle."

"He will side with his son," Tristan said.

"Nay, he is a fair man." Malcolm trusted his uncle to always do what was right.

"Laird!" A young maid rushed to him, red-faced, as she hurried with skirts pulled up to keep from tripping. "She is missing, Laird. Gone." The girl bent over and gasped for breath.

Malcolm took the maid by the shoulders. The girl, Maggie, was prone to hysterics and often lost her breath. "Breath, Maggie. Be calm and tell me what ye speak of."

After several gulps, she nodded. "Miss Elspeth. She is not in her room. I searched the entire keep…well not the servants' quarters. I suppose she could be there. But I did ask Lily and she had not seen her…"

"When did ye last see her?" Malcolm tried to remain calm, but already he sensed that Elspeth had gone. Either taken again or escaped.

"Ugh!" Tristan swung a fist, hitting nothing but air and Maggie yelped. "It could be she is the one who freed McLeod. I knew it was a bad idea."

Malcolm looked to Maggie, doing his best to keep his temper in check. "Go find the servants and search the keep. Go to Ian's rooms. She could be there checking on him. Report back to me immediately."

There was a commotion at the gate. The guards called down and whoever it was responded.

"What now?" Malcolm asked no one in particular. He closed his eyes and puffed his cheeks, blowing out a long breath as a young lad rushed to him to report.

"My laird, the family is here."

"What family?" he snapped, too angry now to keep from yelling.

The boy looked over his shoulder. "For the ceremony, Laird. Yer wedding is to be today, is it not?"

Tristan groaned and looked up at the sky.

"Tell the guards to allow them in."

Chapter Twenty-One

Unlike the last time she'd been taken from her bed, this time Elspeth was handled with care. She'd been placed atop blankets in the back of a cart. Although her hands were bound and she was blindfolded. That in and of itself didn't bode well.

"Allow me to go please," she repeated. There was a man next to her whose voice she did not recognize, and another managing the horses. Neither replied.

It felt as if they'd been riding in circles for hours and she'd been through so many emotions it left her exhausted.

At first, Elspeth had cried, then pleaded, lastly she'd been so angry some of the words that she'd screamed were ones she'd overheard her father and older brother say. They'd not be proud of her in that moment. Or maybe they would be.

This had to stop. Her life had been turned upside down since meeting Malcolm Ross. It was his fault and that vendetta of his. Now, she was paying the price.

The men were probably going to ask for ransom guessing he would care enough to pay.

"He doesn't care what happens to me. If it is a ransom ye seek, he won't pay."

The man on the bench cleared his throat. "I had not thought of that. What do ye think, Sean, a bit of coin would be good?"

They laughed as if it were the funniest joke and Elspeth gritted her teeth.

If she got out of this alive, she would never have anything to do with men again. They were all idiots.

News of her disappearance would harm her family the most. Her grandmother would be affected most of all, if she continued to be sick. Elspeth shuddered at the thought.

It had to be mid-morning by now as she'd felt the progression of the sun since rising across her face while trying to figure out what direction they were headed.

"Can ye walk?" the man beside her asked.

"Aye," she replied slowly. "Why?"

Instead of a reply, he whistled and the wagon came to a stop.

"Off ye go then," the man, Sean, said, untying her wrists and removing her blindfold.

He climbed down and took her around the waist as Elspeth struggled to keep the blanket around her body.

Sean set Elspeth on her feet and gave her a gentle nudge. "Be with care, there are brambles about."

She stood dumbstruck as he jumped back onto the wagon and they left.

"Wait, where am I?" she called out, but they did not reply. Elspeth turned and her mouth fell open. She was outside her village.

This had to be the most bizarre abduction ever. She hurried toward her house, hoping her family had not left for the ceremony yet. However, guessing by the position of the sun, they were probably already at the keep.

She hurried inside the house, letting out a sigh of relief at the familiarity of it all. It seemed as if she'd been gone for so long and yet only a few days had passed.

Once inside her small bedchamber, she quickly dressed and yanked a comb through her hair. She'd have to find a horse so that she could return to the keep at once.

Although her stomach growled in protest, she ignored the food on the table. There wasn't time. Elspeth rushed out the front door and to the right. Ceilidh lived just a few yards away. Hopefully, her friend had not gone with her family and planned to go later.

When Ceilidh opened the door, her mouth fell open and her eyes popped just as wide. "What are ye doing here? Did ye run away from the wedding?"

"Nay," Elspeth replied. "I need to return to Ross Keep immediately."

Her friend looked past her. "Why did ye not go with yer family?"

Taking her friend's arm, Elspeth yanked Ceilidh out. "I do not have time to explain. Can we take yer horse?"

"Who is it?" Ceilidh's mother came to the door and duplicated the same look as her daughter's. "What are ye doing here? Yer mother is headed to Ross Keep. I just left from yer house a bit ago."

"I need a horse. I must go there now. Can ye allow Ceilidh and I to go now please?" Elspeth was on the verge of crying. How could things turn into such a mess?

The older woman waved her hand dismissively. "Nay, twill not do for two lasses to be out alone during times like these. Let me ask Fergus to go with ye." The woman came out and hurried toward the carpentry shop where her husband worked. Having no choice, both Ceilidh and Elspeth followed.

Like Ceilidh's mother, her father was kind and caring. The man had nary an unfriendly bone in his body. When he frowned in their direction and shook his head, Elspeth started to cry.

"I'll go alone then," she said, stalking back toward her house.

"Wait," Ceilidh said, running after her. "Tis not that Da didn't wish ye to go. Tis that his horse is at my brother's house."

At a loss, Elspeth stopped in front of her house and scanned the houses. "Surely there is someone who would allow me to borrow a horse."

"I have an idea," Ceilidh said, taking her hand. "Hurry, before my mother comes looking for me."

They raced across the dirt road and in between two cottages. Finally, Ceilidh stopped behind the tavern. "We can take Eagan's cart and horse. He won't mind."

The tavern owner's son swore to marry Ceilidh every time he saw her. As if beckoned, he appeared around the corner and his face lit up.

"What are ye two doing here?"

They explained to him the urgency of the matter and, to Elspeth's delight, not only did he agree to allow them use of his horse and wagon, but he also volunteered to guide the horse.

Within moments, the trio was on their way. Along with cider and tarts that Ceilidh's mother insisted they take.

⇶⇷

THE ROSS MESSENGER sat at a table looking particularly uncomfortable as McLeod guardsmen surrounded him. Unlike the messenger they'd last sent, he would return unharmed with a response.

"How can we agree to a truce? They imprisoned ye." Ethan's face was twisted in a snarl. "We should skin their messenger and send back portions of what's left."

Remaining quiet, Alec studied his brother and waited for their father to speak.

The laird scowled at Ethan. "Ye should not have an opinion," he snapped. "Alec went there of his own free will. If one of them came here, we would do the same and throw the person in the dungeon."

Ethan dropped into a chair and crossed his arms. "No truce."

Laird McLeod ignored his youngest son. "Tis for the best that we agree to meet with the man who comes representing Clan Ross. He is the advisor and was once a trusted right hand to the now dead laird."

"We must bargain for Paige's release," Alec said. "She cannot continue there as a prisoner."

His father pressed fingers to the bridge of his nose. "Again, she went there voluntarily. I am not sure what she hoped to gain in going to ask for a truce without any kind of guard or missive."

"A bargain." Alec would not drop the subject. Truce or not, Paige would not remain in the Ross' hands.

"Go speak to the messenger," his father said as he signed a parchment, folded it and after pouring wax, sealed it with his signet ring. "Ye may have him ask about the girl, but it is not to be written. Twas yer choice to associate yerself with that village girl."

Alec followed the messenger out, already formulating how best to word his request.

He refused to consider that she was lost to him. It wasn't inconceivable for a clan to give a woman prisoner to a member of the clan to claim as his own. Especially a woman who went to them of her own volition. Paige was beautiful so it would not be hard to find her a willing husband.

Alec pushed the thoughts away as it made him want to rush to the closest horse and return to Ross lands. This time, the clan would not be as accommodating if he reappeared. Besides, there wasn't anything a single man could do against many.

Walking out with the messenger and escorting the man to his horse, Alec met his gaze. "Tell Laird Ross that I ask as a function of good will that he release the woman, Paige, back to me."

The man seemed to understand the underlying reason and nodded. "I will."

Chapter Twenty-Two

Verity ran a comb absently through her long, wavy hair while sitting in front of her looking glass. Hollow brown eyes looked back as she studied her reflection. With a round face and thin lips, she'd been cursed by inheriting her mother's looks and not her handsome father's. Unlike her brothers, she was never called fair of face. Why hadn't she been born male and inherited the gift of her father's features?

Not that she hated her mother. Quite the contrary, she'd withstood her presence over that of her father, who seemed to find fault in everything she did.

Just months before his death, he'd finally deemed her worthy and tried to speak to her, ask her about her day. But she didn't have the time for him; it was too late for a bond between them. Now it seemed Malcolm was much too absorbed in his battles and revenge to care what happened to her.

"I wondered why ye were not at first meal," Aiden said, startling her. He walked to where she sat, stopping just behind her. His hazel eyes met hers in the looking glass. "Ye should be downstairs. There is much to see."

"No doubt in part to yer doing."

He didn't reply. Instead, he picked up a strand of her damp hair and studied it for a long moment. "Ye should thank me. It leaves ye free to do as ye wish for a few hours at least."

A shiver of awareness trickled down from her neck. It was as if he touched her skin and not just the lock of hair. "We will be caught one day." But her gaze moved to the bed as if on its own accord.

Taking her by the shoulders, Aiden pulled her to stand, his gaze glued to hers in the mirror. "I do not wish to go to the bed," he whispered, placing his lips just below her ear. "I want to watch ye come undone by my touch alone."

The warmth of his mouth at her neck made her eyelids drop.

"Open yer eyes, Verity," he commanded. "Or I will stop."

She made sure to open them wide, watching with interest as his hands pulled up her chemise, displaying her pale legs and stomach. The way his hands slid up and down her inner thighs seemed surreal. The hitch in his breath, as he too watched, made her tremble.

He pulled the chemise higher and draped it over her shoulder, her entire body now on full display. "I like yer breasts," Aiden said, cupping them with his large hands while circling the pink tips with his thumbs.

Verity whimpered, heat pooling in her core, she needed more than just his touch. And yet this particular game was always the same. He brought her to completion with only his hands. Never kissing her on the mouth and never ever disrobing himself.

Finally, as she was about to plead, unable to withstand it any longer, Aiden chuckled. "Touch yerself. Take care of it."

She did as he asked, hand sliding between her legs, fingers teasing at her core. The release was almost immediate and she bit her lips to keep from crying out.

The entire time, he held her shoulders and watched, his eyes now darkened, lips parted and breathing hard. A lock of dark hair fell over his brow and she considered brushing it back. He would not allow it, of course, so she pushed the thought away.

His disinterest was almost immediate. Aiden strode to the window. "I suggest ye dress and go downstairs. Ye will be delighted at the turn of events."

"My brother celebrates a wedding, while I'm not allowed to find a husband. Why should that delight me in any way?" Verity had already pulled her chemise down and was once again seated and combing her hair. Her entire body hummed, needing more, but she'd be damned if Aiden would know. He needed more, she knew for a fact that after every encounter like this one, he bedded the first maid that he came in contact with.

"It seems the bride is missing," Aiden said in an amused tone. "Perhaps she ran away, or perhaps taken. Who is to know?"

She whirled to look at him. "It was ye."

With a lazy shrug, her cousin went to the door. "Why would I bother with trivial things like that?"

"Because ye hate Malcolm. Ye hate all of us. Why do ye even come here to my chamber?"

His lips curved, the smile not reaching his flat gaze. "Because ye cede to me every time." With a chuckle, he opened the door and walked out.

Verity cursed. This would be the last time.

THE DOOR OPENED and Paige looked up from the mending she was doing. She'd asked for something to do to pass the time. Days were beginning to blend together even though she hadn't been there more than four or was it maybe five?

Upon a tall, dark-haired man entering, she stood and backed up. Immediately, she didn't like him. "Who are ye? What do ye want?"

"I am Aiden Ross, cousin to the laird. I heard ye were a wee bit bored." He didn't move closer, but his gaze traveled from her face down her body, making it seem as if he was much too near.

Paige hitched her chin in an attempt not to look intimidated although her heart pounded. "I am not bored, I have mending to do. I am waiting to speak to the laird once again."

"He is much too busy for ye. What is it ye wish to say?"

Although she doubted this man had any influence on Laird Ross, it was best to keep talking. The servant was due to return and bring her more mending. Paige prayed it would be soon. "Would ye please ask the laird to consider releasing me? I hold no value to the McLeods. I am but a simple village woman."

"And yet ye came as a messenger?"

"Nay. I came to ask for peace. My brother died when he came with a missive. I didn't wish anyone else to die."

"Especially not Alec McLeod?" His lips curved. "I do believe ye are important to him."

She took another step backward, the back of her leg hitting the small cot. It was a mistake to trust this man. Paige considered screaming, but he'd not done anything to threaten her safety. Not yet.

"I do know Alec McLeod, but have only met him briefly."

"Hmm." He rubbed his chin and moved closer. Cupping her chin, he lifted her face up. "What does he see in ye? Did ye know he came to barter for ye? Ended up in the dungeon."

Her eyes rounded. "Ye lie."

"Now, now. Ye do not want to insult yer hosts. I do not lie. He was here."

"Was?" If she'd been the cause of his death, she would never be able to live with herself.

"Escaped," he said, studying her for a reaction. "Seems someone let him out."

Despite herself, she let out a shaky breath. "It was solely my idea alone to come here."

"Yes, but ye care for him. I think…" he paused, his gaze moving to her mouth. "Ye owe me payment for allowing his escape."

Paige had a hard time swallowing past the dryness of her throat. "I will not."

"Ye seem to think I am giving ye a choice in this matter." Taking her by the shoulders, he turned her, dragged her closer to the small cot and then pushed her head down so that she was bent at the waist.

"Let me go!" Paige struggled, kicking and flaying her arms in an attempt to hit him. He was much bigger than she was, his arms like vises pinning her arms to her sides.

"Be a good lass and allow it." His words came out guttural, his breathing harsh. "Stop fighting, ye will not win."

Paige let out a scream and it seemed to stun him. There were footsteps out in the hallway and the sound of male voices. Aiden shoved her away until she fell onto the floor on all fours, hair covering her face.

"What happened?" someone asked as she scrambled from the floor to the cot. Paige pulled her legs up, wrapping her arms around them.

"I do not know," Aiden replied. "I was walking by and noticed the door was open. I looked inside and she screamed. Must be touched in the head."

The guard didn't look convinced. He looked at her and she tried to convey to him what had actually occurred.

"I will remain outside the door until she calms," the guard told Aiden who glared in her direction.

"Very well. Tis a waste of time being there is much to do today." He stalked off and Paige worried for whoever he would take his frustration out upon.

"Are ye well, Miss?" the guard, a young man, asked.

Paige nodded, knowing very well the guard would not stand up to a Ross in her defense. He'd already taken a big chance by even stating he'd remain.

"Thank ye." Paige couldn't help the tears that flowed as she remained on the cot, thankful for the young guard at her door.

⫸⫷

A WHIMPERING MAID hobbled out of his bedchamber and, still, Aiden wasn't satisfied. He wanted more, needed more. Perhaps he'd return to Verity's chamber and take her this time.

He went to the window and noticed the guards were lining up. It was time for their daily reporting to Kieran and Tristan. His self-important cousins who would spew some useless nonsense meant to motivate them and then divide them for sword practice and such.

Pushing away, he cursed and turned to the doorway. A male servant entered, the male's eyes moving to him before going to the fireplace to place wood in a neat pile next to it.

"Where is my cousin, Malcolm?"

"In the great room, Sir. He is speaking with visitors." The young man waited for any other instructions.

"Is my father present as well?"

"Aye, he is."

"That will be all."

Of course his father was there. Forever the lap dog waiting for the next bone tossed to him by Malcolm. Aiden wanted to throw up when his stomach lurched at the idea that he was expected to follow suit.

Deciding it was best to ensure that no one considered him a suspect in Alec's escape, he adjusted his clothing and walked out.

It lifted his spirits to find Malcolm being confronted by the parents of his not to be wife.

Aiden strode into the great room and sat upon the high board. He motioned for a servant to bring him ale. The situation was worthy of a drink.

His lips curved as he focused on the interaction.

CHAPTER TWENTY-THREE

"YE WILL FIND my daughter. I do not care if it takes every guard. Not only are ye telling me she was taken and injured, but that, once again, she is missing?"

The huge blacksmith was beyond addressing him as "Laird", nor did the man seem to care that armed guards surrounded him.

Malcolm had to admit the combined presence of the blacksmith and his equally muscular older son would make most of the guardsmen hesitate before attempting to restrain either one.

He looked to the lead guard to ensure that the man remain back. "I was as shocked as ye are when I was informed. I assure ye, we have sent men out to search."

"I saw about four leave this morn," his damned cousin piped up. "They will find her."

"Four?" The blacksmith bellowed. "Four?" He inhaled sharply and every guard leaned forward in expectation. "I can beat four with my bare hands." As if to prove it, he pounded a fist on the closest table. The cracking sound of wood guaranteed his point was made.

Malcolm let out a breath. "What if she left of her own accord?"

"She would have been home by now." Elspeth's brother spoke this time. "Elspeth knows the forest better than most. She spends many hours gathering herbs and can make her way."

Instantly, the memory of the day she'd thrown a branch at him at the loch's edge came to mind. Malcolm nodded. "I am aware."

"We should go and gather men from the village. We must find my daughter," Elspeth's mother said between sniffs. "Let us go." The grandmother was content to glare at him.

"Wait," Malcolm held up a hand. "I will come with ye and bring my guards."

"And leave the keep unprotected?" Aiden, the ever not so helpful idiot spoke. "I do not think it is wise."

As much as he wanted to punch his cousin in the face, he held back. "I suggest ye find yer sword and stand with those that remain."

One of his personal guards provided a sword to Aiden.

Malcolm turned to face the blacksmiths. "Let us go."

"WHAT EXACTLY DO ye plan to say?" Ceilidh asked as the fortified Ross Keep came into view. "Tis not as if they will open the gates in welcome."

Elspeth frowned. Too weary to care other than to assure her parents, she wanted nothing more than to return home with her family and sleep for days. "I do not know. My parents are inside. They cannot turn me away."

"True, but the archers may fling arrows and ask questions later," Eagan said, sounding worried. "I do not know what it feels like and am not of an ilk to find out."

"Do ye think they will do so?" Ceilidh asked. "They do have archers atop the gates that keep an eye out for trespassers."

"Please be calm. Ye're both starting to make me wonder." She studied the fortress and let out a breath. "Slow down the horses, Eagan, so they can see we mean no harm."

"As if a cart with two women in the back poses any kind of threat." Ceilidh shook her head. "Since the day ye took in Ian, there has been naught but strife. I do believe Malcolm Ross is deeply infatuated with ye. And feeling just as strongly, someone else wishes ye gone."

"His mother does not fancy the idea of a village lass with her laird son. Tis understandable and I wish he would listen to her."

"Why should he?" Ceilidh insisted. "He is Laird of Clan Ross and may do as he wishes."

They came to an abrupt halt and all three looked up to a large warrior who called down, "Who are ye and what do ye seek?"

Both Ceilidh and Eagan looked to Elspeth and she stood, wobbling a bit from the unsteadiness of the cart. "I am Elspeth, who was taken last night. I come for my family who are inside with yer laird."

The guard made a motion for them to remain and disappeared. The archers went from looking down to talking to one another. A man appeared and looked down. "Who took ye?"

She recognized him as Kieran, Malcolm's youngest brother.

"I do not know," Elspeth replied, not wishing to publically divulge it was his mother. Although she'd not seen or heard her this time, it had to be the second attempt directed by the woman, as the first had not succeeded.

The immense gates opened slowly, pulled back by men on horseback. Elspeth not only found Malcolm standing in the courtyard, but her father and older brother as well. The three looked ready for battle.

Exchanging a look with Ceilidh, she wasn't sure what the first thing to say should be. Seeming to understand her thoughts, Ceilidh shrugged.

"Come down from there at once," her father said, stalking to the wagon. He looked up at Eagan. "Thank ye, ye may return to the village."

Eagan nodded, looking about the courtyard with curiosity. It was obvious he did not wish to leave, but to remain and see what would happen next.

Everyone remained silent while Eagan disappeared behind the closing gates, Ceilidh was sent to the kitchens and Elspeth walked into the keep flanked by her father and brother. Other than meeting her gaze for but a moment, Malcolm had not uttered a single word.

They entered the great room where her mother and grandmother sat with Malcolm's uncle. Both jumped to their feet upon seeing her.

It broke Elspeth's heart when her mother rushed to her, arms open and sobbing. Her grandmother was right behind.

"I am fine. The men who took me did not mistreat me in the least. They left me just outside the village." Elspeth met Malcolm's narrowed gaze over her mother's shoulder.

"What men?" he asked, crossing his arms. "Can ye describe them?" Malcolm's flat tone made her glare at him.

She shook her head. "They wore cloths tied about their faces. I only saw their eyes. Both spoke in low whispers, but I got the impression by their movements both were young. One was named Sean."

"It was two then?" he asked in the same tight tone.

Elspeth scowled. "What do ye want to say to me? That I left of my own accord and stumbled about the woods all night? It would take until late today to reach my village by foot and ye know this."

"Perhaps yet met someone?" he said, lifting an eyebrow. "A planned escape."

Ignoring the others in the room, she stomped to stand but a few inches from him. "Why would I escape? Can ye explain to me what I would gain from it?"

He looked past her to her father. "I am asking because ye left the same night my prisoner disappeared."

"The girl? Is she gone as well?"

"What girl?" Malcolm and her father both asked. Then exchanged looks as if she were daft.

"The girl that came to bargain for a truce. The poor village girl ye locked up somewhere."

His uncle came forward and took her elbow. "Why don't we all sit and have a glass of mead. Ye need to rest and arrangements need to be agreed upon."

Elspeth allowed the man to guide her to a table where her mother and grandmother were also brought. "What kind of arrangements?"

"The wedding of course," her mother replied, wiping her eyes. "Now that ye're found safe, there is nothing to stop it."

It took a great deal of inner strength not to stomp her foot in frustration. "I will not marry him. There will be no wedding, no marriage."

"Ye spent many nights in his bed. Ye will," her grandmother said, shaking a gnarled finger at her. "He must make things right."

"Nothing happened between us," Elspeth said, but no one listened as guards entered the room along with a young man who carried a piece of parchment.

"A message from Laird McLeod," one announced.

Elspeth rolled her eyes when Malcolm walked away to meet with the messenger.

Her mother pulled her into a tight embrace once again. "We should take ye home immediately." She glared at her husband. "Perhaps there is no need for her to remain here. Tis obvious they cannot keep her safe."

Lady Ross, who up to the point remained silent, cleared her throat loudly. "If the lass would stop stealing away with God knows who, it would be easier to keep an eye on her."

Before her mother could reply, Elspeth whirled to face the woman. "It was ye that had me taken the first time. I heard yer voice instructing them."

"Nonsense. Although I do not agree with this marriage," the woman said, waving her hand dismissively, "my son is laird and may do as he pleases. Tis not possible to keep a wayward girl like ye safe while in the midst of battle."

"My daughter is not wayward," her mother spat out. "Yer son would be privileged to marry such a lass as my Elspeth."

Elspeth met Malcolm's gaze, which grew wide when his mother walked toward her mother. Both he and her father stepped between the angry women.

"Why don't we sit and talk," Gregor Ross said, pointing to the table where they'd been seated earlier.

Malcolm remained standing as did her father, an obvious ploy not to cede to the other. Elspeth wanted to scream in frustration. No one listened to her, nor did they ask what she wanted or felt. True, at the moment, she was quite disoriented and confused. Upon coming to fetch her family, her mind was made up that she never wished to see any Ross ever again. However, upon seeing Malcolm, she wondered how it could be that such a pull to another person could exist.

In that instant, he met her gaze for a moment and his lips curved just a bit. No one probably noticed, but she felt her cheeks grow warm. Malcolm met his mother's gaze. "If I find ye did, indeed, intend harm on Elspeth, ye will answer for it. I will not have any guest of mine treated in such a vile manner."

Lady Ross' mouth fell open and her hand went to her chest, but she did not speak.

"Now," Malcolm said as his gaze scanned every face at the table, stopping upon looking at her father. "Do ye wish me to marry yer daughter?"

"Aye," her father responded without hesitation. "Tis a matter of honor."

Her mother sighed, Lady Ross groaned and her brother glared. For a long moment, no one spoke. The awkward silence was only broken when Gregor Ross motioned for a servant to come. "Pour ale for the men and honey mead for the women. Oh, and bring some tarts if there are any left."

Malcolm neared Elspeth and took her arm. "Let us speak for a moment." He guided her to stand and brought her away from the others. From where they stood, they were out of earshot and yet she could feel every eye on them.

"Can we go out to the garden please?" Elspeth asked.

"Yes, of course."

It was a pretty day. The afternoon sun was hidden by tall trees, giving the garden a pleasant shading. Elspeth let out a long breath. "This has certainly been an extraordinary time."

"Yes, it has."

Dressed in a green tunic with the Ross plaid around his body, he looked every bit the laird. She studied the burnished brown waves that curled at his shoulders, the only part of him that was soft. His expression, darkened eyes and the set of his jaw all told her that he pondered too many things.

"Ye have a lot on yer shoulders." Elspeth placed her hand on his lower arm. "It cannot be easy, I imagine."

When he looked at her, she was glad to see a slight softness. "And yet with one touch ye put me at ease."

"Who escaped? Why did ye think I would free the person?"

"Alec McLeod. He came to ask that I free the village lass," he replied. "Seems he feels strongly for her."

Elspeth nodded. "Would ye have done the same for me?"

Malcolm scowled, meeting her gaze for a long moment. "Aye, I believe I would."

"Then I am glad he escaped. I only wish she would have as well."

"Ye are bold to say that to me." The corners of his mouth twitched. "I could throw ye in the dungeon as a suspect."

"But ye will not." Elspeth became serious. "Ye do not have to marry me, Malcolm. Father will grumble, but he will soften if I tell him I do not wish to remain here."

He cupped her face between his palms, his brown eyes boring into hers. "Is that truly how ye feel?"

Elspeth closed her eyes, unable to continue to look into his. "I do not know what I wish for, if I am to be honest." The only thing she could think of at the moment was how much she wished for more of his touch.

"A kiss?"

She couldn't help but smile at him reading her so easily. "I did hope for that."

It was as if strong currents pulled her under water when his mouth clashed over hers. It was impossible to surface from the depths of sensations Malcolm brought out in her. Her fingers dug into the rough fabric of his tunic as she fought not to melt to the ground. The heat intensified when his tongue dove into her mouth and she reached up and wrapped her arms around his neck, pushing her body into his, wanting to be closer despite the fact they were plastered against one another.

"Ye take it all away, Elspeth." His harsh whisper in her ear was a combination of balm and fire. "Be mine. Remain with me. I beg ye."

The plea made her heart stop. He needed her. Malcolm Ross actually needed her.

It was impossible to think further when he took her bottom and pulled her up so that their sexes lined up. The thick hardness of his erection rubbed at her core, and she should have exclaimed, but instead she kissed him.

There was so much more that happened between a man and a woman. Elspeth was well aware of it and, in that moment, Elspeth understood need, want and frustration all at once. They would not go further, but she was on the verge of begging.

Malcolm moved his hips, the length of his sex sliding up and down between her legs while at the same time she wrapped her legs around his midsection. "Oh."

"I need ye so very much," he repeated.

"Sorry to interrupt," said a male voice. It was like a bucket of ice-cold loch water thrown over her and, instantly, Elspeth dropped to the ground. At the same time, Malcolm pushed her behind him, hiding her from whoever it was.

She peered around him to find it was his brother, Tristan. The man met her gaze, a slight curve to his lips. "The family wishes to know what ye have decided. They thought ye were taking a wee bit long."

It was obvious Tristan found the situation humorous. When he looked down to Malcolm's body to his midsection, he lifted a brow. "Take a moment and then come inside." He held out a hand to Elspeth. "I will escort ye back inside."

"Go," Malcolm said, his gaze on her. "I will be in momentarily."

She allowed Tristan to take her elbow and guide her inside. Just a few steps in the doorway, she stopped. "One moment please."

He waited, his large body blocking the view as she used her fingers to smooth her hair and straighten her dress. Once finished, she tapped his shoulder. "Thank ye."

"My pleasure," he replied. "I think ye and my brother are a good match."

The words shocked her. It was good to know someone in Malcolm's family was not against her.

She returned to the table, every pair of eyes boring into her.

"So what is going to happen?" her mother asked.

Before Elspeth could reply, Malcolm spoke from the doorway.

"There will be a wedding today. A celebration to follow once the assuredness of a truce is in effect."

Chapter Twenty-Four

"Come along," the maid said from the doorway, startling Paige. "There is to be a wedding and my laird wishes ye to be present. Miss Elspeth, his soon-to-be bride, requests that ye come to her chamber."

Relieved at the reprieve from being cloistered, she hurriedly grabbed her shawl and rushed after the young girl. They walked past a great room where she eyed the entrances. Each was guarded by an armed warrior.

In the great room, servants hurried to and fro, sweeping rushes, washing down tables and placing fresh greenery on the hearths.

Chilly wind blew in from open doorways, refreshing the room, and it felt as if it were giving her new breath as well.

Up the stairs and down the corridor, they continued until stopping at a doorway. The maid knocked and then entered with Paige behind.

Inside the room was another flurry of activity. Two women were in a heated debate, neither of which Paige recognized. Then again, she'd never ventured so far into Ross lands to know anyone.

By a looking glass, a woman of about her age sat. Her reddish-brown hair was bring brushed back and then braided by a maid, while a blonde woman looked on and spoke in low tones.

"Tis a mistake and yet I remain here to support my son," one of the arguing woman said.

The other lifted both hands in exasperation. "Ye are here in hopes of ruining something. I can sense these things," the other said.

"Can ye stop this, I feel faint," a younger woman with a round face stood between the arguing women, looking like she was about to faint.

The woman who was seated, who Paige guessed to be the bride-to-be, met her gaze in the mirror. "I am so happy to see ye. I am Elspeth."

At the comment, the older women stopped their debate and looked to Paige.

"I am glad to be out of the room I've been locked in for days."

The woman Paige presumed to be Lady Ross narrowed her eyes. "And who allowed ye out?" She pinned the maid with an annoyed look. "Who ordered ye to let her out?"

"My…my laird," the maid stammered. "He…said…to bring her."

"I will speak to him now," the woman stormed past, brushing Paige aside. The round-faced girl remained behind, looking from the door to Paige and finally to Elspeth. "My brother is affected by ye. Ye must be a witch." With that, she followed her mother out.

Elspeth rolled her eyes. "I tire already of this family. I am not sure this is wise."

"But ye agreed nonetheless," the older woman left behind grumbled. "Why did ye, Daughter?"

Elspeth looked to Paige. "This is my mother, Eileen Muir, and this is my friend, Ceilidh." She motioned to an elderly woman who sat by the window. "That is my grandmother. She is a wee bit ill. We come from Kildonan and ye?"

"The McLeod lands. My home is just outside the gates of the keep. I do not…did not live in a village."

"Poor girl, why are ye here?" Eileen Muir took her by the shoulders and gave Paige a hug. The warmth of the woman's gesture made her press her lips together to keep from weeping.

Paige told them of her coming there in hopes of bartering for a truce. She left out the part of fearing for Alec, although being that Elspeth was a villager about to marry the Ross laird, it was possible they'd understand her feelings for him.

"I will find a suitable dress for ye," the maid said. "There is a wardrobe with Miss Verity's discarded dresses that are kept for such matters." The maid hurried away.

Paige could only sit and watch, enjoying the company of women as they continued chatting and preparing for an evening of celebration.

Despite the situation, the clan battles, not knowing where Alec was, and missing her family terribly, Paige relaxed. For the first time, she learned how healing the company of other women could be.

The maid returned with a clean dress and helped Paige change after she freshened up at the washbasin. She donned the simple cream-colored frock that was a bit too big. However, it was nice to have washed up and wear clean clothing.

Elspeth stood in front of the looking glass, dressed in a simple but flattering green dress that fell in folds to the floor. A tartan of the Ross colors was carefully draped over her left shoulder and held in place with a beautiful broach. Her hair was done up in a flattering crown of braids with ringlets falling to her shoulders.

The young woman was breathtaking. Paige could barely wait to see the expression on her soon-to-be husband. Not that he deserved such a kind wife.

Perhaps before her stood the one person with the power to stop the clan wars. Yes, Paige was certain. Elspeth would be the key to peace in the region.

Her lips curved at meeting her new friend's gaze. "Thank ye for allowing me to attend."

"Nonsense," Elspeth replied, taking her hands. "I will demand ye not be locked up any longer. Tis a thing of men, imprisonment of innocents. What threat can ye possibly be if allowed to return home?"

Paige looked to her interlocked hands. "I do not have a home to return to. However, I thank ye."

MALCOLM STOOD INSIDE the chapel, flanked by his brothers. Kieran, as usual, scowled, his eyes locked on the door as if wishing to escape. Tristan kept vigil, his attention moving from Malcolm to their mother and then to the doorway. During times like this, it was impossible to relax. They'd yet to discuss Laird McLeod's missive and decide how to best move forward.

His uncle had stated it was best to get the wedding ceremony completed and allow for a short meal and celebration.

They would meet afterwards with council members to discuss how to proceed. Just then, someone walked in. It was the woman who'd come to plead for a truce. The one Alec McLeod was willing to chance death for. She sat in the back of the chapel. He had to admit she was quite lovely although gaunt. She kept her gaze downward.

Elspeth had demanded for her release and Malcolm could not deny her anything. Not that day. For the first time in his life, a woman affected him like none before her. There was a desperate need within him for Elspeth and he would not deny it to himself.

Somehow, she'd become the one person he could be with and not hide his thoughts, feelings or weariness. Elspeth listened without judgment. True, she did not agree with everything he said, but despite it, she accepted him.

His mother and sister sat stiffly with identical expressions of disapproval. Lips in a tight line, eyes straight ahead. Even when Elspeth appeared at the entrance, they did not turn to look. Everyone stood, leaving his mother and sister as the only ones seated.

Malcolm lifted his gaze to the entrance and his breath left. Elspeth was dressed in a beautiful, moss green gown, the Ross tartan draped over one shoulder. Beside her, her father walked. The blacksmith wore a plain brown tartan, effectively stating no affiliation to a clan.

There were murmurs as his woman walked forward, her beautiful green eyes locked on him as if for support.

"I am here for ye." He mouthed the words and hoped to convey the message. When her lips curved just a bit, he knew she'd understood.

Once at his side, the clergyman began to speak. "State yer name and make yer promise."

"I, Malcolm Patrick Ross, accept to be tied in marriage to ye today and for always." Malcolm took her hands with his as both their mothers wrapped a strap of fabric around them.

She swallowed visibly and looked to him. "And I, Elspeth Clare Muir, accept ye to be my husband for always." Her voice trembled a bit and her hands shook.

Finally, the clergyman finished whatever he said. Malcolm did not hear a word of it. His entire concentration was focused on the woman whose hands were bound to his.

He leaned forward, ensuring only she could hear. "I will never betray ye."

When she smiled, his chest expanded.

Soon, everyone made their way to the great room. The atmosphere was lighter than usual, especially once the people began to drink ale. He saw to it that everyone, even those in the courtyard, were well fed and had plenty of ale. Lively music wafted from outside as people began dancing around small fires.

Inside the great room, a separate set of musicians entertained, the candlelight making it seem much more intimate. Although guards remained at each entrance and at their appointed posts, it was the most enjoyable day since his father's death.

Tristan pulled Verity to dance, his sister finally relaxing enough to do so, her face brightened by a smile when his uncle joined in.

Malcolm looked to his mother. She watched, her face devoid of expression and he wondered what she thought.

"Go speak to her," Elspeth whispered. "She must be terribly lonely on a night like this without her husband."

Malcolm recognized that he'd not given his mother much attention in the months past. There was so much to do then and even now. However, he could, for one night, allow time to do other things.

When he settled next to his mother, she gave him a startled look. "Should ye not be with her?" There was bitterness in her voice that had not been so evident when his father was alive. Although his mother had never been a mild-mannered woman, she had been fair and he'd never a doubt that she cared for him.

"Now that I am married, I hope ye find it within ye to get to know Elspeth. She is a kind and caring woman. She is who I choose, Mother."

Lady Ross nodded. "I know that full well. Tis not that I do not wish the best for ye. Tis that she is not who yer father would have chosen."

"I believe he would have once meeting her."

"A peasant, a villager as the laird's wife? Ye make a mockery of our family, the entire clan."

Malcolm took a strengthening breath to not yell at his mother. "Is that why ye had her taken?"

Her eyes grew round and slowly narrowed, a scowl appearing. "If I did, it was to save this family from having to withstand yer marriage to that pauper." His mother glanced toward his bride. "She barely knows how to hold a cup properly. Have ye noticed the roughness of her hands, the lack of knowledge of even the most rudimentary of things?"

He'd had enough. "And yet her presence is so much more pleasant than yers or Verity's."

"Tis not with yer head ye are thinking. Soon ye will realize the error of yer ways. But tis too late."

"Enough, Mother."

Instead of relenting, his mother turned her attention to where Paige walked to sit with Elspeth's mother and grandmother.

"And now what happens? Even the prisoners are allowed to celebrations?"

He fought to keep his voice even. "The woman is not a prisoner. She will be released to go once I am assured of her safety. Things have to change, Mother."

"And what about those responsible for yer father's death. Are ye forgetting…"

"I am not." He didn't wish to argue, nor attempt to convince his mother of something she'd not change her mind about. "Try to enjoy yerself." He stood and returned to where Elspeth sat.

Not wanting to ruin Elspeth's night, Malcolm took her hand. He guided her to where his brother and sister danced. They joined in as the musicians started a new lively song.

"Tis not a race, Husband," Elspeth grinned up at him. "If ye do not slow down, I will faint."

Malcolm had to laugh. He'd not realized how fast he'd been guiding Elspeth about the room.

Tonight, he would enjoy his wife and in the morn, would face whatever came next.

CHAPTER TWENTY-FIVE

ELSPETH WAS FLUSHED and happy. Although she'd never ever expected marriage to a man like Malcolm, so stern, stubborn and relentless in his pursuit of vengeance. At the same time, he enthralled her.

The side he revealed to her in private was what made her sure in the choice to marry him. Now as the night progressed and it came time for the marriage bed, she became anxious for what was to come. There was no fear of what would occur between them. As a matter of fact, she was ready for the next step that came after the culmination of so much need.

The only portion that was worrisome was the bedding ceremony. With him being the laird, it was expected. The annoying tradition had to have been the idea of men. Women had no desire to see bloodied sheets. At least she didn't.

In her village, it was fathers of the groom and bride that sometimes demanded it. For the most part, the wedding night was private between the newly married couple.

She eyed Malcolm, who sat next to her. He spoke to his uncle and looked to be relaxed. When he nodded and chuckled at something the man said, it made her glad to know he was in good spirits.

There had been so many bad days.

"We should see about getting ye to the bedchamber," her mother spoke into her ear and, immediately, her stomach tightened and her eyes grew wide. Malcolm turned and took her hand. He squeezed it gently and then turned away.

Some comfort he was. Elspeth stood and allowed her mother, Ceilidh and Maggie to lead her away. To her chagrin, Malcolm's mother and sister hurried to follow. No doubt ensuring they didn't try to cheat in some sort of way.

Elspeth turned to look at her new mother-in-law and smiled. The woman responded with a stern nod.

Once in the bedroom, the bedding was turned down. Elspeth changed into a newly made white chemise and her hair was brushed out.

She wanted to tell everyone to leave, as it was silly for so many to help someone to prepare for bed. Traditions like these made her glad to have lived in a simple village her entire life.

Just as she sat atop the bed refusing to lay back, the door burst open and Malcolm entered, obviously pushed forward by his brothers. Behind him were his uncle and his cousin. She was relieved her father and brothers remained outside the door. When the clergyman entered, her wide eyes clashed with her mother, who had the same shocked expression.

"Very well then. Let us get the required formalities done with," the clergyman stated matter of factly, his disapproving gaze on Elspeth. "Ye must lay back, lass."

"I am perfectly aware," Elspeth snapped. She swallowed, her throat bone dry. "This is most distressing."

"Lay back," Lady Ross said, pushing her shoulder. "It will be over quicker if ye cooperate and do not simper."

"I am not one to simper," she replied and gasped when Malcolm took her ankles and pulled her to the edge of the bed.

He pushed her legs apart, and then moved the chemise up to her stomach. Without hesitation he then reached through the folds of his tartan to take his sex in hand.

"Relax," he said softly.

Elspeth wanted to laugh at the absurdity of it all. Here she was, bare to a room full of strangers with her legs apart, about to be taken for the first time and he wanted her to…

"Ouch!" She yelled as he pushed his erection in, causing a piercing sensation that took her breath. "Stop!" She pushed at his hips. "That really hurts."

He pulled out and she scrambled up to the headboard pulling her chemise down over her legs. Perhaps she looked a fright but, at the moment, she cared little.

"There, darling, it's done." Her mother came up and attempted to hug her. But Elspeth was much too mortified to move.

"Go." Malcolm said. "Everyone please leave."

When he looked at her, she was sure he saw how much she did not like him in that moment. Whatever he'd done had nothing to do with lovemaking. It hadn't brought any feelings other than pain and embarrassment.

As the room emptied, to Elspeth's horror, she began to cry.

She peered up to Malcolm through wet lashes expecting that he'd be turned away. Instead, he watched her with guarded concern. It was as if he were at a loss as to what to do.

"Elspeth," he finally said, coming to stand beside the bed. "I am sorry that I hurt ye. It was required. Do ye understand?"

It wasn't in her to reassure him, not in that moment. Elspeth glared at him. "Ye could have said no. Ye are Laird Ross after all." She sniffed and wiped away tears with the back of her hand.

She watched with fascination as he pulled the tunic up and over his head displaying a beautifully sculptured, masculine body. It was impossible to look away and she studied him. Wide shoulders, broad chest that tapered to narrow hips. His legs were well built from horse riding and his biceps bulged from sword handling. She purposely kept from looking at his sex, the stark reminder of pain and humiliation she'd just gone through.

Fully nude, he slid between the covers. "Come here. Allow me to hold ye."

For a long moment, Elspeth hesitated. Torn between needing comfort and being upset, she wasn't sure to trust him fully yet. And still, she was tired of all that had happened since the night before and what was still to come.

Finally, she went to him and Malcolm pulled her into his arms. "I understand why ye are cross with me. But tis tradition. One that has nothing to do with us. Not really."

"The only purpose is to ensure we join? I do not understand. We said vows. It should be enough."

He nodded and rubbed her arm absently. "True. But without consummation, the marriage can be annulled. Families want to guarantee it cannot be so."

"Tis only the wealthy that hold to it. In my village, it is not done."

When he pressed a kiss to her forehead, she relaxed against his warmth. "True, our marriages are often agreements between clans, for reasons of survival. We have to ensure the well-being of our people."

Elspeth bit her tongue as she was on the verge of reminding him how he'd not exactly done well by his people lately. She didn't want to argue on this night.

"Will ye allow me to show ye how it should be between a man and a woman?"

His hand slid down her back, leaving a trail of anticipation. She shivered despite the warmth of the bedding and his body. He took her chin and tilted her head up to press a kiss onto her lips. "Let me show ye," he murmured.

"Aye." Elspeth was breathless, her heart thundering at the thought that they'd be joined and it would be different than just a few moments earlier.

At least she hoped it would be.

Traveling from her mouth, Malcolm licked down the side of her throat, his hand making quick work at sliding her chemise off her shoulders and down past her hips, until it was finally completely off. He trailed his tongue from her shoulders to her breasts, his mouth taking one tip in while cupping both with his hands.

She gasped at the unfamiliar sensations that surged up and down her entire body. Already, the kisses, licks and caresses were proving to overwhelm her senses and she wondered how it was possible to continue.

"Mmmmm." Elspeth threw her head back and threaded her fingers through Malcolm's hair.

With the tip of his tongue, he circled the tip of one breast and then the other, while she writhed beneath him. He wasn't completely atop her, just his upper body and she wanted more. What she needed was his full weight, the pressing of his body completely touching every inch of hers.

When he sucked in the tip of her breast, she gasped and dug her fingernails into his shoulder. "Oh."

"Ye are perfect," Malcolm said and lifted his head to look into her eyes. "When did it come to be that I cannot consider a day without ye?"

Elspeth wasn't sure if a response was necessary. His confessions astounded her. Why did he feel so strongly about her? It made little sense, especially when he was so heartless and distant most of the time.

Thought evaporated when one of his hands slipped up her leg and inner thigh. He circled his fingers on the sensitive skin until she couldn't help but moan loudly. Every single sensation was multiplied when his lips pressed over hers, his breathing just as quick as hers.

Finally, he moved over her. The weight of him was as exquisite as every touch and kiss.

Elspeth ran her fingers down his broad back, rewarded by a low deep moan. He pressed his hips to her center and then slid up and down, his hardness rubbing just at the precise place where heat pooled.

"What do ye feel?" His husky voice at her ear made Elspeth's eyes open. When he moved again, he once again caused so much arousal in her that she feared fainting.

"Too much to explain," she whispered. "Tis like I want for it to end and to continue forever at the same time."

His throaty chuckle made his stomach ripple and she felt every bit of it. It was as if her skin were on fire, sensitive to the touch, every sensation pronounced.

Once again, he took her mouth, this time with so much fervor she couldn't breathe. And yet if she were to die in that moment, it would be a wonderful ending. She gasped when he probed past her lips with his tongue and, at the same time, one finger pushed into her sex.

Moving in and out with both his tongue and finger in the same rhythm, Malcolm brought her to a point where she cried out. The elusiveness of whatever was to come was too much to bear and she grabbed at his hips. "End it please."

"Ye are ready," he replied and she wasn't sure what he meant.

Once again, his sex prodded at her core and she spread her legs instinctively. He pushed in, the intrusion of his thickness filling her completely. Elspeth's hips lifted and she took even more of him.

"Ye are so perfect," Malcolm said and then slid out and slowly pushed back into her. He continued the movements at first slow and then faster.

"More," Elspeth said, her hands cupping his buttocks and pulling him into her. "I need…"

He thrust with force, sliding out and then again, the pace taking her by surprise and, at the same time, not seeming enough.

Suddenly, the room began to spin, her body quaking as she felt herself floating. Strange streams of heat traveled from her core down her legs and she screamed as she fell from nowhere.

His hoarse cry was loud as his entire body trembled while, at the same time, heated seed spilled. Elspeth pulled his face up and took his mouth, needing the closeness between them to continue.

Malcolm responded, kissing her as if his life depended on it. The intimacy of the moment sent trembles through her. They were to be together the rest of their lives. For whatever reason, Malcolm Ross needed her.

And she needed him just as much.

When they continued kissing, he hardened against her stomach. "I will not take ye again. Tis too soon," he told her. "But I want ye."

Elspeth sighed and met his gaze. "I want ye, too. Can we try?"

Lifting his hips, he slid into her slowly and she cringed. It hurt just a bit at first, but when he began to move, she no longer cared.

CHAPTER TWENTY-SIX

CEILIDH SAT AT the kitchen table cutting potatoes. Although she hated not having seen Elspeth since the night before, she hoped all was well.

The couple had first meal in their chamber and had not come out as yet. It was early afternoon and she kept vigil, listening as the servants came and went. No one seemed at all preoccupied about the marriage, most were relieved for the quiet. The drinking of the night before meant most of the household remained in bed.

"Are there more, Moira?" Ceilidh asked the cook as she cut into the last potato. "If not, I will go see about Ian. I need to check his wound. Does he still remain abed?"

"Tis more than enough, girl," Moira replied, her plump cheeks flushed from scurrying about the kitchen. "He is in his chamber. Ye may take him a light meal. I am sure he will be glad for the company."

She'd not seen him since returning from the village. It was unseemly to go to a single man's room. However, going as a healer, it would not be thought of as wrong.

With a tray that held only a cup of tea and freshly-baked bread, she made her way down the familiar corridor to the small room that housed some of the guard. Cautious to not make much noise, she kept her footsteps light. It wouldn't do to be caught by a guard who'd think she was there for more than just visiting a sick man.

Unable to knock properly, she tapped on the door with her elbow.

"Go away," came the response from within. "I do not wish to see anyone."

"Ian, tis me, Ceilidh." She kept her voice soft, hoping he'd hear her. "I bring ye something to drink."

There was no response and she decided to take it as a welcome. Managing to rest the tray against the door, she opened it slowly.

He sat in a chair turned away from the door and facing a small window. From where he sat, it was impossible to look out and see more than a patch of sky. He didn't react to her entering, so she proceeded to place the tray on a tiny table.

"Tis lovely thistle tea Moira sweetened with honey," she said in a light voice. "I nipped a bit of fresh bread for ye, too."

He didn't turn to her, but kept his gaze straight ahead. "I am not hungry."

"Ye're lying. Moira said ye barely ate this morning. She is worried about ye."

After helping Elspeth with healing for so many months, she'd grown used to the different ways men like him reacted to life-altering injuries. In losing his arm, he would fear he'd lost his ability to continue his life as a warrior.

She rounded him and was shocked at how gaunt he'd become. His bearded face was barely recognizable compared to the handsome man who'd first come to be under her care.

"I won't have it," she barked. "Ye look like a forest man."

Ian's brows moved closer in a scowl. "Leave me be, Ceilidh. I am not in the mood for company."

"I am not here to visit ye, but to ensure ye are taking care of yer wounds." She went to the washbasin and found it was dry. "Why is this empty?"

By the set of his jaw, she knew he'd been turning people away. She crossed her arms and once again went to stand so she could look at his face. "I will return shortly. Ye will not bar the door or I swear I'll have it broken down." Ceilidh moved the table and tray closer to his right side.

"Both best be gone when I return. Eaten and drank." She hurried toward the door. "I cannot believe someone did not come and see that ye were well. I must speak to whoever the lead servant is…" She stopped talking when she walked out. He wasn't listening anyway.

When Ceilidh returned, she was surprised to find Ian had eaten the bread and drank the entire cup of tea. However, he remained in the chair not looking to the doorway.

Behind her, two lads carried buckets of water and a servant girl followed with bandages and drying cloths.

Not waiting for him to move from where he sat, Ceilidh instructed the lads to place the buckets next to the chair. She stood in front of Ian and took the bottom of his tunic and pulled it up. "Lift yer arm." She left no room for argument although she expected him to ignore her.

To her surprise, he lifted his arm. The entire time, he kept his gaze directly forward.

He was stubborn, she knew it, but so was she. "Now, I will remove yer bandages. If they are stuck in any way, I will use water to soften them." As she spoke, she unwrapped the stump that remained of his left arm. The wound was healing well, but remained red and jagged. She was not as well trained as Elspeth, but it looked healthy in her estimation.

Once that was completed, she commanded him to lean forward and she cut the bandage around his midsection. This wound was a bit more worrisome; it oozed and the bandages were stuck.

He winced as she used the warm water to wet the bandages. Then looking over her shoulder to the servants, she spoke to the lads. "Can ye bring more water?" She then directed her gaze to the girl. "Refill the basin and take the bed linens to be washed."

Once the wound was free of the bandages, she went to the window and opened it. "Did ye come to this chair without help?"

"Aye."

"Ye tore yer wound open a bit. But I think it will heal without need for more stitching."

She continued in her work, cleaning the wounds with clean water and dropping the dirtied cloths into an empty basket.

Once she felt it was done well and the cloths were no longer bloody, she began to clean Ian's face and neck. When the lads returned, she continued to his chest and arms. "Clean each of his legs."

"I am perfectly capable of cleaning my own body," Ian snapped, but then looked away when she leveled a glare at him.

Without waiting, the lads did as instructed.

"Now stand," Ceilidh instructed.

"I will not let ye clean me there," Ian said, placing his right hand across his private area.

"Fine." She dipped a cloth into the water, wringed it out and shoved it into his hand. "Lads, help him stand."

She walked around him, hovering when they did as instructed. He groaned just a bit, but then washed himself. The lads rinsed the cloth and gave it back to him as Ceilidh washed his back.

"To the bed with ye," she instructed just as the maid finished stretching clean linens onto the narrow cot.

Refusing further help from anyone, Ian lowered to sit on the bed.

"Take the dirty water and leave the one bucket with clean water. Rinse the cloths and leave them in one of the buckets. I will see about washing them."

When she turned to Ian, he had pulled a sheet across his lap. When a man worried about modesty, he was feeling better. A man in agony cared little about propriety.

"I'll finish bandaging yer wounds and then see about a clean tunic so ye can rest."

As she continued with wrapping the injured areas, he watched her with interest. "Why do ye do this? We have a healer here at the keep."

She met his gaze. "Tis obvious it has been days since he's come to see about ye."

"There are many injured worse that require care."

"I do this because I care for people." Ceilidh spoke the truth in part. The main reason she was there was that Ian rarely left her thoughts.

When she finished, Ceilidh looked to a trunk, the only item that seemed personal in the space. "Is there a clean tunic in there?"

"Aye," he replied as he nodded.

She helped him dress, noticing his eyes were beginning to droop with sleepiness. "Ye have not slept well?"

Ian shook his head. "Nay. Ye do not understand. I am not worthy to remain here. I cannot fulfill my duties as the laird's guard. Once I can go about easier, I plan to leave."

"And do what?"

The corner of his mouth curved just a bit. "Perhaps to become what is it ye called me? A forest man?"

"Ye have purpose and skills. I have no doubt that ye will do whatever it is that ye set yer mind to."

When his eyelids fell, Ceilidh smiled. "Let me help ye to lie down."

He didn't require much help to move to the bed. "I will return later this afternoon and ye will eat and leave this chamber."

She picked up the last bucket and took her time walking about the room, lifting up dirty clothing and then the tray. She carried everything to the door and placed them just outside.

Finally, she returned to the bed and peered down at Ian. He'd fallen asleep, giving her an opportunity to study him. His hair was the color of dark golden sunrays. It had grown to his shoulders since she'd first seen him.

That afternoon, perhaps he'd allow her to cut his hair and trim the beard as well. She touched a soft lock of hair and then took a step backward.

What would it be like to lay with him, to place her head on his broad chest? When it lifted and lowered, she followed its rhythm wondering if he had a lover.

Shaking her head, Ceilidh went to the door and quietly slipped out.

IAN WOKE WITH a start. Disoriented, he didn't remember getting in bed, nor opening the window. A light breeze filled the room, making it both chilly and fresh. The smell of the outdoors filled his lungs and he closed his eyes, relishing it.

Ceilidh had said she'd help him go outside. In truth, his midsection hurt quite a bit when he moved. However, he would not lay about waiting to be assisted. He was a warrior after all. Had been a warrior all his life.

As he struggled to sit, the pain of his wounds annoyed him. It would be a long while yet before he'd be able to walk upright and without pain. Not one for patience, he forced himself to move painstakingly slow. If he tore the wound open, it would be even longer before he'd be well enough to complete some of his duties.

There was a strange twinge down what remained of his left arm. Upon noting the clean bandages, Ian thought about Ceilidh. She was a willful lass.

Her having ministered to his wounds, bathed him, had been exactly what he'd needed but had been too proud to ask for help with.

Raking his right hand down his face, he groaned. Thankfully, he'd managed to keep from becoming aroused. It had been a struggle because he was not immune to her beauty. To wanting her.

This was not the time to think about a woman. No lass in her right mind would want a man with a missing limb. He'd wanted Ceilidh since first seeing her upon waking from the battle. The reddish-golden hair had captured his attention, her bright, sparkling, blue eyes his thoughts and those plump pink lips all of his imagination.

There was a soft knock.

"Yes." Ian wanted to tell her to go away, but he knew she'd ignore it.

Once again, Ceilidh entered, accompanied by the same two lads, one carrying a tray of food, the other went to work clearing his room of the bedpan and dirty clothes. Both boys seemed in good spirits. Funny how the presence of a beautiful woman put males in good moods.

Her bright eyes met his as she went to the window and pulled the shutters, leaving them just a bit cracked. "How do ye feel?"

"Well." He didn't mean to, but his reply was curt. He wanted them all to leave, to not look upon his wounded body and think him weak. And yet, since he'd not been eating or trying to do more than sit, he felt every bit a weakling.

"I see," Ceilidh replied and continued looking at him.

While he ate, Ceilidh made busy work of tidying his stark room.

"I thought we'd go for a walk in the garden. Tis not good for ye to remain cloistered for so long. Can ye manage?"

He nodded even if the thought of going outdoors and perhaps catching a glimpse of the guards at swordplay would make him physically sick.

The lads scurried to help him as he slid to the edge of the bed. Once his boots were laced, he allowed them to help him stand, but then shook his head.

"I can walk on my own."

With Ceilidh beside him and the lads following, they made slow progress toward the kitchens. The familiar surroundings seemed anything but as he saw them differently now when having to move so slowly. He'd never paid much attention to the tapestries the servants had made and hung to cheer up their area, nor how clean the floors were inside the kitchen despite all the activity.

Moira's face lit up at seeing him. "There ye are, lad. I miss ye coming in and stealing my food." She walked over and not caring that she might hurt him, gave him a tight hug.

The pain was nothing compared to how her touch made Ian feel, less than the sickly man he was. He managed a smile at her. "I will only be able to steal half as much now."

The cook shook her head. "That I doubt." She made shooing motions with both hands. "Go on now. Sit outside with the lovely lass. I will send ye some tarts in a bit. I know how ye like them."

Once outside, he took a deep breath. The warm afternoon sun was enough to dispel the chill. He was instantly glad that Ceilidh had insisted on this. Although a bit breathless, he wasn't ready to sit. Instead, he stood and looked to the courtyard. As per usual, there was plenty of activity.

Women were gathered in circles outside tents that had been set up for them. Some mended, while others tended to young children. The stable master and his helpers stood by the corrals talking as they watched over the horses.

Although he couldn't see the guards practicing, the sounds of metal clashing came from the side courtyard.

Atop the walls, archers and guardsmen stood. Some intensely keeping watch while others moved about looking into the courtyard. Keeping guard was an important job, but it could get extremely boring.

"Ye could do that," Ceilidh said. "Tis work that does not require two arms."

"And how would I defend if enemies come?"

Her shoulders lifted and lowered. "Ye could defend the gate with yer sword. Ye are right handed are ye not?"

Despite a bit of embarrassment at her so openly pointing out his lack of a limb, he nodded.

"And ye can push ladders away from the wall. Ye can…"

"Ye have made yer point," he interrupted and turned his attention away from her. "Ye do not have to remain with me. One of the lads will do."

Her eyes twinkled and her lips curved, making him want to kiss her soundly. "I am going to trim yer beard and cut yer hair. Once that is done, I will let ye be."

Ian started to argue, but decided against it. The idea of her so close to his face had merit.

Chapter Twenty-Seven

After having sent everyone out, only Malcolm, his brothers, uncle and four council members remained in the great room.

Just as they began to discuss the message sent by Laird McLeod, Aiden entered and sat to listen. If he was the one who'd double-crossed them as Malcolm suspected, he didn't want the man present. However, being a member of the family, Aiden was in his right to be there.

"Laird McLeod has once again requested a truce. There is not a request for the return of the girl. Not in writing," Gregor informed those present.

Kieran huffed. "Tis not time yet. My father's killer remains alive."

"And yet by continuing to battle, it is perhaps more difficult to kill him," Tristan said. "He is elusive and does not often face us in battle."

"I agree," Malcolm said. "If we stop fighting, we can concentrate on finding Ethan McLeod. He will pay for what he did." Fury began to build and he pushed it away. He had to think about his people and the effect of the clan wars on them.

When the council members began talking at once, Gregor held up a hand. "Winter will be here soon. Tis best to have at least a temporary truce in place."

Malcolm nodded. "The messenger brought a verbal plea for the woman's release directly from Alec McLeod. Not that it matters to me what he wants, but I do not see any reason to continue to keep her here."

"If she matters to him, she should remain," Kieran said.

"To what end?" Tristan asked. "She did nothing except come and plead for a truce. We killed her brother."

At the silence, Malcolm spoke. "A small party will go with my uncle to the McLeods to discuss the terms of our truce. The lass will travel with them."

He looked to Kieran and then to Tristan. "Tristan, ye, ten and four of yer best men go at first light."

Kieran stood and stormed from the room. Malcolm watched him leave, deciding he'd speak to his brother later.

Although it was understandable for Kieran to harbor so much fury over their father's death, he had to be made to understand that he alone would be the one to put the final strike and see to it that Ethan McLeod was dead. It would be the only way to sate his youngest brother's fury.

He stood and stretched, planning to go in search of Elspeth.

"Tis a bad idea and ye know it," Aiden said, coming to stand beside him. "Why a truce when our vengeance is not complete?"

"Our vengeance?" Malcolm met his cousin's gaze. "Since when do ye fight with us?"

Aiden huffed and gave him a droll look. "I tire of having to prove myself to ye and yer brothers. No matter what I do, tis never enough."

It was pointless to list the number of times Aiden had found excuses for not going to battle. He'd even gone to the extreme of lagging behind and remaining in the forest until the battles were well over. At that time, he'd appear and sit on the sidelines pretending to have fought.

Instead, Malcolm shrugged. "If we go to battle again, ye will lead the guard. I have not seen ye fight in a long time."

"What do ye mean?" Aiden had the audacity to shove him backward. "I am as much a warrior as any man in this room."

Malcolm looked to the empty room. The council had followed Tristan, who went to meet with the guards.

"If ye consider yerself my equal then I challenge ye to a sword fight."

Aiden spun, noticing they were the only two who remained. He regained his composure. "I do not have time for this."

A sensation trickled up his spine and Malcolm paid heed. In the past, his sense of foreboding was rarely wrong and had saved his life many times.

Once he spoke to Elspeth to ask that she inform the woman, Paige, that she'd be returning to McLeod lands, he would once again speak to Tristan and Kieran to confirm the party would be well prepared.

He'd make sure they left early in the morning, allowing for travel there and back during daylight.

Across the courtyard, Malcolm spotted Kieran brushing his horse. His youngest brother always insisted on caring for his own steed. It worked well since the beast barely tolerated anyone else near him. The huge black horse pawed at the ground as Kieran continued to groom it.

Deciding it was best to speak to Kieran, Malcolm made his way through the courtyard. Once he moved closer, healed wounds on the animal's sides and front chest area were visible. The horse had been to every battle, fighting as courageously as Kieran. Malcolm studied the duo for a moment, noting that perhaps the horse was the only being that truly connected with his troubled brother.

"I hope ye can understand my decision, Kieran," Malcolm said. "I want vengeance as much as ye. But not at the cost of our people's well-being. Father would not have wanted to be the cause of so much death."

Kieran remained with his back turned, soothing the horse that did not care for Malcolm's presence. "I know what ye're doing. But the anger inside me will not go away. I want them all gone."

"We will capture Ethan Ross and ye will see to his demise. Ye have my word."

When Kieran turned to look at him, there was pure hatred in his gaze. "What of Laird McLeod? He should pay as well."

"Perhaps his death would quench the fury inside ye. Although I doubt it."

"Nay, ye're right, nothing will."

Malcolm studied his brother for a moment, but did not go any closer. The horse was as dangerous as his brother.

"See that ye go after the first party. With at least ten archers."

"I will. I've also sent replacements for those at the northern border."

"Good." Malcolm turned and walked away, knowing that no matter what was said Kieran continue to be filled with rage. His brother would never accept that it was not his fault that their father had been killed.

Back inside the keep, Malcolm hurried up the stairs to find Elspeth. When her room proved empty, he went to the sitting room where his mother and sister were. The women looked up at him once he entered.

"Son?" His mother studied him. "I wish to speak to ye. We need to send a messenger to Clan Munro. Tis time for Verity to find a husband."

His sister looked to them with a bland expression. "Tis useless, Mother, he cares nothing about me."

"It is not true," Malcolm, said, resigned to the fact that he would have to remain with his mother and sister for a bit. "We are seeking a truce with the McLeods. A party goes in the morning. Once that is done, I will send word to Clan Munro."

Although Verity didn't smile, he could see her mind turning the information.

His mother's lips curved. "Very good news."

Chapter Twenty-Eight

The late morning brought perfect weather for herb gathering. Elspeth and Paige walked along the woods' edge under the watchful eyes of two guards and two archers.

Excited that she'd finally felt up to activity, Elspeth did her best to ignore the men who took turns huffing to show their boredom at being there.

"What will ye do when ye return to Ross lands?" Elspeth asked the other woman.

Paige frowned. "Find my place among the people who are seeking refuge within the walls. I have nowhere else to go."

"There are many at Ross Keep as well. I am hopeful the battles end for good." Elspeth bent to pinch leaves from a small bush. "War is the way of men. A barbaric way to settle a score."

Elspeth looked up at the sky when a flock of birds flew by.

"Ye are yerself now a Ross. Can ye not influence yer husband?" Paige studied her with interest and lowered her voice. "How is it that ye can be with such a heartless man?"

"I cannot explain it. I, too, considered him to be ruthless and without care for innocents. And perhaps in some ways he is. I believe the brothers, all three of them, act out of grief for their father."

"That doesn't make it right," Paige said, her voice harsh. "That so many had to die and will continue to do so."

"I agree," Elspeth replied, letting out a long breath. "I have spoken at length with Malcolm about it. But as ye know, women have little say in these things."

"Does yer mother have say in what yer da does or doesn't do?"

Elspeth's lips curved as she considered the question. "Many times, aye. He does as she wishes if he is to sleep in their bed." Elspeth giggled at recalling her huge father following behind his wife trying to appease her after she'd lost her temper.

Paige nudged her shoulder. "I do not wish to make ye feel badly. Ye're just barely married. I suppose a part of me wishes I were a man and had more of an opinion."

One of the guards huffed and both women turned to glare at him. The man looked up to the trees, pretending interest.

"What about ye?" Elspeth asked. "Alec Ross seems to have taken great interest in ye. He came so far as to try to exchange himself for ye."

A light blush crept up Paige's face. "I do not know why he would do that."

"I do," Elspeth replied. "He cares very deeply for ye."

"I am angry with him. He sent my brother to his death and because of it, my grandfather soon died as well." When Paige sniffed, Elspeth took her hand.

"We will be friends."

Paige's lips curved. "Aye, we will. I wish to be yer friend."

They continued down the path, each with a basket on one arm and hands held.

"Would it not be interesting," Elspeth began, "if ye married Alec Ross and we demand to see each other?"

"I would not take no for a reply," Paige said solemnly. "Tis my right to have ye as a friend."

Elspeth laughed. "I wish it for ye then."

Paige considered it for a moment. "His family will not allow it. However, the thought of two village girls married to powerful men does make for an interesting turn, does it not?"

"Malcolm's mother doesn't like me." Elspeth sighed. "I must admit, I have not made an attempt to get to know her better. I will make a better effort."

"Ye should. Tis best not to have strife with one's husband's mother."

Elspeth looked to the guards. "We can head back now. Ye can stop yer huffing."

The men pretended not to hear her, neither one responded. Elspeth met Paige's gaze and rolled her eyes.

They continued toward the keep at a slow pace, neither wishing to be inside the gloomy interior on such a nice day.

"Have ye been in the cook's garden?" Elspeth asked. "Tis wonderful. I like to go and help. Tis replete with vegetables and fresh herbs."

"Nay," Paige replied. "Tis only since yer wedding day that I have been allowed out of the chamber."

"Then let us go there. I will show ye where it is." They walked a short distance in silence.

"Once I return, it will be impossible to see ye." Paige sighed. "Ye cannot travel far, not when there is not a truce in place."

"Perhaps when I visit my family. My village is not part of either clan. Ye can come there."

Paige nodded. "Aye, that would be good."

The women hugged and upon separating, Elspeth noticed Malcolm approaching. The man emanated power, strength and by the flat look in his eyes, a lack of emotion.

After meeting her gaze, effectively sending tendrils of awareness through her body, he nodded in acknowledgement to Paige. Then he turned his attention to the guards, who were suddenly animated.

Elspeth narrowed her eyes at one of them.

"Anything of interest?" he asked one of the guardsmen.

"Nay, Laird," the man replied.

"Very good." Malcolm came to Elspeth's side. "We must speak, come with me." He took her elbow and then as if remembering Paige's presence, took hers as well.

Malcolm looked to Paige. "Ye will be returning to McLeod lands in the morn."

Paige and Elspeth exchanged looks. Scared for her friend's well-being, Elspeth peered up at her husband. "Will it be safe for her?"

"I will ensure it. She will travel with my uncle and ten men."

Still, it didn't bode well. Only twelve people traveling during a time with no peace between them was not enough if they were to be attacked. "Only ten?"

"Aye, we…" he stopped midsentence. "We will discuss it further in a bit."

Once inside the keep and in the small area outside the kitchens, Paige took the two baskets. "I will place these in the shed."

Elspeth nodded. "Thank ye."

She allowed Malcolm to guide her inside and through the great room. They went up the stairwell to their chambers. Once inside, he seemed to immediately relax.

"Tis best for her to return." He tipped Elspeth's face up to him.

"I like her and we wish to remain friends."

"Ye can become friends with Verity."

That he cared about her having female companionship made Elspeth smile. "I will try. She does not seem to care for me."

Pulling her into his embrace, he nuzzled her hair. It never stopped amazing her, how the man seemed to require her presence in such an intense manner. "Is something wrong?"

He kissed her temple and placed his chin atop her head. Elspeth wrapped her arms around his waist, loving the feel of her strong husband's body against hers.

"I do not know. A feeling of foreboding came over me. Perhaps I will reconsider allowing my uncle and brother to go forward with the travel. Wait a few days."

She nodded. "Trust yer instincts. Although I do wish for peace more than anything, not at the cost of bad things occurring."

"Elspeth," the hoarseness of his deep voice flowed over her and she knew what he wished.

"Come." Elspeth took his hand and led him to their bed.

Once beside it, she slid her hands under his tunic and pushed it up. He pulled it over his head and waited, watching her with interest.

She untied the fastening around his waist and his breeches were easy to remove then. Other than the hardening erection, he remained calm, the intensity of his gaze following her every move as she pushed him to lay on the bed.

There was so much power in knowing she alone could affect him in such a way that she was at once aroused, needing him.

Elspeth climbed on the bed straddling him. Reaching under her skirts, she found his sex and guided it to her entrance.

Slowly, she lowered onto it, allowing her body to stretch and take him in. Her breath caught at the feel of it.

She lifted a bit and lowered, every single movement bringing glorious sensations.

Head tilted back through half-closed eyes, Malcolm kept his attention on her face. "Take all of me," he said and then moaned when, once again, she took all of his length.

Up and down she moved, using her thighs until they began to burn and even then she could not stop. Malcolm's chest expanded and the tendons of his neck bulged as he neared completion. Needing more, he took her hips and held her as his hips lifted and lowered, his sex pumping into her with vigor.

Every single inch of her body responded and she flew like a freed bird. At the same time, Elspeth struggled to not lose total control as she enjoyed the view of Malcolm's handsome face.

She loved the sight of him coming undone as she reached peak after peak. Finally, she lost all control and fell from invisible heights, crying out his name.

At the same time, Malcolm continued moving in and out of her until his hoarse cry told he, too, found release. His masculine body shuddered as he thrust into her one last time.

"I do not think I can move," Elspeth gasped out. "My legs are trembling."

Malcolm's chuckle was prideful. "Lie here with me for a moment." He ran his hands down her back when she lowered to lie atop him.

"What did ye wish to speak to me about?" Elspeth asked once she regained her normal breathing. "Is something wrong?"

He let out a long breath. "Nay, not really. I needed time with ye. Are ye comfortable here, Elspeth?"

Considering for a moment, she decided it was a good time to broach the subject of her standing. "Will I be allowed to travel to my village and see my family?"

"Nay. For now they must come here. They can stay as long as they wish."

She considered it. "What about my duties. Yer mother manages the servants. What will I do?"

"I have been considering it. My mother is very close to Verity. She may wish to go with her once my sister marries."

"Until then, may I take responsibility for the kitchen?"

"Aye. I will inform my mother."

How easily he agreed made Elspeth suspicious. Her father readily agreed to things if he had something planned that would displease her mother.

"There is something else?"

His wide shoulders lifted and lowered. "Yer younger brother,

Conor, wishes to join the guard."

"Nay!" Elspeth pushed away and sat up. "He cannot."

"He is a man full grown, Elspeth."

"He barely is. Just ten and six. My older brother Gil, is maimed because he fought for ye. Why would Conor now wish to fight for this clan. We are not Ross'."

"Ye are now." He sat up, not bothering to cover his nudity. It was difficult for her not to take him in and yet she stubbornly kept her eyes locked to his.

"I will not allow it. That my brother go to battle and perhaps die for a cause he has nothing to do with doesn't make sense."

"There is much training yet for him to do. As ye said, he is still young. I do not foresee him going as of yet. Besides, we are negotiating a truce."

"No." Elspeth scrambled from the bed. "Where is he?"

Malcolm stood and attempted to pull her into his arms again, but she resisted. "Nay, Malcolm, do not try to dissuade me. My brother will not fight." Tears fell from her eyes and she sniffed.

"He will not then. I promise ye."

She looked up at him. "Swear it."

"I swear it. He will be given other tasks. Guarding the gates or up on the turrets, but not the battlefield."

Looking into his eyes, she could see the truth of his words and she finally relaxed. "Do not forget this, Malcolm. If my brother goes to battle, I will leave ye. Disappear forever."

His eyes widened just a bit, and Elspeth knew he feared just that. She would not threaten him like that again. But this once, she was glad for it.

CHAPTER TWENTY-NINE

Morning came and, with it, a light drizzle. The cloudy sky would hopefully give way to sun in a few hours. Or so Tristan hoped as he mounted. He would ride in front with Begawan, a seasoned warrior. Behind him would ride two men flanking the woman and then his uncle flanked as well by two men. Additional guards would follow the group.

A scout had been sent ahead. The man would return to them at a predetermined point. If the scout was not there, they would know something was amiss. His brother had not had a good feeling about the trip, so he'd sent a scout ahead the night before.

"See to it that ye return with haste," Malcolm said, meeting his gaze. "The sooner this is done, the better."

Tristan nodded. He wished for peace more than his two brothers and perhaps that was why Malcolm had chosen him to escort the group.

He looked over his shoulder to where Kieran and several archers stood watch. They would follow after a while, as additional aid in case of wrongdoers.

"Let us go then," his uncle said with impatience. Tristan smiled. Gregor sounded so much like his da, it was uncanny at times.

"Aye, Uncle. We go." Tristan signaled the guards atop the gate and the immense doors began moving.

Once they were outside the gates, they took the horses to a canter and the party began the half-day trek.

IT WAS LATE morning when they arrived at the meeting point. Tristan motioned for the party to remain behind as he rode forward with Begawan. The huge warrior lifted a hand to signal they should not speak and motioned toward a copse of trees.

Tristan narrowed his gaze, noting a horse tied to a tree. Perhaps the scout was relieving himself. If so, they would give him a moment and then make their presence known.

After a moment, Tristan whistled. There was no reply.

"Something is wrong," Begawan whispered. "The horse is alone. It could be it is not our scout's."

Tristan urged his mount a bit further into the trees. "It is. We must turn around."

Just then, a scream sounded and, with it, the pounding of horses.

Both Tristan and Begawan lifted their swords and kicked the horses to a gallop back to the party.

There were at least twenty McLeods. Already, two guardsmen lay on the ground, while the rest, including his uncle, fought. They were outnumbered, but Tristan often took three men at once. A guttural yell left his lungs as he rushed into the fight.

Swords clashed against his, but he managed to keep from falling off the horse. One of his opponents sliced across, the tip of the sword barely missing his neck as Tristan leaned back while striking against another opponent.

"We come in peace," his uncle screamed. "To speak to yer laird in response to his message."

The man that fought Gregor barely hesitated before thrusting forward. Thankfully, his uncle was a seasoned warrior and was able to keep from harm.

Begawan fell from his horse, bleeding from his side. He managed to kill the man who'd struck him before turning to defend against another.

The pierce of a sword into his back made Tristan howl in pain. Unable to see who it was, he swung blindly, relieved when striking someone.

Stumbling sideways, he refused to fall and blocked the downward swing of a battle-ax. His breathing became labored and he fought not to lose consciousness.

"Son of a dog," someone said as a hard hit came from the side, sending Tristan stumbling into the woods.

He fell face forward, unable to remain upright while the fighting continued.

Just then, movement of the ground accompanied the sounds of horses racing closer. The hooves pounding gave Tristan the strength to push up.

In the distance, he recognized the Ross tartan. At the same time, the attackers saw them, too. Grabbing a couple of injured warriors, the McLeods mounted and left.

When Tristan looked in the opposite direction, he saw a man dragging Paige into the woods. He struggled to his feet and followed, barely able to lift his sword.

His brother and archers rode past in pursuit of the attackers. Kieran would not allow for any survivors. There would be no truce now.

"Help me," Paige's scream was followed by silence as Tristan continued forward. His vision was blurring and he knew that even if he did come upon whomever it was that took her, he'd be unable to defend the woman.

The sound of water took his attention as he was unable to focus. He thought that it would be best to stop. Instead, he listened intently for the woman's voice. If nothing else, he would point the guards in the direction in which they went.

Tristan swooned and everything tilted. It became impossible to keep his balance and he fell sideways. The fall seemed to continue forever and Tristan realized he'd fallen down the side of a slope. He attempted to get up only to once again fall. It took several more rolls and thumps down the side of a hill until finally coming to a stop on his stomach.

For a few moments, he would rest before making his way back. His eyes were so heavy now and breathing was almost impossible.

He would pass out, there was no doubt. "I...I am here," he called out but his voice was like a whisper.

CHAPTER THIRTY

THE THUNDERING OF horses' hooves followed by shouts made everyone at the evening meal stop speaking. Malcolm got to his feet and Elspeth did as well. Lady Ross rushed out, but Verity remained at the table seeming to be frozen in fear.

Elspeth didn't hesitate to run after her husband. Her throat constricted upon reaching the courtyard and seeing injured men barely able to ride. There were two men thrown across horses. Gregor Ross was helped down from his mount and carried into the great room.

With loud shouts, people scurried to get out of the way, most sent away by Malcolm's mother. Not stopping to see what else happened, Elspeth raced to find the healer who lived in a set of rooms next to the stables.

She found that a guard had already alerted the older man who was grabbing bandages and throwing instruments in a wooden medical box.

"There is a basket there," he said to her. "Fill it with bandages and follow me, hurry." He pointed at several bottles that she had no idea what they contained.

Elspeth and the healer hurried toward the main house and into the great room where four injured men lay upon tables and two others, who'd not been wounded as badly, sat on benches.

"What happened?" Elspeth asked a guard who stood at one of the tables placing pressure on an unconscious man's wound.

"Our party was ambushed by those sons of dogs," he said, lips twisting in fury. "We were outnumbered by more than double."

She looked to the other three injured men. None were Tristan and she let out a sigh of relief.

Recognizing the warrior as Begawan, she looked up to his face after scanning him for injury.

"See about him first," Begawan ordered as he motioned to a warrior.

They tore away the young man's clothing to find he'd been pierced through. The sword had sliced through his ribs. He couldn't breathe and was bleeding profusely, his lips already turning blue.

Elspeth swallowed and looked to Begawan. "There is nothing to be done for him." Not wanting to dwell on it, she motioned for a servant to come close. After she placed a thick, folded cloth on the table, she laid him back upon it. "Press down on the wound. If his bleeding stops, we may be able to save him."

Begawan moved back, allowing the servant to continue as he hurried out to the courtyard.

On the next table was a warrior writhing in pain. He'd been cut on the upper leg and thigh. The angry slashes were deep but not life threating. The bleeding had already stopped.

Elspeth poured tincture directly from the bottle into his mouth. She motioned another servant. "Once he calms, pour water into the wounds and clean them thoroughly. I will sew them shut once that is completed."

"I can sew wounds, Lady Ross," one of the maids informed her. "I have done it many times."

Startled at being addressed as "Lady", Elspeth was struck silent for a moment. "Very well. See that the wounds are thoroughly washed and call me to look him over before doing so."

The third man was being looked after by the healer, so she moved to the last one. This man suffered from deep cuts to his midsection. Elspeth cut away his tunic and began washing out the wounds. She kept an eye for where the bleeding came from and began to sew internal wounds shut. When the man convulsed, she waited for a few moments, maintaining pressure on the wounds until he calmed.

When she completed cleaning the injury, she packed the opening with clean cloths and instructed servants to cover him up with blankets to warm his body.

"What are ye doing?" The healer came to stand next to her. "Why did ye not sew his wound shut?" He seemed both interested and annoyed.

She let out a breath, watching the injured man intently. "I am not certain I have found all that is wrong with his inner wounds. They continue to bleed. I will wait to see if they stop. If not, he could die."

He followed her back to the first young man who remained alive. The servant who'd continued to apply pressure spoke into his ear.

"Seems he has a strong will to live," Elspeth said as she approached. "Let me look." When the servant girl removed the cloth, blood oozed, but it wasn't as much. Elspeth peered at the small wound. "Should we sew him up or leave it be?" she asked the healer who shook his head. "Leave it be. If he lives through the night, he may recover."

Once again, thick bandages were placed in the front and back of where the warrior had been pierced through. Then Elspeth and the healer wrapped a strap around his midsection tightly.

"Remain with him," Elspeth instructed the servant girl and looked to the healer. "Where is Gregor Ross?"

"He is over there, refuses to be treated."

Elspeth left the healer to see about Malcolm's uncle.

"Just a head knockin', tis all," the older man waved her questions away. "When someone hit me from behind, I was passed out for the fight. Tis not right." He scowled. "It was Tristan. I am sure."

"Why would Tristan hit ye?" Elspeth knew the answer before she finished the sentence. No doubt, his nephew sought to protect him by making it look as if an enemy had felled him.

"Because he is a fool," Gregor snapped. "Now he is gone."

Her eyes rounded. "Gone? Did they take him?"

"Nay. At least I do not think so." Gregor looked to the door. "I tried to remain awake. Just before passing out, I saw someone come and take the lass. I could not make out who."

Heart pounding, Elspeth looked around the room. Malcolm had yet to return from the courtyard. She let out a long breath. The battling would continue now. Malcolm would not stop to consider that perhaps the party who attacked were robbers, or perhaps not from the McLeod clan at all.

"I must speak to Malcolm." She rushed from the room, not stopping even when the healer said something.

For a moment, she stopped to allow her eyes to adjust and then scanned the courtyard. Other than the usual people, Malcolm was nowhere to be seen.

Elspeth hurried to the stable master who guided two horses closer. One of them was the monstrous black beast that Kieran rode. "Where is my husband?"

"In the keep I assume, Lady Ross."

She hadn't seen him enter but, then again, she'd been distracted. Once again, she went inside and made her way to his study.

Inside stood Kieran, Begawan and Malcolm. They were deep in discussion so they didn't hear her approach.

"We should go now. They will not expect it," Kieran said.

Malcolm shook his head. "Tis best to plan. First, we must send men to search for our brother, in the forest and the surrounding land. He may be injured and hiding."

"I do not think so, Laird. I searched," Begawan said. "They must have captured him."

"But ye said that ye watched them taking only their injured."

"True," Begawan replied.

Kieran shook his head. "Those dogs do not deserve for us to think on it. We have to attack."

"What of the lass?" Elspeth spoke up. "Yer uncle saw someone take her away."

The men turned to her and only Malcolm spoke. "Leave us, Elspeth."

"He is in the great hall. He's been injured by a blow on the head." Elspeth wanted to glare at him for acting as if she were but a mere messenger. "He is well, just needs a wee bit of time to rest."

"He could have been killed," Kieran said between clenched teeth. "Like our father."

Malcolm held up both hands to quiet his brother. "Begawan, ye and six men go and search for my brother. In the meantime, Kieran, ye will plan for two sets of warriors. One group will ride westward and then north and the other the opposite. We leave just as soon as they are armed and ready."

We. Elspeth's throat constricted as Malcolm came to her. Taking her elbow, he led her away from the room. "Come, we must speak."

By the set of his jaw and flared nostrils, he was angry. But was he furious at the situation or at her?

"Ye are hurting me," Elspeth complained as she attempted to pull her elbow from his grasp. In truth, although the grip was tight, it didn't actually hurt. However, since her arrival there, he'd never been so rough with her and she didn't like it.

Malcolm softened his hold on her elbow. "I did not mean to." Although he said the words in a soft tone, his expression didn't change.

At the top of the stairwell, they ran into his mother. Her face was blotchy from crying. "Are ye not going to find yer brother?"

"Begawan and several warriors leave now. Kieran and I leave soon after."

She seemed satisfied with the reply and wiped her eyes with a wrinkled cloth. "I must see about Verity, she is unwell at the news."

They continued into their chamber and, finally, Malcolm released her arm. "Ye are not to come to the study when I meet with my men, ever. Do ye understand?"

"And why not?"

"Tis not a place for a woman to speak on clan…"

She huffed. "I will do as I please. Ye are not my master. I am not yer slave or servant."

"Elspeth…" he let out a long breath as if to stop from losing his temper. "As my wife, ye have vowed to obey me."

He had a point. Elspeth considered it for a moment. "Up until now, ye have not given me any order to stay away from yer study. Tis not to my liking, but if ye ask, then I shall refrain from it. Even if we are in the midst of attack."

For a long moment, she met his gaze.

"I leave to go find my brother. Remain here. Do not leave the keep no matter what."

Every ounce of her being wanted to protest. What of the injured? It was in her nature to be at the battlefield where essential needs were most important.

He took her by the arms and peered down at her. "Do not disobey me on this, Wife. I will not forgive ye if ye do."

It was inevitable, her eyes rounded and her mouth fell open. "Consider the wounded. Tis what I do."

"Nay. There are wounded here for ye to care after." He released her and went to his trunk. After removing his clan tartan, he spread the Ross colors onto the floor and pleated the fabric as she watched.

"Malcolm. I know ye have to go. What if someone misled the McLeods? Tis unlike them to attack first."

He looked up at her. "Why would someone lie to them?"

"To keep the clans at war." She tapped her chin. "Paige said she was very afraid of Aiden. He is nowhere around…"

Jumping to his feet, Malcolm stalked to the door. Not seeming to care that he only wore a tunic, he rushed out and down the stairs. Elspeth followed but remained at the top of the stairwell. Instinctively, she knew their conversation was not yet over.

"Where is Aiden?" Malcolm asked one of the guards. "Bring him here."

The man shook his head. "He left after the group earlier. Just behind."

"Find Kieran. Tell him to come to me at once." The warrior left and Malcolm stalked back up the stairs.

This time, he rushed to lie atop the pleated fabric and tied it securely around his waist. Upon standing, he pulled the corners up and over his left shoulder, holding it in place with a crest. His gaze never left hers.

Elspeth neared and placed a hand on his chest. "Promise ye will return to me."

At once, he pulled her into his arms, his face nuzzling into her hair. "I promise." He pressed a kiss to her temple. "I need ye more than ever, Elspeth."

When he lifted his head, the expression on his face was hard, reminding her of first meeting him. "Please see about the injured here. Upon my return, if there are more, ye will be needed."

"Do not worry, I will do as ye ask." Every word tasted bitter, but Elspeth understood. She didn't wish Malcolm to be worried about what she did while he was fighting. He needed to be fully focused. "There is one thing I ask."

"What is it?"

"Attempt to find out the truth first."

"What truth?" Kieran stood at the doorway. Also in Ross colors, he was as intimidating as he was beautiful. Every inch of the warrior promising swift death, from the daggers at his waist to the huge bow strapped to his back and finally the broadsword on his left hip. His sharp hazel eyes took them in. For a moment, his gaze hesitated where Malcolm's hand touched Elspeth's upper arm.

Malcolm didn't move away from her. "Aiden is missing. I am told he left soon after Tristan and his group."

Kieran was slow to react. Narrowed eyes moved from Elspeth back to his brother. "Why would he betray us?"

"Tell him," Malcolm said to Elspeth.

"Perhaps Paige. He came to her several times when she was locked in. Once, he tried to have his way with her. A guard interrupted. She told me to be wary of him."

The brothers exchanged a look. "Let us go," Kieran said and left.

Once again, Malcolm brought Elspeth against him and tipped her face up. "Be here when I return."

It struck her as odd how vulnerable he seemed when they were alone. A protective urge overtook her. "I will always be here, Malcolm. Be with care. I beg of ye to find a way to know the truth. Battle is not always the answer."

CHAPTER THIRTY-ONE

ALEC STALKED ACROSS the floor, his footsteps crumpling the fresh rushes that had just been spread. "How could this happen? Why did ye attack?"

Four warriors stood lined up facing the front of the room. Each one was the leader of a group of men who'd gone to intercept the Ross group headed their way.

His father pounded a fist on the table. "If ye saw they were few in number and had a woman with them, obviously they were not coming to attack, but in response to our request for a truce."

"The bastard double-crossed us," Ethan gritted out. His narrowed eyes met Alec's. "I should never trust a Ross."

The last thing Alec needed at that moment was some sort of remark about trust from the one person responsible for everything that had occurred.

Alec made a slicing motion in the air in his brother's direction. "Stop talking, Ethan. Ye of all people cannot cast blame anywhere."

"Ye know I am right," Ethan persisted.

Before Ethan could utter another word, Alec grabbed his tunic with both hands and shoved him backward. "Shut up, cease with yer nonsense."

"Stop this at once," their father shouted. "We must come up with a response. A way to let them know what truly happened."

Ethan pushed around Alec. "Father, ye know what comes. Clan Ross will attack. We must prepare."

"What of the woman?" Alec asked the closest warrior. "Did they take her back with them? Did harm come to her?"

The warrior looked to his father and shook his head. "Nay. She was taken away just as we arrived."

"By whom?" His heart began to pound. Something in the way the warrior paused made Alec's stomach lurch. "Who took her?"

A different warrior replied, looking to Ethan. "I believe it was Aiden Ross. The man who met with ye."

Aiden Ross had not only betrayed them, but now he meant to have Paige for his own. The bastard would die. He probably thought to get away while the attack occurred and no one would notice him stealing Paige away.

"I will kill him." His teeth ground with fury.

Laird McLeod stood, his face set in a resigned expression. "Ethan, go gather the men. We shall prepare for the inevitability of an attack. Ensure that every area of the wall is protected."

His father continued issuing instructions to the guards, sending some to gather people, others to fortify gates and ensure fires were lit at every archer station. If they were to be in battle, they would fight hard.

Alec went to his father. "If it can be stopped in any way, we should try."

"I agree. However, it will be hard to get Laird Ross to listen to reason now and I cannot blame him. We attacked a messenger party."

"Two Ross' were among those in the group," a guard informed them. "Tristan and Gregor."

Alec spun at hearing the news. The news became worse and worse the more they found out. "Were they injured? Killed?"

"I do not think so..."

"Does anyone know anything for certain?" Alec wanted to toss his younger brother out of the room for everything that happened.

One of the four lead guards replied, "Nay, Laird. Tristan was only injured. I believe the elder man was as well. When we left, they were alive, the both of them."

Alec's father came to him. "We should start by gathering the warriors and speaking to them. Tonight, they will be defending the keep.

"First I must find her."

His father seemed to sense he would not relent but there was a strong set to his jaw. "This is not the time to worry about a woman. Tis our clan at risk."

"Why do ye not place responsibility on Ethan? He remains without worry despite being the..."

His father cut him off. "I know what he has done. And it has been done. Our work now is to stop what is about to happen. Our clan cannot withstand another clash with such a large warrior force."

Over his father's shoulder, for the first time he saw something cross Ethan's face. His brother's brow furrowed and he looked down to the floor, unable to meet his gaze.

Once their father left the great room with the four warriors, Ethan went to follow. Alec stopped him with a hand on his shoulder. "I ask for yer help now, Brother," Alec said. "I must go after Aiden. Help reinforce the keep."

Ethan nodded and met his gaze. "I will."

Moments later, Alec and his mount exited out a side gate that backed up to a steep decline. There was a familiar path for those who lived there. If one wasn't aware of it, a fall down into a deep gorge was inevitable.

Although not quite sure, Alec was hopeful to find Paige and return shortly. He'd met Aiden at a cottage not far from the keep. The small home had belonged to a warrior long dead. Now empty, Alec had kept it for himself and, over the years, had often used it when wishing for time alone. It was furnished with all that was needed, but most of the time it stood empty.

When the hay-thatched roof cottage finally came into view, the hair on the back of his neck stood on end. There was a horse tethered to a tree. It was Aiden Ross' steed.

Alec dismounted a distance away. Although he was sure it was possible to go closer and not be seen, this was not the time to take a chance.

At the sound of a woman's scream, he almost raced to the door, but it could prove detrimental. It took every ounce of self-control not to tear the door down with his bare hands and barge in. What if he was too late and the cause of the scream was a fatal strike?

Low to the ground, Alec hurried to the small dwelling until he was able to flatten against the exterior wall of the house.

Paige was crying. It was both a relief and like a punch to his stomach to hear.

"Ye will not escape, nor leave until ye belong fully to me. Tis not as romantic as I would have wished, I fear." Aiden mocked her. "Unless ye wish me to tear the rest of that rag ye call a dress, remove it now."

"Why would ye want to be with a woman who detests ye?" Paige cried. "I won't undress for ye."

"Do it."

Alec looked in through a small window. Thankfully, Aiden had his back turned. Paige stood in a far corner. Her eyes were swollen, her bottom lip bleeding and there was bruising on the side of her face.

Sword in hand, he crept to the door and pushed it open, praying it didn't make a sound. As soon as he was able, he slipped in.

Aiden threw Paige onto the bed and tried to hold her down. It proved difficult since the wee lass struggled with all her might. Paige managed to slap him across the face.

Out of the corner of his eye, Aiden must have caught sight of Alec because he whirled around. His eyes widened at realizing it was too late to defend himself from a drawn sword.

Aiden immediately straightened. "I rescued her from an attack. Yer clan attacked the Ross party. I was trying to calm her."

Sword pointed at his neck, Alec advanced. "Ye brought her here. Ye also lied to my brother about the Ross' attacking."

He swallowed visibly. "I did not. Did they not come with warriors toward yer keep?"

"Twas but a small party. Ye have caused us great damage." Alec motioned for Paige to come to him. "Go outside," he told her. "Wait for me." Without a word, she scrambled out the door.

"Now, how should we settle this?" Alec asked, circling his sword. "By removing yer head or spearing yer heart?"

"We can come to an agreement. I can help ye. Ye need me to bring information. Now more than ever."

Alec spat on the ground. "Ye are not worth a pig's eye. Ye are a disloyal coward."

The idiot dove for his sword at which time Alec speared him.

Aiden rolled onto his back and used both hands in an effort to stanch the blood flow. It was useless, of course, but just to be sure, Alec speared him through the heart.

After a few gurgling sounds, Aiden Ross was dead.

Alec stared down at the dead man. If the Ross' found out he killed Aiden Ross they would have no mercy on his clan. How much could his small clan withstand?

Heavy with burden, he walked out and found Paige sitting on the ground, weeping.

"There is nothing to cry about now." Alec pulled her to stand and held her against his chest. As he comforted the crying woman, reassuring her, he wished there was someone who'd reassure him.

Alec grabbed Aiden's horse and headed for his own. Lifting her up to the horse's back, he mounted behind her. Paige could not stop trembling and he knew it would take time for her to get over what had happened. Women were emotionally strong when they needed to be, but because they lacked the physical strength, they were too often the recipients of mistreatment.

How he hated his gender right now.

They headed back to the keep, his woman tightly wrapped within his tartan as drizzle began to fall. Two of his warriors came into view, obviously sent by either his brother or father. Alec met their serious gazes. "Bury the body."

The men nodded and continued on past to the cottage.

Within moments, Alec and Paige arrived at the heavily-fortified walls of the keep. Paige finally moved enough to look up at him. "Thank ye. I am sorry to have caused ye trouble. I feel…"

"I thought I had lost ye." Alec lifted her face to him and kissed her.

"Are ye coming in?" a guard asked from atop the gates with a smirk.

Alec couldn't help but grin at the older man. "Aye, we are."

Once inside the gates, the people were eerily quiet. Groups were huddled around fires and under tarps waiting to hear the sounds of approaching horses. Not even the babes cried.

After dismounting, he released his horse and Aiden's to the stable master who walked away without speaking.

"Son, ye found her." His mother met them just inside the doorway. She looked over Paige who hid her face in both hands. With torn clothing, and little in the way to cover up, she remained tucked inside his tartan.

"Let me take her. I will look after yer lass." His mother's sympathetic gaze moved to Paige. "Come here, lass. I have a cover for ye. What ye require right now is a hot bath and warm food."

Paige turned and met his gaze for a long moment. "Speak to Laird Ross. He is not what he once was."

"I will try," Alec said, even if he had no idea how to bring a conversation with his enemy to happen.

When the women walked away, his father neared. "Let us go up to the wall and see what happens. The Ross' will probably not be in sight. They will not come until nightfall. At that time, they will attempt to attack from two sides."

"How do ye know?" Alec asked as they made their way up a side stairway.

His father pushed a finger to his right temple. "Tis what I would do. At night, they will hope for cover of darkness."

"The archers will not see them."

"There is a way to light the path. But we must be sure they are there. I pray we can get through this night without bloodshed."

He would not burden his father with the knowledge blood had already been shed that day.

CHAPTER THIRTY-TWO

SOMETHING WET FELL onto Tristan's face. It was not unpleasant. The cool liquid eased the heating of his skin.

"Can ye open yer eyes?" A sweet voice floated over him, somehow reaching his ears, but at the same time seeming so far away.

Once again, cooling liquid oozed over his face, chest and arms. It could be it was raining and a wood nymph was upon him. It was said they appeared and stood by waiting for death to come.

"Use the tincture. Tis best to keep him asleep," a male voice said. "He is not of yer clan. He could be dangerous."

A vile taste filled Tristan's mouth and he smacked his lips in disgust. If only he could muster the energy to open his eyes and find out where he was. There were no forest sounds, nor that of a fire. It smelled fresh, almost as if he were outdoors but without a breeze.

"Thank ye for yer help," the sweet voice said. "He is quite braw. I wouldn't have been able to carry him here."

The man made a throat clearing sound. "Yer family will be searching for ye."

"They are busy with the business of battles and such. My brothers, too. They believe me to be abed. Since I found him, I returned to last meal. I told mother I was going to my chamber, as I feared for what would happen. Our clan is once again at war."

"What if something does happen and here ye are away from shelter?"

"Please keep watch over him. Ye are right, I should return."

Tristan could not figure out what they spoke of. Although the voices were clear, his mind was not. The sound faded and lifted, each word sounding new.

Once more, he tried to lift his lids and, finally, they parted enough to see a bit. There was, indeed, a fire in a hearth, but it was on the other side of the room.

Wisps of red hair blocked him from seeing more. Soon, a heart-shaped face came into view. Clear blue eyes met his. "Do ye see me?"

It had to be a wood nymph, as he had never seen any human woman with such fine, delicate features.

"Grier, look." She turned away. "He has awakened. But just a wee bit."

There was no reply and Tristan tried to look to where she did, but his eyelids began to close. Once again, he looked at the woman who continued to peer at him with curiosity. "My name is Merida. What is yers?"

He tried to speak, but his throat would not allow for sound. "T-T-Tr..." Tristan gave up.

"Do not worry. Ye will be well enough to speak soon. Rest." She pressed a cool hand to his jaw.

He fought to tell her he did not require rest. Whatever happened earlier was not clear. Had the McLeod warriors slaughtered everyone? Was his uncle dead?

There had been too many against them. He hoped they'd been tricked to think his uncle was felled and allowed him to live. Tristan groaned at a stinging pain from his back.

The woman, Merida, and the man rolled him onto his stomach and turned his head to the side.

"Ye have a large wound; I must clean it. Twill hurt," she warned, placing a warm hand onto his shoulder. "I am so sorry."

Whether it hurt or not, Tristan did not feel anything at first. As long as the woman continued to talk, he could concentrate on the soft lilt in her speech, the sweet sound of each word. Suddenly, excruciating pain seemed to pierce him in half and he cried out and then, thankfully, lost consciousness.

"THE BATTLES WILL continue." Elspeth shook her head and Ceilidh, too, felt the heaviness of what was to come upon her shoulders. How could it be that the clans could not meet to discuss an agreement to stop?

"Surely Clan McLeod cannot continue to want this. Their numbers are quickly dwindling."

"I do not know," Elspeth replied and looked across the garden where they'd sat to rest after spending hours treating the injured and ensuring their wounds were clean and the men well fed.

Two remained on the brink of death, one young warrior stubbornly hanging on to life. Ceilidh hoped he would live. But not to ever have to fight again.

"I best see about Lady Ross. She is caring for Verity who developed a fever. Tis most worrisome."

Ceilidh didn't wish to go back inside. The fresh air and birdsong reminded her of life in the village of a time before the battles.

Deciding to go for a walk, she slipped out a side gate and made her way to the tree line. The sounds of the water from the loch nearby were soothing to her senses.

There were other things to consider as well. Eagan insisted on courting her and although she cared for him a great deal, Ceilidh couldn't bring herself to think of him as her husband. He was too…what? She pondered. What exactly was it that made him unattractive as a partner?

"Ye will fall if ye don't watch yer steps here." A male voice startled her.

Ian stood next to a thick tree, his face devoid of expression. It had only been two days since she last saw him and he'd barely been able to walk unassisted.

Hurrying to him, she looked around for servants or whoever had helped him outside. "Why are ye out here alone?" She frowned up at him. "Ye could fall."

"I am capable of walking on my own. Tis an arm I am missing not a leg," he snapped.

"Ye were cut through several times. Barely healed. If ye tore the stitches open, I will not care when yer guts spill."

The corners of his lips lifted. "Ye will."

Of course she would. Upon seeing him, her pulse had raced and continued to do so. It was hard to keep from allowing him to see how hard it was to keep her breathing normal. Pretending to be angry with him helped hide the fact her hands trembled just a bit.

"Why do ye care so much?" His expression became serious. "I am but half a man now. Tis unlikely I will ever fight again."

She neared and frowned up at him. "I think ye will be just fine. Too stubborn to remain pitiful." Taking his hand, she led him down a slight decline to the water's edge. "Like me, ye have been inside too long. I do believe being cloistered brings dark thoughts."

"My fellow warriors are preparing for battle and here I am walking about without a care," he grumbled. "Tis not the way it should be."

Ceilidh had never been one to coddle and she turned to him and motioned with her finger for him to come closer. When he leaned forward, she motioned again. "Closer."

"What?" He wasn't in the mood for games and it made it so much more delightful. "This I have to whisper," she lied.

When he was but a hair's breadth away, she wrapped her arms around his neck and pressed her mouth to his. At first, he stiffened, seeming to consider whether to move away or not. Then ever so slowly, Ian's lips softened, his arm wrapped around her waist and he responded to her kiss.

Tracing his lips with hers, Ceilidh had never felt so free, so wanton. It was as if he were meant to be the one man she could allow such behavior with.

His mouth traveled down the side of her neck sending tingles throughout her body. "Oh," she murmured and then repeated.

"Tis not what ye really want, Ceilidh," he whispered in her ear. "Not me."

"Only ye make me feel alive. Look at me and see I am being truthful."

He lifted his face and peered into her eyes but did not keep her gaze for long. His eyes traveled down to her lips and then downward.

"Do it," Ceilidh challenged, her chest expanding with each breath. "I want ye to."

When he continued looking at the fastenings, Ceilidh untied the lacings and pulled her top apart, exposing her breasts. Ian's breath hitched and he covered one with his hand, kneading the fleshy mound gently before circling the tip with his thumb.

"Ah," Ceilidh gasped. How was it possible that the simple touch could bring so much pleasure? She gripped his shoulder. "Tis wonderful."

When he lowered and took the tight bud into his mouth, she gasped and dug her fingers into his shoulder and threaded the other hand through his hair. "Oh, yes."

He lifted and trailed kisses back up to her jawline until pressing his lips to her ear. "Ye and I have much to discover. Will ye allow me to be with ye, Ceilidh? Not now, for I cannot satisfy ye well, but soon?"

"Aye, Ian. Ye are the man for me."

"Ye give me hope," he said, meeting her gaze. "Make me feel whole."

Ceilidh couldn't help the curve of her lips; she pressed a kiss onto his chin. "Do not forget it. I am not willing to share ye."

When Ian chuckled, it was the first time she'd heard him laugh. The sound was both reassuring and melodious to her ears.

"I would not dare cross ye," he teased.

Taking her hand, he led her to lie upon the soft grass. "Just because I cannot make love to ye, does not mean we cannot explore other pleasures."

"Aye, I wish to see more of ye as well." She pulled him down for another kiss as he palmed her bare breast once again.

Chapter Thirty-Three

"WE CANNOT CONTINUE forward," Malcolm finally admitted as rain pelted down over them. "Tis best we turn to the forest and search for my brother."

The horses were barely able to get traction on the muddy slopes as they turned around to find shelter in the forest.

"Over there," a man shouted. "Someone comes."

A lone rider came into view. Malcolm lifted a hand to shield his eyes from the downpour.

Finally, the man neared, not at all intimidated by the fact every man was heavily-armed.

"I come to talk," the sodden man called out.

Malcolm recognized him immediately and was shocked to see Laird McLeod unaccompanied.

The older man met his gaze for a moment. "Malcolm, how fare ye?"

Looking to his men, he motioned for them to move away. "Retreat to the trees. I will speak to him alone."

The men exchanged confused looks, but then obeyed.

Malcolm waited for them to be out of earshot. "How is it the laird is out and without escort?"

Clyde McLeod looked over his shoulder toward his keep. He was soaked but it didn't diminish the air of power that emanated from him. He remained straight upon his steed. "When fortifying for battle, they do not expect the laird to sneak away. Much less alone."

"Ye are taking a great chance in thinking I will not strike ye down." Malcolm met the man's gaze directly. "We are enemies, after all."

"Aye, we are. I do not fear death. I am confident my son Alec will make a good laird when I die."

There were so many questions Malcolm wanted to ask. The man and his father had been friends at one time. In their youth, they had often competed in the games. "What do ye wish to say to me?"

Once again, the laird looked over his shoulder. "We were misinformed by one of yer own. Aiden Ross said ye were masking as messengers to catch us unaware and charge my keep. We now know it was not true. I have no proof of this other than my word. I did not give orders for yer party to be attacked."

He believed the man. "Yer younger son did."

"I take responsibility."

At least now it made sense since they'd requested a truce to begin with. "Where is my cousin now?"

"Alec searches for him. He has taken the lass. The one he cares for."

"What of my brother, Tristan. Do ye have him captive?"

"Nay. My warriors did not bring anyone. One did say he saw him having fallen in the forest. He was not sure if yer brother remained alive."

It was not possible that Tristan was dead. Why was he gone? If an animal had dragged him away, there would be tracks. Tristan was alive. The question was where.

"I cannot promise a truce," Malcolm admitted. "Not fully. Yer son killed my da. That cannot go unpunished."

"Tis understandable. My son acted without thought. There is

naught I can do about it now."

"Ye will not do what is right because he is yer son."

Laird McLeod nodded. "And one day when ye have bairns of yer own, ye will understand."

It was as if the rain poured harder and Malcolm had enough of it. "A temporary truce. But if any McLeod so much as steps over into our land, it will be over."

"I accept," Clyde McLeod said without hesitation. "And Malcolm," he said as he reached for Malcolm's shoulder and squeezed it. "Ye will be a great laird to yer people one day. Think of them first, always."

The words, much like those his father had once spoken, made Malcolm clench his jaw. Laird McLeod did not consider him a good laird. Not at the moment. Not that he should care what his enemy thought.

He could only nod. "Be with care upon yer return. My brother and his warriors approach from the east. I will send a scout to stop them. Hopefully, he will reach them in time."

"I thank ye." McLeod turned away and urged his mount to a gallop, making Malcolm wonder how the man could travel so fast when the rain made it hard to see. He remembered something his father once told him and his lips curved. Clyde and his father had competed blindfolded to a specific destination. It honed their skills, but it was difficult. According to his father, Clyde usually won.

He returned to his warriors. "That was Laird McLeod. We have agreed to a temporary truce. Two of ye go and find Kieran. Tell him to return to the keep at once. Ten remain with me to go in search of Tristan. The rest of ye, go home."

CHAPTER THIRTY-FOUR

THE RAIN CONTINUED without ceasing and Elspeth hated that she could not see through it as she peered out the window.

What was happening now? Were Malcolm and his men battling out there, rain, mud and blood mixing under their feet?

"Why are ye in here?" Verity asked from the bed. She lifted a hand as if to send her away, but it fell back onto the bed limply.

"Yer mother is resting. Ye have been ill since yesterday." Elspeth neared with a cup of water and lifted Verity's head. "Drink."

The woman drank greedily, gulping every last drop. Her round face was wet with perspiration, hair sticking to it. "How do ye feel?"

"Weak and unable to stay awake."

There was a strange yellow tone to her skin. Although Elspeth had noticed it before, now it was starkly apparent. Whatever ailed her was not something Elspeth knew how to cure. If only she could once again see her tutor. He would know what to do. But she'd not seen him in a very long time. It was as if he disappeared into thin air. She could not even find the small cottage he'd lived in.

Mentally inventorying each herb in the drying building, Elspeth did her best to remember her lessons. Once in passing, he had mentioned yellowing of the skin. She would have to look to her sketches to find which herb was best.

"I will return shortly."

Milk thistle. It was hard to find. Elspeth looked at the drawing and racked her brain trying to remember if she had some at her parents' home. She'd been so overtaken by everything that she'd not thought of them as of late. Perhaps someone could be sent to go and fetch it.

Putting her notes down, Elspeth left the chamber she shared with Malcolm and hurried down the stairwell.

Thankfully, the rain was finally slowing. She slowed upon entering the great room where Gregor Ross sat at a table with ledgers. He looked up, his gaze warm. "Tis too dreary to work in my rooms. I prefer here where there is a bit of noise at least."

"Is it possible to send someone to my village? To my home? I require milk thistle to give to Verity. She is quite ill."

His brow lowered. "So her mother said." He stood. "Come, let us go seek a young lad who can ride swiftly."

Soon, they found an eager volunteer. The lad, much too young to fight, was eager to prove himself.

"Make sure they find the right herbs. If they're not sure, then bring as many as ye can." Elspeth held out a sack. "There are more sacks inside, bring what ye can. Thank ye."

The lad nodded and hurried to find a horse.

"Will he be safe? I hope no harm will come to him."

Gregor nodded his head. "Warriors are too busy at the moment to bother with him."

Holding her face up to the light drizzle, Elspeth was glad that it had slowed. She mentally pictured Malcolm returning to her. To their bed and into her arms. She concentrated on the closed gates.

When Gregor placed a hand on her shoulder, she met his gaze. "Do not worry, he will return. I am hopeful the battle did not take place because of the rain."

"I pray ye're are right."

Hours later, Elspeth could barely remain awake. In the sitting room with her, Ceilidh held mending on her lap, the needle long forgotten, a soft smile on her lips.

"When will ye tell me what happened today to have ye in such good spirits?"

Her friend sighed. "Ian, he and I...we kissed."

Elspeth couldn't help but chuckle. "Ye did more than that by yer expression."

Her friend attempted at a serious expression, but failed when her lips curved. "Must I remind ye that he remains injured? We will take our time and allow for time to get to know one another."

"A courtship then? Wonderful." Elspeth would have wished for the same with Malcolm although she tried to picture it and failed. He was much too direct and distant for such dalliances.

Her lips curved. "I am getting to know my husband more every day. I hope he returns soon." She yawned and stood. "I am going to check on Verity once more and retire."

Although Verity remained very ill, her coloring was improving. Elspeth woke her and, once again, made her drink from the cooled milk thistle tea.

Lady Ross watched from a chair, her gaze moving from Verity to Elspeth. "Thank ye for helping her."

She and Malcolm's mother would never be close, but at least now, hopefully the woman would be a bit kinder. "She will recover. I am sure of it."

Moments later, in her and Malcolm's bedchamber, Elspeth slid between the bedding and instantly lost any interest in sleep. What was Malcolm enduring at the moment? Was he sleeping in the wet forest? Could it be he was injured and unable to return?

Just as she was about to slip from the bed and go to the window, the door opened.

She watched in silence as her husband went to the washbasin and, dipping his hands into the water, washed his face and hands. Then after undressing, he took a cloth, dipped it into the water and ran it over his body.

The candlelight did an exemplary job of highlighting the dips and valleys of his perfect body. Elspeth could stand it no more and she slipped from the bed. "Are ye injured?" She went to him.

"Check for yerself," Malcolm invited, standing perfectly still.

Panic set in and she ran her hands from his shoulders to his chest and then rounded him and did the same to his back. "Where does it hurt?"

"Here." He took her hand and placed it over his erection. "It's excruciating."

"Malcolm!" Elspeth drew her hand back. "I am being serious."

With quick motions, he brought her against his body and took her mouth with greed.

"I missed ye, Wife." There was a hunger in his voice that was followed by a hard kiss. He tore her chemise off and lowered her down to the floor onto the rug. "I want to have ye now."

She acceded, taking his sex in hand and guiding it to her entrance. "Then take me."

With a hard thrust, he drove into her and let out grunt. His hips moved slowly at first in a gentle rhythm, sliding in an out of her with precise movements.

"More," Elspeth gasped, needing him to move faster and sink deeper. "More."

When she attempted to take his hips, Malcolm took both of her hands and pulled them up over her head. "What are ye feeling, sweet wife?" He moved slower. "Tell me."

"Desperation," Elspeth gasped out the word. "Need. Please…"

He covered her mouth, silencing her pleading and continued the slow, sweet assault. Each time seemed to take longer until she writhed beneath him, struggling to free her hands and have him the way she wanted.

He chuckled in her ear, releasing her hands only to groan when she managed to get free from under him and prod him onto his back.

Malcolm's darkened eyes rounded when she straddled him. "My way," she demanded.

With one hand she held him down and with the other took his erection. He was thick, hard and moist. The skin felt silky as she stroked him once and then again, enjoying the feeling of control.

Elspeth was fully aware she only did what he allowed, but that he gave himself so completely. The control gave her a feeling of power.

Lifting her hips, she once again guided the hard member to her core and lowered until he filled her completely.

This would not be slow, not any longer. Elspeth rocked her hips, rising and falling back atop her husband with hard, sharp movements. Malcolm matched her drives by lifting his hips and thrusting up until she could not take it any longer.

Skin slapped together as the pace became frantic, the movements no longer rhythmic or controlled.

"Ah!" A hard climax sent Elspeth spiraling, gasping, and screaming as she became lost in a sweet abyss. In the fog of release, she knew Malcolm had rolled her onto her back and lifted her hips so that he could continue taking her body. Every time he drove in, her body trembled in response.

Finally, he shuddered and cried out as he spilled his seed. When he collapsed over her, they both fought to breathe, their wet bodies remaining joined.

"Ye came back to me," Elspeth whispered between harsh breaths.

"I promised I would," Malcolm lifted just enough to meet her gaze. "Ye would make me crawl back if I had to."

She stroked this hair and kissed him. "Is the battle over?"

"There is a temporary truce." Malcolm rolled to his back and pulled her to lay on his chest. "Tis not over, but for now I want to concentrate on finding Tristan."

He slid a hand lazily down her side. "Winter will be here soon. The people need a respite."

Elspeth let out a long sigh. "Spoken like a true laird." She placed a trail of kisses across his chest. "What do ye think happened to Tristan? He must be near where the battle took place."

"Someone said they saw a bearded man in the forest. Perhaps the man took him in. We are searching for him."

"Could it have been a monk?" Elspeth sat up. "I know a monk who lives in the forest, but he lived closer to my village. Perhaps it is the same man."

"Perhaps," Malcolm replied and yawned. "Should we go to bed, Wife? I must leave right after breaking my fast in the morn." He lifted up to rest his upper half on his elbow.

"There is something I must tell ye," Elspeth said. "Yer sister, she is very ill."

"Verity?" Malcolm asked as if he had another.

"Aye."

"She has always been of a strong disposition." He lay back down onto the rug. "What happened to her?"

Elspeth lifted up and held out a hand. "Come to bed, I will tell ye."

As she finished telling him about Verity, they began to speak of Ian and Ceilidh. "Ye are aware, Ian should remain in the guard. He only has one arm, but he can still fight. He right handed."

Malcolm pressed a kiss to her temple and let out a long breath. "I will speak to Ian once things settle. I wonder if it was like this between my mother and father. How the lady of the home brings order and keeps her husband informed. Tis one of the many reasons I need ye."

Once again, he repeated the words. Elspeth met his gaze. "Tis not only ye, Malcolm. Today, I realized how much I need ye as well."

Lips curving, he shook his head. "Do ye realize what I mean when I say it?"

Elspeth frowned. "Of course. Ye require my presence to set ye right. To feel as if all is well here in yer home."

"Aye, that is part of it. The other part is different. When I saw ye come to the battlefield that day and care for Ian, ye stood up to me. Like a warrior who could easily beat me in battle, ye did not do as I demanded."

She wasn't sure what to say, so she remained silent.

"Ye were exactly what I needed in that moment and what I need every day. A beacon of peace and rest."

"Rest?" She reached between his legs and his sex reacted to her touch. "I would not expect too much repose."

"Tis rest for my mind and body at once," he replied and then closed his eyes when she began to stroke him.

"Tell me, Husband, what will we do now?"

Malcolm's eyes opened, his lips parted and his breathing caught when she traced the tip of his erection with her finger.

"For now, we wait to see what tomorrow brings."

When he rolled over her, Elspeth wondered how many tomorrows would come. And then she gasped upon being taken completely.

It was so different waking up with his wife tucked against his side. Malcolm didn't want to move and disturb her. Every morning since marrying her was the same. He lingered in bed, arriving late for first meal and enduring his brother's knowing looks.

Yes, he had many duties as laird and was expected to be up early and ready to deal with all the preparations for the upcoming winter season.

Malcolm let out a breath thinking about Tristan. There was a ravine near the place where they'd been attacked. Warriors had gone down and found no trace. And yet, he had a feeling the only reason Tristan had not been found initially was because he'd fallen and remained hidden.

If the men who'd been searching through the night had not found Tristan yet, Malcolm would return that day and continue the search. He would not allow winter to set without his brother being accounted for.

He placed a kiss on Elspeth's brow and slipped out of the bed. After donning clothing, he hurried down the stairs and found that only his uncle was at the high board.

"Where is Kieran?"

"He didn't return last night. I heard he joined the search for Tristan."

"Aye, I will go as well as soon as we discuss what to do about the people. It is safe for those who have homes to return. Organize with the men and ensure homes are built in the nearest village for those that require one. If the rest insist on returning elsewhere, they can, but I am not sure we have time to help them rebuild."

"I will meet with Ruari to discuss how to divide our supplies and the workforce. Do not worry. Ye should concentrate on finding yer brother," his uncle said.

Malcolm met his uncle's gaze. "What of Aiden? Do ye have any thoughts as to where he is?"

His uncle shook his head. "Nay. He is either gone to avoid the wrath of two lairds, or dead by a McLeod's hand. Either way, he is no longer welcome to return. If he does, I will not begrudge ye whatever punishment ye see fit."

It was interesting that the only thing Malcolm felt for his cousin was pity. No matter what happened to Aiden, at the moment, in Malcolm's opinion, being ostracized from one's clan was the worst punishment.

Just then, Elspeth appeared. She glided down the stairs and walked over to where he sat. There was a poise about her that came naturally. Although born humble, there was nothing lowly about his wife. From the moment he'd met her, she'd exuded strength of character.

When she lowered to sit next to him, she nudged his shoulder with hers and gave him a playful smirk. "Ye should have woken me."

"I wanted ye to rest."

"I have much to do today. Once I have eaten, I will check on the wounded and on Verity." She continued speaking and he was glad she'd found her place there at Ross Keep. It was her home now and Malcolm could not imagine life without the willful woman.

A plate of food was slid in front of him and his cup filled. Malcolm scanned the great room, noting guards had begun trickling in for first meal. At another table, a family sat eating and speaking in low tones. A baby toddled into the room and his mother rushed in after him, looking up to the high board. Malcolm smiled and she visible relaxed. "How fare ye, Laird?" she asked, lifting the baby to her hip.

"Well and I hope ye are the same," he replied.

"Aye, Laird. We are happy to be returning home." She hurried to a table and joined the family already eating.

Perhaps it was time to allow the people to be happy, he considered. His father's death would be avenged, and he wondered who would be the avenger.

Malcolm had a strong feeling it would not be him.

The End.

About the Author

Most days USA Today Bestseller Hildie McQueen can be found in her overly tight leggings and green hoodie, holding a cup of British black tea while stalking her hunky lawn guy. Author of Medieval Highlander and American Historical romance, she writes something every reader can enjoy.

Hildie's favorite past-times are reader conventions, traveling, shopping and reading.

She resides in beautiful small town Georgia with her super-hero husband Kurt and three little doggies.

Visit her website at www.hildiemcqueen.com
Facebook: HildieMcQueen
Twitter: @HildieMcQueen
Instagram: hildiemcqueenwriter

Made in the USA
Columbia, SC
28 February 2020